All At Once, Then Not At All

Caitlin Bowden

For Peter, who I loved all at once, then again and again and again…

One

When Sebastian Clarence is sixteen, his father finds out he kissed one of the other boys on the lacrosse team. It wasn't even a very good kiss. The boy's tongue was sloppy and insistent, seemingly trying to find the answer to one of life's great mysteries in the back of Sebastian's throat.

Sebastian can't remember exactly what his father says when he finds out, only the vague sounds of Ivan, the family head of security, trying to get his attention in the aftermath. His head is heavy and slick with something hot. Blood, he soon realises when his brain catches up and the delayed thud of something hard against his right temple pounds through his skull. He supposes that's what skulls are for at the end of the day. If his skull is hurting, then his brain is probably fine.

His brain is not fine in the end.

When he wakes up in the hospital two weeks later his father comes to see him. He doesn't even get angry when he reaches down to take Sebastian by the hand and Sebastian flinches away (it's the wrist his father broke a few times when he was a child, so it's a force of habit by now). He takes Sebastian's hand and he says that he only did it because he loves him and he won't let Sebastian throw his life away for some *fucking sissy*. He knows Sebastian isn't a *fucking sissy*, couldn't be because he's *his son*, and he *understands what's at stake here*, what *that sort of shit* does to a family's reputation. Reputation is important, because the company is bigger than just *their* family, and there are thousands of people *relying on them*. His father tells Sebastian to get well soon. He adds that he had to give Sebastian's doberman pinschers, Poppy and Nuca, away—they were too much of a nuisance.

Sebastian asks Ivan if his father really did give Poppy and Nuca away or if he had them euthanised. Ivan looks him dead in the eye when he lies and says they're safe with someone else now. Sebastian thinks it's strange because Ivan doesn't usually lie, but he doesn't question it. That night in the hospital bed, he wishes for the first and last time that he was dead; like his *whore mother*, like Poppy and Nuca.

He mustn't wish hard enough because they discharge him the next morning. His father says he has to get back to school.

His father misses his high school graduation. He says there's little point in attending, seeing as Sebastian barely managed to scrape his way into the 90th percentile. He expects *nothing less than perfection*, he says. It would give the wrong impression if he goes along and claps in tandem with those other *idiots* cheering on their children's *bland mediocrity*. Sebastian is better than that, because *he's his son*. Sebastian ends up skipping graduation too.

It's bad enough in general when he gets the pitying *I'm so sorry your mother threw herself off an 80-storey building* head tilt. He doesn't need the accompanying *isn't it terrible your father doesn't give a fuck about you* sigh.

For Sebastian's twenty-first birthday, his father decides to throw him a *real shindig*. He says Sebastian is spending too much time holed up studying. If the degree is so difficult then maybe he shouldn't be wasting his time and his father should be looking for someone with more than *half a fucking brain* to run the company some day, he says. It's nice to give the tabloids something to *sink their teeth into, keep the family name relevant, all publicity is good publicity.* And fuck knows what damage Sebastian had been doing all those years behind his father's back at that all boys school. No doubt the *hush money* will be pouring out soon to conceal the number of *fluttering sissies* his son has entertained.

Sebastian wonders if his father can see the irony in saying *all publicity is good publicity,* then despairing about *hush money* in one breath. He doesn't ask. The old injury behind his right eye twinges in protest every time he questions his father's logic.

In the run up to the party, he does as his father suggests. He starts attending his fraternity's parties. He drinks copious amounts of cheap liquor, repulsed by the distinct difference between Jack Daniels and the Laphroig his mother used to rub on his gums to help him fall asleep. He fucks girls, all moist curves and cheap shampoo that smells like coconuts. Enough of them that he garners a bit of a reputation as a heart-breaker, but not enough to imply he sees them as disposable.

Sebastian doesn't really *see* them as anything— he keeps the lights off and only fucks them from behind.

When the invites go out then, for his twenty-first birthday party, there are people to actually accept them. His father seems pleased which makes Sebastian pleased. He says he's going to need his own security team, that Ivan doesn't have time anymore to be splitting himself in two trying to manage everything. Ivan hires someone new, says they'll be in attendance at the party. His father thinks it will be amusing to see if the new guy can keep tags on his son during the festivities; the *spitting image of me* at this age, he says. Nothing like his *whore mother*. He asks Ivan to corroborate this fact. Ivan agrees, and his father seems pleased again.

Sebastian glows with the praise; his father tells him to wipe the *shit-eating grin* off his face.

The night of the party arrives. Sebastian watches from his father's side on a stage as a thousand people he doesn't know salute him with champagne flutes. His father waxes lyrical about how proud he is. He even gets a little misty in the eye, slapping his hand firmly over his son's wrist and dropping a subtle joke about his sexual prowess as he winks at the masses. They laugh in unison, like they're at a church service, like they believe every word coming out of his father's mouth. In the end, Sebastian supposes that they do. How easy to just lap it up, let it wash over you and then drain away again because none of it fucking matters. It never has.

Sebastian doesn't matter. His *whore mother* didn't matter, Nuca, Poppy, Ivan doesn't fucking matter, whoever the fuck he's found to follow Sebastian around like a shadow doesn't matter, the lacrosse boy who he didn't just kiss but let throat fuck him in the locker rooms until he spat bile on the floor doesn't matter (and that *especially* doesn't matter because Sebastian's not a fucking *faggot*).

Sebastian suddenly realises the room has gone quiet. The faceless mass poised to toast him appears to be looking his way. His father's grip on his wrist tightens infinitesimally. An echo of something deep inside him makes Sebastian's heart lag for a moment as fear paralyses his brain. It wanes enough to be subdued by his good sense, and he clenches his jaw, rearranges his features into a brilliant smile. He surveys the shimmering crowd, the lights above catching on every diamond, every facet of the crystal glasses which cast rainbows across their dreary black ties. He relaxes as he lets an easy laugh leave his body, mouth stretching into a grin. He winks at his father. The grip on his wrist loosens and the panic recedes along with it.

"Dad told me not to sample the champagne until his speech was over," Sebastian says, raising his own glass to mimic the toast. "So forgive me if my mind was elsewhere." There is a soft swell of laughter as everyone absorbs his words. Sebastian inclines his head towards his father, smiling his most golden smile. "Thanks for everything tonight, dad. I wouldn't be the man I am today without you—the older I get, the smarter you seem to be!"

The crowd makes the same rumble of laughter, their gazes never shifting. Sebastian's father brings his glass to his lips.

His father tells him *happy birthday son*, and together, they sip delicately at their champagne. He lets go of Sebastian's wrist. Sebastian retreats from his side, a subtle lean in the opposite direction.

Off the side of the stage, he can see Ivan scanning the crowd, a younger man with glossy black hair at his shoulder speaking into an earpiece. Sebastian watches a moment longer until the man's narrow, hooded eyes meet his; they are beetle black and focused.

He blinks, and then suddenly the man is at his side, body pressed solidly against Sebastian's as he pushes him to the floor of the stage. He feels the impact of the hard wooden boards on the backs of his shoulders, his hips, the force of it shoving the air from his lungs. His champagne flute slips from his fingers, but the accompanying shatter of it hitting the ground is swallowed by the unmistakable bark of a gun.

Sebastian gazes up at the dark hollows of the man's eyes in the breath of silence which follows.

Then the crowd dissolves into hysteria. The cacophony feels as if it's happening in the next room over, Sebastian's ears still ringing with the sound of the gunshot. They scrabble over one another at the edge of his vision like rats, their only instinct self-preservation. The smooth filter over their faces drops as they grab at each other's hair, yanking and pulling and stepping on each other to exit the ballroom. Sebastian wants to watch it all unfold, but the dark-eyed man is grasping his shoulder, getting his attention.

"—go, sir. We have to go," he's saying, and he's tugging Sebastian to his feet. He keeps his body between Sebastian and the crowd as he moves swiftly across the stage, hand pressed to the small of Sebastian's back. He twists his head to get a glimpse of his father. Ivan is bent over him, and there's blood staining the stage at his father's side.

"Dad's been shot," Sebastian says, his words coming out in a burst of exhilaration and shock. His stomach feels strange, like it's full of worms scrabbling to escape.

The dark-eyed man shakes his head, fingertips pressed sharply now into the space just above Sebastian's tailbone. It makes his spine tingle.

"Just grazed him. He's going to be fine. The rest of our men are trying to apprehend the shooter but our top priority is making sure you're safe," he says, never pausing for breath as he leads Sebastian through the stage door and down into the service corridors the staff use to ferry champagne to the ballroom. His earpiece buzzes every now and then with static, probably security still searching for the gunman. Sebastian's legs feel like they're going to give way underneath him as a giddy thrill rushes through him.

"*I'm* your top priority?" he asks coyly. "I like the sound of that."

The dark-eyed man still doesn't stop, but he does throw Sebastian a quizzical look. He quirks a thick eyebrow, his sharp jaw set as he tries to deduce what on earth Sebastian could mean by that. Sebastian grins at him, the flurry of nervous energy in his stomach and limbs finally, *finally* reaching his brain and he nearly collapses.

He's caught mid-fall, pressed against the wall as the dark-eyed man props him up in an uncomfortable slump. He leans back from Sebastian and mutters something into his earpiece, but Sebastian can't quite make it out. Is he speaking a different language? Sebastian opens his mouth to ask but his tongue feels like a ball of cotton wool, spongy and unresponsive. The man touches his face and his fingers feel hot, like the tips of cigars branding his skin (Sebastian's father burnt him with a cigar once. The burn had healed horribly, so from then on Ivan made sure to always have an ashtray on hand). Sebastian shivers again, can hear his own teeth chattering. He winces, trying to force his jaw to still and bites the end of his tongue instead. He hisses at the pain, clutching the bottoms of his arms as he tries to warm himself up.

"I'm Ren," Ren says, taking his suit jacket off.

"Bet you don't know who *I* am," Sebastian tries to say, his joke coming out as little more than huffs of air thanks to the chatter of his teeth. Ren frowns. Sebastian rolls his eyes. Opens his mouth to explain his joke to Ren, who is apparently an *idiot*, but nothing comes out.

Ren wraps his suit jacket around Sebastian's shoulders then, tucking it in where his hands are white-knuckled, clenching his elbows in tight to his body.

"You're going into shock, sir," Ren says, but his voice is starting to sound far away like the people in the ballroom had. Sebastian blinks back against the words slowly, shaking his head from side to side as Ren says something else, trying to slide him further down the wall. Sebastian jerks away from his touch, the heat from his fingertips unpleasant. He can feel his heart trying to bang its way out of his ribcage, and it seems to be having some effect on his ability to breathe. It's as if his lungs won't do it. He shouldn't have to breathe *manually*, they should just *do it* for him.

He recalls vaguely feeling this breathless just once before. He'd been fourteen, at boarding school, and Ivan had called to say his mother had killed herself. Sebastian was initially rather surprised it had actually worked, given all those previous attempts and subsequent stints in the clinic. Ivan said she threw herself off the roof of their apartment building. Seemed like she really meant it this time. Sebastian agreed.

His chest had felt similarly tight then as it does now, the connection between his lungs and his brain seemingly cut off altogether. Shutting down, as he pushes away the feelings he's uncertain how to deal with.

Sebastian therefore can't resist Ren when he plants his hands on his shoulders and forces him down again. He's got his long fingers flush with the hollow of Sebastian's throat, clumsily unfurling his bowtie and yanking the top button of his shirt off in his haste. He drops the button and it gets lost between the folds of the shirt and Sebastian's skin. Sebastian can feel the mother-of-pearl digging into his flesh.

How *aggravating*, he thinks as Ren continues to loosen his shirt. The back of his head is on the floor now, and Ren is tucking his own jacket around Sebastian snugly, constantly yapping into that earpiece. What is he even saying?

Sebastian's eyelids feel heavy, his line of sight bleary as he tries to focus on Ren's empty, dark eyes. He'd thought they were black, but they're actually just a very dark shade of brown. He lets his eyes wander between Ren's other features, distracting himself from the way the edge of his vision seems to be darkening with each second that passes. Ren has a long, proud nose. He's exceptionally clean shaven, not a whisper of hair on any smooth expanse of his face. His jaw is sharp though, masculine. Sebastian wonders vaguely what his collarbone looks like and scandalised laughter escapes him.

It brings something else with it, but he manages to tilt his head to one side as he starts to vomit. Maybe setting the worms in his belly free is a better idea than trying to keep them down? But what if his father finds him?

Sebastian tries to sit up, a new wave of panic suddenly clenching his throat, like fat fingers holding him down and forcing him to smell the bile as it seeps into the carpet. (His father says it's a waste of the whiskey which is *damn good stuff*, and if Sebastian wants to be *respected like a man* and not treated like the *sissy he acts like* he needs to *learn to like it*.)

Someone is rolling him onto his side so he doesn't choke, but he tries to shove them off. Sebastian doesn't need their help, doesn't want it, it's worse if he doesn't just deal with it on his own, he can *deal with it on his own*.

"Sir, can you hear me? The paramedics are on their way sir, just hang in there," the person—what did he say his name was again?—the person with dark eyes, hollow eyes, so black (no, not black, *very dark brown*) is above him. His hair is tickling Sebastian's cheeks; he's so close, and the man smells delectable, like he'd taste just as good if Sebastian ran his tongue along the length of that sharp jaw. But he's covered in his own vomit, (how fucking embarrassing), and so is this man—so is this man's jacket. *Covered* in Sebastian's vomit. His father is going to fucking kill him.

Sebastian feels the press of something dry over his mouth, wiping vomit and spittle off his chin, feels a steady hand reach to grasp his own. He twitches away instinctively, self-preservation intact despite all else. The hand doesn't give in, and hot fingers twine around his own. He can feel the unfamiliar warmth of someone else's palm. It's sturdy and a little rough.

"Just hang in there, sir," the same voice says, as hair is brushed from his forehead. It's sloppy and wet with perspiration.

Ren, Sebastian thinks then—his name is *Ren*, like the little brown bird. Their hands are entwined together, fingers interlocked as Ren leans over him. He can feel Ren's pulse humming at the edge of his palm, like a bird's—like a wren's.

Sebastian wonders how bad he must look right now, sweat slick and gasping, as Ren's perfect features swim in his view. Then, darkness corrodes the edges of his vision and quite suddenly, he cannot wonder anything at all.

Two

Sebastian wakes up in his bed.

His head throbs, the backs of his eyes burn. His mouth, sour and dry. A hangover. No. He rubs at his face, picking apart eyelashes which are glued together. The curtains are open and the light which pours through stings. Must be a hangover. *No.*

He recalls the bang of the gun ripping through the air first, the feeling of his back hitting hard wooden boards next. His head had been protected though, wide hands sheltering him as he tumbled down and his champagne sloshed over his suit. His father had blood on him. *Just grazed him*, the hollow-eyed man had said.

Sebastian blinks through the blear, his sunshine soaked bedroom coming into focus, the door slightly ajar. He frowns.

He doesn't sleep with the door open, ever.

"You're awake, sir?"

Ivan steps into the room, sensing Sebastian's subtle movements with ease. He's as unassuming as ever, dressed in the same boring suit he'd worn to the party last night. Fair hair slicked back, collar appropriately stiff, tie still ramrod straight. He's got these eyes like a shark, Sebastian thinks, pale and watery. They display the appropriate level of concern, bushy brows furrowed as thin lips curve in almost-amusement. There's a scar which splits the right corner of his smile open further than it should.

"We had Dr Warren give you something to help you sleep once she'd looked you over. How are you feeling? Do you remember what happened last night?"

Sebastian's mouth curls into a grimace and he rubs at the inner corners of his eyes.

"What time is it? Did you have her give me pills or hit me over the head with a fucking iron?" he asks dryly, running a hand through his already dishevelled hair. It's matted and unkempt. He's bare chested. He lifts the duvet to check he's not been stripped naked under the sheets by that over enthusiastic doctor his father keeps on staff. He's wearing the same briefs he'd worn last night, so that's something.

Ivan smiles.

"It's just gone midday. She said given how bad the panic attack was in conjunction with your previous head injury, you might feel a bit worse for wear today. Do you remember what happened last night? Dr Warren was very clear that I should test your recall."

"*Yes*, Ivan," Sebastian snaps, looking back up from where he's studying himself below the covers. "I remember what happened. Is something funny about my birthday party being ruined and my father being shot?"

Ivan's smile doesn't drop, he just shakes his head.

"Not at all, sir." Sebastian jerks his chin in frustration.

"Then what are you smirking about? Did I piss the bed or something?"

Ivan barks out a laugh.

"Not this time, sir."

"Fuck off, old man," Sebastian groans, leaning back onto his pillows and gazing up at the ceiling. The chandelier needs to be dusted. He can see the whisper thin tendril of a spider's web connecting one crystal teardrop with the next. His head hurts. "If you're not going to say or do anything useful, then get the fuck out."

"Do you want to hear about what happened last night? Beyond what you remember?"

Sebastian lets his eyes slide shut, trying to focus on the feeling of the soft down pillows enveloping his head rather than the shooting pain behind his right eye.

"I thought I was very clear about what I want," he mutters. He hears Ivan shift a little where he stands, weight moving from foot to foot. He's getting impatient, which is mildly entertaining.

"I can have Ren brief you later, if you'd prefer. I had hoped to introduce you formally last night, but he tells me you've been well acquainted with each other now," Ivan says smoothly. There's silence for a moment as Sebastian lets his eyes peel open again. The spider's web sways.

"Ren," he says.

There's silence again. Sebastian sits up straight, bed sheets rustling below him. Ivan nods.

"Yes, your new personal bodyguard. He'll still be reporting to me, and therefore ultimately the president, but he'll be your point of contact going ahead for security needs. Ren," Ivan raises his voice just an increment on the last word, and Sebastian watches as Ren slips easily into the room.

The same hollow eyes as last night meet Sebastian's, their owner bowing his head in a show of respect. Ren wears inexpensive cologne, subtle but resinous, like the remnants of incense. It makes Sebastian's nose tingle. He's as well turned out as Ivan is, similar unremarkable charcoal suit, no jacket. Sebastian watches the way his muscles shift below his crisp shirt as he stands up straight. His shoulders are broad, enough to shield an entire body from a potential shooter lurking in a crowd. No jacket…?

Sebastian remembers then.

"I threw up on you," he mutters, pressing his palm to his forehead and trying to force the fucking stabbing out of his brain.

"I won't hold it against you, sir," Ren says, his voice a monotonous rumble. Sebastian raises an eyebrow, the lack of expression on the other man's face bizarre. Is he trying to make a joke? No. The tone of his voice is utterly without inflection.

"I wouldn't think so," Sebastian replies immediately, eyes flickering to look at Ivan's smug features before land-ing back on Ren's passive ones. "I've pissed the bed on Ivan before, haven't I, Ivan?"

One time, after a sorority party turned feral rave; anoth-er after a nightmare so vivid he'd woken himself up yelling. Sebastian can't remember what it was about now.

"Not in a long time, sir," Ivan says graciously, like he's doing him a favour. Sebastian rolls his eyes.

"No need to grovel quite so ferociously. I'm still not even vice president," he adds, watching Ivan's sharklike gaze twinkle with amusement. Ren doesn't let his stare drop from Sebastian once, and it's impossibly unnerving. Sebastian tugs the duvet up a little further, concealing his bare chest from view and shooting Ren the most syrupy smile he can muster (given the stabbing pain in his head). "He hasn't blinked once since he came in here. I think he likes what he sees, Ivan. Are you sure he'll protect my virtue? What if he takes advantage of me?"

Sebastian lets his voice teeter up in pitch, squeezing his eyes shut like some kind of hysterical maiden in a pantomime.

"Just giving you a once over, sir. You weren't well at all last night," Ren says solemnly, tucking his hands behind his back. Sebastian frowns, sinking down into the mattress as his expression drops.

"Oh, you're no fun at *all*, are you?" he says.

Ivan claps his hands together.

"On that note, I'll leave the rest to you, Ren. Sir, the president would like to see you when you're feeling up to it. He's already been awake for some time. Perhaps after you're cleaned and dressed?"

Sebastian watches Ivan sweep out of the room, instruction sitting pretty in the stiff air he leaves behind. He hears the words left to linger unsaid; *get out of bed, make yourself presentable, make sure it's in the next hour.*

He flops back on his pillows, jaw clenched.

"I need a fucking Advil," he mutters, reaching over to his bedside table to call for a maid. Ren twitches forwards.

"I can grab you some if you tell me where they are," he says. Sebastian snorts at him.

"You're not a man-servant, *Ren*," he says, rolling the name leisurely across his tongue. It's pretty, like the man himself. Simple, no fuss. "You're security. Stand there and shut up and make me feel secure."

Sebastian dials the phone by his bed and has someone bring the painkillers and coffee. When he's finished, he frowns over at Ren, immovable in the same position as when he first entered the room.

"Where did you put my jacket? I need a smoke," he says. Ren frowns.

"Your jacket is being dry-cleaned. I didn't know you smoked," he responds. Sebastian clicks his tongue against the roof of his mouth impatiently, but Ren is already reaching into his own pocket and producing a pack of cigarettes and a lighter. They're not the brand Sebastian likes, some cheap imitation, but nicotine is nicotine and his veins are positively humming at the thought of it.

Ren just continues to stand, staring at him. Sebastian watches him for a moment more than he should do, face creasing in confusion.

"What the hell is the matter with you? Give me a cig-arette," he snaps. Sebastian wonders if Ren will challenge the blatant antagonism of his conflicting instructions. *Stand there and shut up and make me feel secure.*

Ren just raises a careful brow—they're well groomed. Does he wax them or pluck them—?

"Sorry, sir," Ren says promptly, crossing to his bedside and tapping a cigarette free of the pack. Sebastian leans forwards, letting the duvet slip out of his fingers and fall around his waist. He meets Ren's hollow gaze as he parts his lips, tongue peeking forth from between his teeth. The edges of his mouth twitch up.

"Put it in my mouth," he instructs carefully, gazing up through his lashes. Some of Ren's shiny dark hair falls forwards into his eyes as he looks down at Sebastian. He sets the cigarette between his lips without further hesitation, tucking the pack away and swiftly igniting his lighter. He shields the tip of the cigarette with a cup of his palm, which is criss-crossed with dry skin and blisters. *Rough,* just like Sebastian remembers it feeling last night.

Sebastian takes a deep breath, steadying the cigarette with his index and middle finger and reclining back all at once. Ren hovers at his bedside, expression neutral, unprovoked.

It sets a spark of annoyance alight in Sebastian's chest. He is well equipped with how to interpret the quiet fury of his father. These days, it's almost entertaining to see how far he can push before he runs the risk of retribution. He can comfortably absorb the constant idiotic babble of girls at parties, so desperate to be different from their peers. He makes sure to tell them what they want to hear, makes each one feel as individually special as the other. He understands the potent smell of desperation pouring out of the middle management in his father's company when he's presented to shake hands. He knows how to simultaneously inspire fear and respect, which ones to banter with and which ones to purr at. All of it comes easily to him, years of his life spent training every muscle in his face to portray exactly what he wants it to, when he wants it to (because he's *his father's son*, and he *understands what's at stake here*—).

Ren betrays *nothing*. Not a hair out of place, no twitch in his jaw. No matter what Sebastian has said so far, he's garnered no reaction and it's downright *fascinating*. Perhaps he's just as skilled as Sebastian is when it comes to the mask he wears.

Sebastian wonders how far he'll have to push to watch it crack.

He offers up a poisonous grin as smoke pools out either side of his mouth.

"So? Tell me about yourself, Ren," he says evenly, as a maid raps her knuckles gently on the door and carries in a small tray with the coffee and Advil. Ren steps out of her way as she lays it out on Sebastian's nightstand, pours the hot liquid with meticulous care. Sebastian catches her gaze wander over to him, sees the pert pink blush smother her squishy cheeks. He takes a drag on his cigarette, smiling luxuriously around the filter as she looks away.

"About myself?" Ren asks. "Don't you want me to debrief you on last night, sir? Before you meet with the president?"

Sebastian runs his tongue over the points of his canine teeth, reaching over to lift the coffee cup and delicately replacing it with his cigarette on the saucer. He snatches up the two Advil, swallows them dry before chasing the bitter pills with espresso. He taps the cigarette free of ash, takes another drag, all the while watching Ren coldly.

"My my," he hums. "Ivan made you in his fucking image, didn't he? He's got a nasty habit of telling me what I want as well."

Ren blinks, unperturbed.

"What would you like to know?"

Sebastian chews the question over, mouth flooded with the tang of black coffee. Cigarette smoke lingers on his tongue, lungs burning with the cheap tar. He wrinkles his nose.

"Why do you smoke this brand of cigarette?" he says. "They're disgusting."

Ren tilts his head, like a bird considering an insect it wants to swallow. It's the first indicator he's given that there's anything going on inside that pretty head of his.

"Aren't all cigarettes disgusting?" he replies, tone edging towards curiosity. Sebastian's temper flares like the glowing amber tip of the cigarette as it steals his breath.

"Don't answer a question with a question," he snaps, smoke rushing from his nostrils, and then, "But yes. I suppose they are."

A beat passes as Sebastian flicks ash onto the saucer again. Smoke curls up between the two of them to caress Ren's face like a beckoning finger.

"They're reasonably cheap, but strong," he tells Sebastian. "I'm trying to quit."

"No point," Sebastian informs him, stubbing the end of the cigarette out in his half-drunk coffee. The pain behind his eye is fading, now only surging every other minute. It's as if someone is snapping an elastic band repeatedly against his optic nerve. He grins past the sharp snap. "What if I misplace my own again? It's better if my personal security smokes too, no matter how shitty his taste is."

Silence falls across the room again. Sebastian can hear the faint noises of the city far below the penthouse apartment. He sighs deeply.

"Like blood from a stone. I'm bored of you now, I need to get ready," he says, pushing the duvet back and off his legs and standing to make his way over to his ensuite to shower. He slides his thumbs smoothly across his stomach as he goes, hooking them into the waistband of his briefs and tugging as he reaches the bathroom.

Sebastian turns the faucet on, palm extending, retracting, extending until he's satisfied with the temperature. The soft hiss of the water accompanies the smell of his shampoo as he lathers his greasy hair up. He feels it clumped together on one side. He scrubs harder, tries not to linger on the fact it's probably congealed vomit. A laugh escapes as he thinks of himself—poised below Ren on the bed, mouth pink and wet and waiting as he teased him for the cigarette and the whole time he's had fucking vomit smeared across his head.

He takes his time cleaning his face, lathering his hair with conditioner, before brushing his teeth. He supposes it's been about half an hour since Ivan told him his father was expecting him. That leaves about twenty-five minutes to waste before he cuts it *just* fine enough.

"Well then?" Sebastian asks, as he exits the bathroom, towel wrapped around his waist. Ren is sitting up straight in the armchair by the floor to ceiling window, the door still ajar as another maid makes Sebastian's bed and takes his breakfast tray away. Ren stands when Sebastian addresses him, like he's a fucking drill sergeant or something. Sebastian snorts.

"At ease, dickhead," he says as he opens his wardrobe and considers what to wear. His hair drips freshly scented drops of water onto his bare shoulders and back. He can feel Ren's eyes hot on his neck—it makes him shiver with something primal. He redirects his thoughts sharply to the matter at hand. "Who tried to shoot my father?"

Sebastian tilts the wardrobe door back a little so he can see Ren's reflection in the mirror there. His stare reveals nothing, glassy, professional.

He shakes his head once, a clear negation of Sebastian's statement.

"We don't think they were trying to shoot the president," Ren says. "We think they were trying to shoot you."

Sebastian drops the towel from around his waist and selects a new pair of briefs. He bends over leisurely as he slides into them, dragging them slowly up his thighs and snapping them in place. He glances back in the mirror. Ren is looking out the window, jaw still set. Sebastian grins.

"And why do you think that?" he asks brightly, idly pawing through his clothes. He's meeting his father, so he wants something well made and expensive. Enough to set his teeth on edge at the potential cost of Sebastian's chosen wardrobe, but that looks undeniably well draped across his lithe form.

"The angle of the bullet. The fact it grazed the president on his left side suggests he wasn't the target. You moved back just before the gun went off, meaning it's more likely the shooter was aiming for you—"

"Yes, yes, that's all fascinating," Sebastian cuts Ren's clipped speech off, sliding a cashmere sweater over his head as he turns. It settles just below his collarbone, thin, low cut. Sebastian thinks he catches Ren's eyes narrowing, but decides ultimately it must be a trick of the light. "But I didn't ask for a play-by-play, I asked *why* you think someone would try to shoot *me*?"

Ren studies him for a moment, mulling over his answer, perhaps. Sebastian watches, waiting for a chink in the armour, *something* to indicate anything going on inside his head, but it doesn't come.

"Any number of reasons, sir," he says carefully. "The impact on the president being a major one—his son, assassinated on stage beside him on his twenty-first birthday could be detrimental to his own health. It could spell major unrest for the company; two birds with one stone."

Sebastian tilts his head, lower lip jutting out as if in consideration of the statement. He grins widely at Ren, finding it difficult to contain his amusement. As if there aren't countless little bastard heirs scrabbling around trying to get on the payroll. His father has plenty of insurance.

"What you possess in analytical skills, you lack in creativity, Ren," Sebastian says, lips curling over his name again. He finds he likes the way it fits in his mouth. He wonders how his name would sound coming from the other man, not just the clipped single syllable of 'sir.'

Seb—a—sti—an.

(Pressed against his neck, *wet* heat—)

"What's the time?" he asks suddenly, the expected flutter of panic shuddering through his core. Ren checks his watch, a simple thing but well looked after.

"Five until one," he says. Sebastian swallows down the butterflies and makes for the door immediately, gesturing vaguely for Ren to follow.

"Have you met my father properly yet?" he asks as they walk, heading to the end of the corridor to the stairs leading up to his father's suite. Ren shakes his head.

"Not officially, sir. He was away on business during my induction."

Sebastian meets Ren's hollow eyes, lips peeling away from his teeth in what begins as a smile, but definitely resembles more of a grimace.

"You won't like him," Sebastian says surely. "No one ever does. He likes that, though. Makes him feel supreme, untouchable. He hates when people kiss his ass, so don't do that."

They finish climbing the stairs to the president's suite, Sebastian's fingers skittering along the shiny brass of the doorknob as he licks his lips in anticipation. There's something thrilling about crossing the threshold here. Poised to toe the line between the begrudging approval that Sebastian can't help but crave and the reminder of imminent peril in the sting behind his right eye.

"Do you like him, sir?"

Sebastian jerks at Ren's question, forehead furrowing in consideration. The man's face is as immovable as ever, but there's something more in the depths of his expression. It's searching, invasive. It makes Sebastian feel sick, like Ren is trying to reach inside him and tug something out—something he doesn't want to let go of.

Sebastian smiles easily.

"Of course. He's my father."

Three

Sebastian tops two red cups of whiskey with coke, each humming with pleasant effervescence, and takes a gulp from one. He tries to channel the bubbly levity of the drinks into his smile as he wanders his way into the crowd and hands the other cup to the first woman he sees. She's wearing a cardigan with Greek letters, some sorority girl playing nice during rush week.

He listens to her compliment his signet ring before she starts telling some meandering story. His eyes fall half-lidded as he watches her lips move, his arm subtly brushing the length of hers when she leans in towards him.

Sebastian sips his drink as he thinks mildly of the meeting with his father after his ill-fated twenty-first birthday party three weeks ago. His father asks him *how fucking long he expects him to wait around* for Sebastian, declares he's too old to still be having those hissy fits. Sebastian watches Ivan subtly avoid his gaze. Ever the president's faithful dog, Ivan reports it all back. Sebastian apologises, says he was just worried about his father. It's gruffly brushed off, a show of sincerity too raw for the old man to take. It makes Sebastian's chest buzz with satisfaction.

They'll simply throw another twenty-first birthday party, his father says, a *show of force*. Business as usual, because you can't let *the bastards* think they're winning. Sebastian's not sure who *the bastards* are that think they're winning and he's certain his father doesn't know either, but he nods along anyway. He's to attend his classes and social events as normal, combine the annual company Halloween party with his reinvigorated twenty-first birthday celebrations—it'll be more cost effective that way. Sebastian wonders when his father started caring about cost effectiveness.

His father gives Ren a once over, says make sure that *new hound* knows what he's doing, Ivan. If Ren dislikes being referred to as a hound, his father's preferred moniker for their security staff, he doesn't emote. Sebastian is not surprised.

Sebastian gazes into the fuzzy brown liquid in his cup, before he catches a stray curl which has fallen from behind the girl's ear. She pauses in whatever she's saying, blood rushing to her cheeks, her eyes glazing over a little. She's got some kind of glitter smeared across her face for the party, an unnecessary addition; an attempt to seem interesting.

Sebastian offers her a coy smile, tucking the curl back and leaning in a little closer to her as her friends seem to finally get the hint, turning away to busy themselves elsewhere.

As he leads her through the crowd, he feels the sting of piercing dark eyes on the back of his neck from the other side of the room. A thrill runs through Sebastian, the game set in motion.

Let's see him keep tabs on me, Sebastian thinks. Let's see.

It's the first chance he's had in the three weeks since Ren's hasty induction to have a little fun. He's done nothing but be annoyingly diligent, lurking around each of his classes and escorting him home.

Sebastian squeezes the girl's hand and makes some show about wanting to give her a tour of the frat house. His family's company owns it, built it in fact, when his great grandfather was president, and he's spent the past two years of university exploring every corner and finding the best spots for he and his friends to hang out in.

Some of it is true, some of it is not. Sebastian finds the best place to spin himself the ideal personality is straddling the facts of it all. *Yes*, his family built the frat house, *sometimes,* depending on his level of boredom he'd explore the floors beyond the private library he studies in, *no*, he has no friends to hang out with.

The girl has given up the game of pretending like she's a demure little madam. She's draping herself over him now, running her finger as seductively as she can muster down the seam of his shirt, darting around the buttons like she wants to pop them open. He doubts she would; she seems like the type to have some respect for fine tailoring.

He decides to give her what she wants, doubling back the way they'd come in the hopes he can further disorient his new watchdog (who he *knows* is following and who he *hopes* is becoming steadily more aggravated as they go).

Sebastian lets himself into the ground floor disabled bathroom, his guest gasping in delight at the impropriety of it all.

The door shuts with a bang behind them and the first thing Sebastian does is cross the room to pull the wooden shutters closed. The girl makes a noise which she tries to play off as a trill of intrigue, but is really rather annoyed. Why doesn't Sebastian want to 'gaze at her in all her womanly glory below the light of the moon?' is what he imagines she's thinking.

He returns to her side, ducking his nose into the curve where her neck meets her shoulder and ghosts the tip of his nose along the skin there. The girl shivers, says something vaguely arousing about how she wants him inside her. Sebastian mouths wetly at her skin, the overwhelming floral notes of her mid-range perfume catching in the back of his throat and making him quietly gag. He conceals it by taking hold of some of her soft flesh between his teeth, sucking a small red mark into it with ease.

He'd have preferred she just go down on him, but supposes that beggars can't be choosers. The urgent way in which the girl is tugging his shirt free from his belt isn't the most sensual thing in the world, but he's only human. Every brush of her warm palm against his cock makes it twitch with intrigue, despite the heavy feeling which settles over Sebastian's body.

Disinterest. Mild dread. A cold twinge of panic.

It all coils up tight in his intestines, tying him in knots as the girl leans up to try to kiss him.

Sebastian deflects by grasping her on either side of her hips and spinning her so she's folded over the countertop and sink. She seems shocked at first, her eyes blown wide as she meets his gaze in the mirror, but Sebastian just sinks his fingers further into the meat of her ass as he uses his other hand to hike her dress up around her hips.

He might have let her kiss him on a good day, but she's wearing some kind of strawberry lip-gloss and the thought of the sticky residue left on his mouth makes him want to vomit. Sebastian *hates* lip-gloss.

The girl takes the hint, reaching around and sliding her underwear down until they're just hooked around one ankle, and in a show of reward for her eager attention, Sebastian reaches around and grasps one of her tits. He continues to lavish the back of her neck with kisses and nibbles, the sharp cries of over-inflated pleasure coming from her mouth irritating. He'll cover her mouth when he starts to fuck her (under the guise of remaining undiscovered, of course). He thumbs at the pebble of her nipple, laments the soft weight of her breast in his palm as he fishes around in his pocket with his other hand, producing a condom. He lets go of her chest, unzipping himself and freeing his erection in one smooth movement. He's tearing the condom open and preparing to unroll it when he becomes aware of the sudden stillness in the bathroom.

The girl is no longer writhing and making little breathy sounds, watching Sebastian intently in the mirror. He pauses in his ministrations, wondering why the fuck she's stopped. She's waiting for something; she cocks an eyebrow in query and Sebastian realises she must have asked him a question.

Fuck.

"Did you hear what I said?" she asks carefully, rising up a little on her elbows to better see him in the mirror. Sebastian stares back into her wide gaze, adjusting to the darkness; he notices for the first time how green her eyes are. He tries not to pay too much attention to her exposed pussy, poised hungrily towards him.

He bunches up her skirt and shields it from view; then offers her his most charming smile.

"I'm sorry, I was distracted," he says roughly, letting his gaze flicker momentarily to where his dick sits barely hard in his hand. The girl raises a brow, a slow grin crossing her features. She's amused by that, Sebastian thinks. Women like it when they think they wield some power over hopeless, sex-crazed men. Sebastian thinks it's rather ironic, her thinking she has any kind of power in this situation, bent over the sink fully clothed as she is. He doesn't say so.

"I *said*, I want you to say my name," the girl says emphatically, coquettishly dragging her teeth along her bottom lip, apparently a repetition of an earlier demand.

Sebastian's erection has all but entirely shrunk away in disinterest now. He lets out a low breath, fighting the barb of annoyance that stings at his pride. There's no way he'll be able to drum up enough arousal to get hard again.

The moment of silence is enough to make the girl jerk up straight.

"What's my name?" she demands then, and her fair cheeks are spoiled with two angry red splotches as she tilts her head. The loose curl Sebastian had tucked away earlier falls free again. He wonders absently if she'd told him her name as he'd traced the shell of her ear. He tucks his dick back into his slacks.

He half-grins to himself as the girl whips around to face him.

"Would it help if I said I was just so overwhelmed by how hot you are, or...?"

The girl is yanking her underwear back up her legs, ugly pink spots on her cheeks having developed into a roaring red blush, which seems to have overwhelmed her ears too.

"Fuck you, *pretty boy*," she manages to spit at him. She draws out the sneer, no doubt reaching around her vocabulary for something more cutting. Sebastian presses his lips together to avoid the laugh which is threatening to free itself from his chest. Not entirely good for his image, forgetting a girl's name after pointedly refusing to kiss her, but he's been in dicier scenarios with these types of women.

There'll be another stranger somewhere at this party who, when faced with the insistence from this girl that he's a piece of shit, will defend his honour with vigour. He might have to eat said stranger out to ensure this happens (which is itself an irritation), but Sebastian supposes he's got no one to blame for that problem but himself.

"*Pretty boy*?" he can't help but repeat as the girl crosses to the bathroom door and yanks on the handle. She nearly tugs it off its hinges in her haste to escape. Sebastian gives up trying to stifle his amusement as he watches her curly head disappear down the hall. "Don't tell me you don't remember *my* name?"

"Fuck you!" she yells again, flipping him off over her shoulder.

"It's not a good idea to disappear into a crowd when you've recently been shot at, sir," Ren's voice comes from behind where Sebastian is watching the girl round the corner, low and pointed. Sebastian turns on his heel to see his watchdog leaning against the wall casually, red cup in hand, as if he's just waiting on the bathroom being free. He's dressed down, all dark colours and man-made fabrics giving away how cheap he is. Sebastian doesn't think it's a good disguise at all, given the average net worth of every member of his fraternity and the company they keep.

His interest is piqued however by the edge to Ren's words, sharp enough that they cut through the buzz of activity around them in the hall. Amongst his otherwise dull exterior, it's enough to make Sebastian forget all about whatever the fuck he's just been doing.

"You don't sound happy to see me, though?" he says, pushing his bottom lip out a little. "Smoke?" Ren raises one of his carefully groomed brows and stands up straight off the wall. He's still half a head shorter than Sebastian.

"Fine. Back patio is secure," he says and then, "you've been trying to ditch me all night, sir." He looks away from Sebastian's pout and into the contents of his cup. He swirls it around as if deep in thought, slamming what's left of it back with finality. Sebastian frowns.

"Have I?" he asks innocently, brushing past Ren and continuing his path down the hall. Ren keeps pace with him, the subtle contact of his arm against Sebastian's eliciting a tingle. The hairs on the backs of his forearms stand on end. Ren sighs.

"You have," he confirms, setting his cup down as they pass a fine marble bust of Sebastian's ancestor (someone-or-other who paid for a new lawn after the football team pissed it into subsidence). Sebastian steps deliberately to one side to put a little more distance between the two of them as they approach the back patio doors.

"And yet here you are. I must not be trying hard enough," Sebastian pulls his cigarette case from his back pocket, unclasping the silver and flipping it open. As they come to lean on the patio railing, he sets a cigarette on his lip, eyes casting a wary glance around the other party goers littered about. It's not busy out here, given the sudden chill that September has started to cling to every leaf with. A few more people disappear back inside when they catch sight of Sebastian, their eyes flitting away when he looks at them.

He frowns, unsure if it's the recent assassination attempt or Ren's enigmatic presence that is driving people away.

Ren produces his lighter without Sebastian even glancing in his direction, holding it out in silent offering. Sebastian leans forwards, inspecting the Zippo more closely than he had the last time, the pale porch light highlighting its weathered appearance.

He meets Ren's hollow gaze over the flame as he snuffs it out, inhaling deeply. Something about it irks Sebastian, invasive and probing, like he's dried up roadkill being picked apart by buzzards.

"What?" he asks, working annoyingly hard to keep his tone even. Ren lights his own cigarette, leaning over the railing and looking out at the lawn beyond. He shoots Sebastian a sideways glance.

"Her name was Philippa," he says.

Sebastian blinks once, twice, before taking another drag on his cigarette.

"Philippa?" he repeats. Ren nods, turning his head to gaze back at him. He's as immovable as ever, unperturbed.

"Yes. Pip for short, she said."

Sebastian waves a hand impatiently between them, that annoyance catching on the edges of the glimmering personality he's been wearing for this evening's festivities.

"*Who*?"

Ren frowns.

"The girl. That you were having sex with in the bathroom," he adds, glancing around the patio carefully, as if anyone at this party gives a flying fuck about what they're discussing. Sebastian snorts.

"I didn't have sex with her, actually," he says.

"Fine. The one you *tried* to have sex with."

Something in the way Ren rolls his eyes irritates Sebastian, that familiar pain pinging at the back of his right eye. He can feel his smooth expression curl into something sharper. He leans in, lets smoke pool from between his lips and fan across Ren's jaw.

"What's *that* supposed to mean?" he asks, perilously close to losing his grip on the conversation. Ren blinks, the tip of his cigarette glowing as he inhales deeply. He very decidedly blows the smoke out the side of his mouth, away from Sebastian. Something plays at the edges of that immovable face, something smug, something *knowing*.

"It means I heard you telling her you didn't know her name and her getting the hell out of there," Ren says calmly, taking a long drag on his cigarette again as his dark eyes flicker across Sebastian's face. Searching for something, trying his best to pull him apart, Sebastian can *feel* it. Ren's mouth quirks at the edge then, a glimmer of a smile. "Very smooth, by the way."

Despite Sebastian's initial appraisal, he suddenly realises there's nothing *impassive* about Ren. He's constantly examining every inch of Sebastian's face for a peek below the surface. It's steadfast determination, not cold indifference.

That suggestion of a smile makes Sebastian feel like his skin has caught fire, set ablaze just by being in this man's orbit. It travels across his body, pools in his gut; his dick suddenly feels heavy and neglected, left wanting by the unsatisfactory encounter before. The tips of his fingers sting, buzzing with electricity.

Sebastian's wrist twinges then, the one his father had broken when he was a very small child, as if in answer to the sudden arousal which chases along after the very blood in his veins. No, he thinks urgently. It's just the sudden chill in the air.

As if in response, the ever-lingering pain behind his eye throbs uncomfortably, a reminder of what it is to succumb to his attraction to other men. What it feels like to be hit over the head with a crystal decanter.

His cigarette has nearly burnt out, so he takes one last drag and kills it. As he stubs it out, Sebastian rearranges his features with ease, tilting his head in amusement towards Ren. He smiles on the side of his face and Ren's dark eyes once again swallow up his senses.

"Philippa, you said? Who the fuck is called *Philippa*? It's 1997 for Christ's sake. How the hell was I supposed to remember that?"

"Pip, for short, sir."

"What are you, her fucking publicist?" Sebastian rolls his eyes, flicking his cigarette butt into the lawn. He sighs and cradles his chin in his palm, leaning heavily on the railing. "So, while you were busy finding out the horoscopes of all the women I might fuck tonight, did you find any leads on who might have tried to have me killed?"

Ren shakes his head, throwing a furtive glance over his shoulder. Sebastian twists his head to gaze up at him, frowning in irritation.

"Relax, Fido, we're all alone," he says. Ren frowns then too, brows squeezing together a little in confusion. The minute swell in expression makes Sebastian's mouth dry up.

"Fido?" Ren asks. Sebastian grins.

"Yeah, like a little dog, right? Fido? Because dad calls you *hounds*," Sebastian explains. He wrinkles his nose in amusement as he straightens up from where he's been leaning on his palm so he looms over Ren. It doesn't appear to faze him, which makes Sebastian's chest positively hum with glee. Ren's mouth curls down at the edge in displeasure. Sebastian grins. "Oh. You don't like that, do you?"

Ren's eyes twitch a modicum tighter.

"No, sir. I don't," he replies bluntly, matching the antagonistic exhilaration of Sebastian's gaze with his own solemn one. Sebastian can't stop his grin from twitching wider.

"I applaud your honesty. That's why dad likes Ivan; he always tells the truth, tells him *everything*, including all the naughty things I occasionally get caught up in." Sebastian fingers the hem of Ren's jacket, toying with the zipper thoughtfully, suddenly emboldened to try to draw more of a reaction from him. His grin fades a little, voice rough when he speaks again. "Are you going to be the same? Report everything I do back to daddy dearest? Is that why you took such care to learn dear old Pip's name?"

"I work for the president, sir," Ren responds immediately, the party line drilled into him no doubt by Ivan from the moment he was accepted into the post. "My job is to protect you and, by virtue, the future and image of the company. I don't have any discretion when it comes to what might or might not cause any of those things harm."

"Of course," Sebastian replies airily, further encroaching on Ren's personal space, barely able to resist the urge to keep falling forwards into the dark brown pits of his eyes. "Makes total sense. I understand."

"I'm sure you do, sir," Ren says. He pauses for another instant, scrutinising the sharp edge of Sebastian's face. He lifts his thumb without a second thought, the pad finding the space where Sebastian's jaw meets his neck. He rubs it against the skin there with purpose. His eyes meet Sebastian's again.

If he notices the way Sebastian's breath has caught in his throat, he doesn't comment. Sebastian feels lightheaded, suddenly enveloped in the heady scent that clings to Ren. It feels like he's stepped into the all-encompassing humidity of a palm house, heat pressing down on his lungs with insistence. Ren's tongue slides along his bottom lip. Sebastian leans in. Not unconscious; deliberate.

"You have glitter on you," Ren says simply. "A memento from… 'dear old Pip.'"

Sebastian doesn't have time to flounder for a response. A bright flash of light yanks the pair out of the smothering tension which has settled around them, going off somewhere in the bushes which line the lawn.

Ren's hand drops instantaneously, Sebastian's stomach following suit.

A camera flash.

Four

"Your meeting with the president has been cancelled, sir; there's a press conference he's been asked to contribute to at the last minute. He won't be flying back until tomorrow night."

Sebastian feels granted instant reprieve from the weight which has lingered on his chest for the past week. It's as if he's been left buried in concrete, freshly set around his body but not yet filling up his lungs with cold, wet sand. He nods at his father's new secretary (he switches them out when they start wondering if they should finally bring the sexual assault accusations to the press—makes them sign fat NDAs in exchange for a final salary pay-off), taking a moment to compose himself. He rearranges his features so they appear more irate, subtle annoyance as opposed to gasping relief.

"Typical," he huffs, shoving a hand into his pocket. "Any idea of a reschedule?"

The woman nods, flipping through the pages of her diary. She's barely a woman, Sebastian thinks, as she taps her polished nails along the paper, in as much as he's barely a man. So recently crowned an adult, despite never having even cooked himself a meal.

"Yes, he had me make dinner reservations for the two of you at Carlito's. Next Monday," the secretary says, flashing Sebastian her most practised megawatt smile. She has a particularly sharp canine tooth, a flaw in her otherwise well-crafted exterior. Sebastian mirrors her expression, watching as she shrinks back a little, her cheeks all of a sudden rosier.

"Thank you. What was your name again?" he asks, dropping his voice as he deliberately leans across her desk, head tilting incrementally. He watches her through his lashes, the great gulp of air she pulls into her lungs before she smiles again—hazier, this time, like she's blinded by how attractive he is.

"My name is Melinda," Melinda says, breathless, enchanted.

Sebastian nods, as if he hasn't already begun to forget it.

"Nice to meet you," he says smoothly. "I'm Sebastian Clarence."

She lets out a nervous little chuckle, somewhere between a bashful sigh and a polite laugh.

"Oh, yes. I know who you are, Mr Clarence," she manages to say, glancing down at her diary again.

Sebastian steps back from her desk, shooting a purposeful glance at Ren who's been lingering at his side like a bad smell. Without another word, they turn and make their way towards the elevators, waiting until they're alone inside before Sebastian speaks again.

"This is good," he says, running a hand through his carefully coiffed hair. He checks it in the reflection of the polished brass interior of the elevator, fixes a strand of gold which has fallen out of place. "This gives us more time. Well," he shoots Ren a sharp look. "It gives *you* more time. *'Back patio is secure,'* my ass. Where are you on finding out where those pictures are now?"

"It's slow moving, sir," Ren says, the same utterly useless excuse he's been giving for a week now. "I don't want to alert any of the other guests to the fact we're concerned about the pictures. And I'm still working on finding out who tried to shoot you, which is naturally a high priority for both Ivan and the president. Can I ask—"

"No, you can *not*," Sebastian snaps, rubbing at his temple in exhaustion. The pain behind his eye has been throbbing consistently since the party. If Sebastian had *felt* the intensity with which Ren watched him as he rubbed the glitter innocently from his jawline, then surely it would transpose onto film? *Fuck* knows what kind of face he was making, swept up in the moment as he was.

He feels the weight begin to settle back down into his lungs, pushing the air out and leaving him suddenly gasping. Ren shifts at his side, infuriatingly perceptive, as always.

Sebastian shuts his eyes and tries to calm down. He can't do this now. Not in front of the hound Ivan has set on him 24 hours of the fucking day. He needs to maintain his composure now more than ever. Now more than *ever* when those pictures are out there, and if his father gets wind of them, fuck knows what he'll do to him. He might not be promoted to vice-president until *after* he's finished this useless degree.

"Didn't you say your job is to protect me and the image of the company?" Sebastian asks Ren, clasping his hand into a fist at his side. His wrist twinges so he drops it, fingers twitching irritably at his side instead. Ren nods.

"Yes, sir."

"Well," Sebastian sighs, attempting to get a grip on his expression before the elevator doors slide open on the bottom floor. "What do you think it would do for the company's image if the tabloids got hold of a picture of my bodyguard caressing my fucking face at a frat party?"

Ren hesitates. Sebastian rounds on him then, the elevator slowing down as it approaches their destination. Ren lets out the barest hint of a sigh. It's almost enough to distract Sebastian from the anger which is quickly overwhelming the panic that has made its home in his gut for the past week. Almost.

"I suppose it wouldn't look good," Ren answers finally. Sebastian throws him a quick look of disgust.

"You don't have to *suppose*, dickhead, I'm *telling you* it wouldn't look good," he says, fishing around in his pocket for his cigarette case. "*Lock up your children, the fag son of your favourite oil baron is fucking his security detail! Does he have AIDs? Will he molest your son at the Christmas party? All that and more on tonight's program!*"

Sebastian's fingers are shaking as he tries to pluck a cigarette free from his case. He fumbles, drops it on the ground as the elevator doors slide open. The onslaught of bodies waiting to crush their way inside pause when they realise who he is, parting as if made up of one hive mind to let him and Ren through. Ren picks the cigarette up from his feet and waits for him to move first, watching him intently.

Sebastian wants to tear his eyes out of his fucking head as he pushes through the lobby towards the doors. The sting in his brain has rapidly become a constant drone of red hot pain. He can't stop the tremor in his fingers. He wants to rip off the skin on the back of his neck where Ren is always *watching* him. He vaguely thinks he hears Ren calling after him, but he presses on, ignoring the increasingly desperate calls for his attention.

There's no reprieve as he steps out and onto the busy pavement, realising all at once that a flock of reporters await him. They swarm, blocking his path to the awaiting car, microphones pushed up to his face. The rapid fire of camera flashes nearly blind him, and Sebastian has to put up a hand to shield himself.

He takes a breath and then struggles for another. Feels his emotions about to swallow him up, remembers what it was like when he sat at the dinner table as a child.

When Sebastian was ten, the tabloids ran a story about how his father was having an affair with Rosie, his dog trainer. She stopped coming to walk the dogs and disappeared from Sebastian's life entirely. At dinner, his father told him that the *ignorant little slut* had gone to the papers herself, in the hopes of *exposing him*. His father said *women are idiots* who don't know what it is they want, so it's better for them if they just *shut the fuck up and take it*. His mother had burst into tears at the far end of the table. Sebastian hated when his mother cried. It used to make the same overwhelming swell of emotion crash over him, used to make hot tears spill down his cheeks before he could stop them. That day, as soon as he'd started to cry, his mother had stopped. She looked angry at him. She asked him why he had to be such a *fucking baby* because it just made everything worse. Sebastian tried to say he was sorry, but his throat was drawn too tight with sadness. His father has grabbed him by the wrist—was that the first time he'd broken it? Sebastian can only remember the panic as his father demanded he stop crying. His mother had left the table, taken her martini with her. His father demanded to know why Sebastian was always upsetting her.

His mother was right— crying did make it worse. If he held his breath and gritted his teeth while his father beat him, then it was over sooner. If he pretends to smile now and evades the paparazzi's questions, it'll be over sooner.

He can hear the reporters yelling about the press-conference his father is attending. This is moderately comforting, suggesting the compromising photos still haven't been sold off.

— *will the company be changing tack?*

— *could you step up and take on a more immediate role?*

— is it time your father stood aside, let the youth take up the mantle?

Sebastian watches security guards from the lobby file out and force the reporters back. A firm hand settles between his shoulder blades, a figure dressed in a dark suit shielding him as he's urged towards the car. Ren reaches around his body, the hard plane of his abdomen brushing Sebastian's side as he opens the door, gently but insistently pushing him down and into the backseat.

As quickly as the racket threatened to overwhelm him, Sebastian is left in the quiet, in the dark. The windows of the car are tinted and thick, swallowing up the clamours of the paparazzi and surrendering him to the silence. Sebastian takes a deep breath, looks at his hands. They still tremble slightly. He thinks about Rosie the dog trainer again, about Poppy and Nuca's slippery soft fur. He hasn't cried in a very long time.

The door on the opposite side of the car opens then, a quick burst of noise following as Ren climbs into the seat beside Sebastian. He shuts it firmly behind him, taking a second to ensure that it's locked before telling the driver they're ready to move. He leans forwards without asking, shutting the partition which separates the two of them from the driver's cab. It makes Sebastian's heart skip without hesitation, the prospect that he wants to be *alone* with him so enticing it makes his mouth water.

He's pretty sure he's going to throw up. He shuts his eyes, tries not to think about it.

"Sir," Ren says, and his tone is painted with enough annoyance that Sebastian peels his eyes open again and watches him carefully. He leans his head back against the brushed leather of the interior, waiting for Ren to follow up his pointed address. "I really must insist you wait for me to clear the street in future before you exit the building. Even without the risk of another assassination attempt, it's not safe for you to just launch yourself into a group of reporters like that."

Throughout his speech, Ren manages to get his tone in check again, back down to his usual inexcitable level. Something about it tingles though, the ends of his icy words glittering like frost. Sharp with concern, despite himself.

Sebastian's shoulders drop as he listens, something warm curling up inside him.

"You're so sweet when you worry about me like that, Ren," he hears himself say, his amusement only heightening when Ren's brows actively furrow. He looks away, out the window. Sebastian instantly mourns the loss of his attention.

"It's my job to worry about you. And you're making my job much harder, *sir*," Ren says through his teeth.

Sebastian finds he likes the begrudging tone of Ren's voice. He very much likes the idea that Ren still faces away from him, staring determinedly out the window in an attempt to manage his frustration, forbidding it from showing on his face. It makes a thrill run through him, one that's not of terror, not triggering that familiar survival instinct.

He wants to keep it going, to feel it again. He wants to put the past week of panic and stress and undeniable intrigue with his bodyguard to one side, forget it all for a while.

"I'm about to make it harder," Sebastian says, smiling broadly when Ren turns to face him again, expression once again dampened, deliberately blank. "I'd like to go out tonight."

*

The table is right at the back of the club. It's close enough to the bar that the waitress can slip back and forth with whatever bullshit Sebastian's guests are ordering, far enough that Ren is satisfied none of the rabble are going to murder him in cold blood. He's standing behind the booth, watching, like he always does. Sebastian wishes he'd get used to the feeling of dark eyes constantly trailing over the back of his head, but it doesn't seem to be getting any easier.

He's not even entirely sure who all has ended up at the table. He'd made a generic call to the president of his frat, offered seats at a VIP booth in one of the city's newest nightclubs and showed up fashionably late. He'd had Ren tip off the tabloids about where they would be (much to his annoying protestation), allowing them to photograph him in a situation which was decidedly under Sebastian's control. Pictures of him eye-fucking the shot girls walking up and down the line to enter the club are prime fodder for the tabloid press. CEO's son spotted partying and not giving a fuck about his father's company? Perfect. It's a show of *support* to Sebastian's father. He's too young to take over, still not ready for all the responsibility. He's no threat, not yet.

Sebastian spends most of the night being fawned over by strangers, thrilled by his carefree exuberance and the fact his credit card is behind the bar. He drinks whatever they hand him, smokes whatever ends up poised between his lips, and before long he's pressing himself back into the safety of his VIP booth. His skin is smeared with his own sweat, hair caught at the nape of his neck in wet tendrils but he hasn't felt this free in a while. It all contributes to his meticulously crafted image, one that he'd almost let publicly slip this afternoon.

The waitress brings over a bottle of tequila, and one of the guys who's ended up at the table with Sebastian starts pouring them shots. Sebastian thinks he's seen him before. Perhaps they share some classes? He's usually not very good at remembering people's faces, and the copious liquor he's ingested up until this point isn't helping.

The guy has fiery red hair, a little longer in the back than at the sides, and a shiny golden hoop in his right ear. The strobe lighting in the club glints over it every time it flashes. Sebastian finds himself inexplicably drawn to it, fingers reaching out to examine it and brushing his smooth earlobe in the process. The guy grins up at him, offering a shot of tequila. His smile swims in Sebastian's vision, the rubbery tug of alcohol now present in every move he tries to make.

Sebastian takes the shot, mirroring Red-Head's actions as he brings it to his lips. His tongue slides along the salt rim, harsh edge igniting the tip of it, before dropping the shot back and swallowing it in one go. It burns in a way that makes Sebastian's heart beat ten times faster, his face screwing up involuntarily against the fierce heat licking its way through his core. Red-Head lifts a wedge of freshly cut lime from the tray to Sebastian's lips, and Sebastian fumbles to do the same. Slick fingers press into his mouth, holding the lime taught for him to bite down on.

The tang chases the warmth of the liquor and makes his mouth flood with saliva. He notices a little too late perhaps, the Red-Head's fingers are still firm between his lips, though the pith and skin of the lime has fallen away to his lap. Sebastian feels the strength of the tequila further ooze into his senses, dulling them just enough that they can't quite catch up with his movements. He sucks the other man's fingers with intent.

Desire races through him, red hot and overwhelming. In the state he's in, it easily stifles the lurid panic. It tries to rear its ugly head regardless, just as it does every time he feels the tug of intrigue in his belly at the sight of a man he wants to fuck him.

Sebastian's good sense is drowned out by the clamour of liquor addled lust pounding through his brain. Realistically, the pictures of him and Ren have probably already been sold off, so what difference would succumbing to temptation in the darkness of this club make? How much worse could his father's reaction be? There's no way he could actually *kill* Sebastian—he thinks Ivan would put a stop to it before it went that far, wouldn't he?

"You want to go somewhere a little more private?"

Sebastian hears Red-Head's gruff proposition brush against the shell of his ear as he leans in and whispers. This way, Sebastian can see over his shoulder, past the back of the booth, and straight over to where Ren is standing.

The neon lights of the club make his raven hair catch a different colour with every pulse of music, the late hour having coaxed a shadow onto his usually clean-shaven jaw. His eyes are not hollow. They are very full of something, Sebastian can see, shiny and dark. They're so dark he can almost feel himself teetering over the shoulder of the man he's currently embracing and straight into them. He thinks he sees Ren give a subtle shake of his head, disagreement. Sebastian's stomach flips, another wave of lukewarm fluidity overcoming his muscles from the drone of alcohol in his veins.

In his mind, he fantasises that Ren doesn't want him to go home with this guy. He's upset at the thought of it. He's *jealous*.

The Red-Head in Sebastian's lap runs a purposeful palm across Sebastian's semi-hard cock, and the warm swell of arousal is enough to make him almost forget Ren exists. He remembers him enough to gesture at him vaguely, telling him to bring the car around the back of the club where they can leave discreetly.

Fuck it, Sebastian thinks resolutely. Ivan and his father are both hundreds of miles away. As long as he's careful, they can do this. Tonight, he wants more than just a fumble in the bathrooms of this club.

It's late, late enough that the dancefloor has started to clear and the streets beyond the club are on the other side of busy. Sebastian doesn't pay much attention to the drive home, distracted by the wandering hands of his companion. Ren sits in the front this time, with the driver. Something about that annoys Sebastian—how the fuck is Ren supposed to keep him safe if he's up front? What the fuck is his problem, anyway? Why doesn't he like Sebastian? *Everyone* likes him, he's a very likeable person. He's worked very hard to be a very likeable person.

The door of the car opens and the night air rushes over him like a bucket of cold water. The sweat beading on his skin has turned frigid in the sudden chill. His companion, with his red-hair and his little gold earring, is pulling him out, bundling him along and through the lobby and into the elevator. It's like he's been to Sebastian's apartment before. Has he?

Sebastian tries to get another clear look at him but can't quite seem to get his features to stop swimming about his pale face.

Ren is there too, in the elevator, as Red-Head kneads at Sebastian's cock through his slacks, muttering things as though they're alone.

"Are you going to be good?" he murmurs in Sebastian's ear, once again pressed up to his side as Sebastian watches Ren stand idly in the corner of the elevator. "Are you going to be good and suck my cock?"

Ren's eyes flit over to meet Sebastian's.

He stares back, tongue sliding out to coat his lips.

"Yes," Sebastian responds, and it's barely a sound. "Yes, I'll be good."

It makes Ren's dark eyes flash darker. He looks away.

Sebastian is salivating, core tight with need by the time they arrive at his apartment, tugging Red-Head behind him and out of the elevator, mouth sloppily finding him in the dark. He doesn't know where Ren goes, finds he doesn't care that much as he feels his way along the hallway to his bedroom, *feels* the press of another warm body up against him.

As they cross the threshold into his room, Sebastian hastily undoes the buttons of Red-Head's shirt, the glittering lights of the city below just enough to see his thin frame by. He's not strong or well-built, just young. It's all pale skin stretched taught over muscle and bone but its hard lines and sharp junctures. Nothing about him is soft or plump or squishy and when he moans, it's a low sound in his chest. It vibrates through the palm of Sebastian's hand where it's pressed against his skin, making his cock strain painfully up against the waistband of his underwear. Red-Head pushes him up against the large window.

"I thought you said you would be good," he's saying, holding Sebastian's chin harshly between his thumb and forefinger. He's shorter than Sebastian (as most other men are), trying his best to seem authoritative. It comes across as forced, and makes Sebastian cringe a bit. Before he can allow the embarrassment to catch up with his raging desire though, Red-Head is forcing him down, hastily reaching to undo his belt as Sebastian's knees hit the floor.

It will probably hurt tomorrow, but for now, all Sebastian is aware of is the wet tip of Red-Head's cock painting his lips slowly. It's a decent size and shape (nothing to write home about), but it's a fucking *cock* and its owner is impatiently brushing the blunt head against Sebastian's mouth, seeking entrance.

He parts his lips, taking the base of Red-Head's cock in his hand and swallowing him up. It's been a while since he's done this, so many hours spent in boarding school with nothing better to do than suck each other off in the showers, and he can feel the back of his throat burning in protest. Sebastian squeezes his eyes shut and concentrates, reaching down with his other hand to free his own erection from the tight confines of his underwear. The relief he feels from stroking himself makes his throat relax a little. Tears pool in the corners of his eyes as he runs his tongue up the underside of Red-Head's cock, a bodily protest to the intrusion.

He's groaning with pleasure, his head tilted back as he fists at Sebastian's hair and the sight alone is enough to make Sebastian's gut twitch with pleasure. He begins to work quicker, saliva dripping down his chin as he bobs his head back and forth, enjoying the heavy feeling on his tongue. An involuntary groan escapes him as he moves, travelling up the length of the other man's cock and as the roof of his mouth tingles.

"Fuck... yes... *take it*," Red-Head's huffing between pants, his fingers beginning to slip and lose purchase between strands of golden hair. He starts thrusting his hips into Sebastian's face then, the tip of his dick hitting the back of Sebastian's throat with vigour and he gags so hard he has to stop jerking himself off. He's certain he's going to throw up all over this man, who doesn't seem to notice Sebastian spluttering for air beneath him. He's chasing his own end, only pulling out enough for Sebastian to breathe when his orgasm hits.

He comes all over Sebastian's face, painting his chin and jaw with his sticky spend and in that moment it takes every inch of willpower in Sebastian's body *not* to choke up vomit.

Red-Head is panting, already tucking himself back into his jeans and giving Sebastian a swift pet on the top of his head.

"Good boy. I liked that," he breathes, catching his breath as he wanders away towards the ensuite. Sebastian just lets his eyes slip shut, willing the darkness to help with the overwhelming dizziness thrust upon him, but he's reached the point of drunkenness where even the backs of his own eyelids are betraying him.

He feels sudden softness, the weight of a hand towel being thrown over his head.

"I was hoping we could hook up for real, but you seem too wasted, man," Red-Head is saying, his voice brittle and irritating. Had he sounded like that in the club? Sebastian can't remember. "I'll give your little guard-dog my number. I was never here, right?"

As soon as he was there, he's gone.

Sebastian's not sure exactly how long he sits in the dark, willing himself not to throw up. His tongue feels dry, his throat fucked out and used. He'd have sat there all night, the stranger's cum growing colder on his skin by the moment.

He feels the towel shift where it's still laying across his head. A hand recoils in disgust.

A sigh.

"Come on, sir," Ren says quietly. "Get into the shower."

Five

Sebastian wonders if he's been in more humiliating situations than this one. He can't think of any right now, stripped down to his briefs and dunked below the faucet by his security guard, but there's bound to have been something. He doesn't have time to be embarrassed about the lingering hardness in his dick, nor the wet patch darkening the front of his briefs. The water is freezing, cold enough to make him hiss like a cat and curl up against the tile, trying to stay out of it.

"What the fuck?" he mutters pathetically, slipping back down the wall where he's tried to pull himself up.

"Wash your face, sir," Ren's voice echoes as flat as the marble surrounding them. Sebastian groans petulantly, the cold spray shattering the hot stupor of inebriation.

"Need my cleanser," Sebastian responds, sitting up straighter as his body adjusts to the shower. It's a little warmer now that he's getting used to it, the steady flow breaking over his shoulders as he just sits on the floor. He hears Ren rustling around the sink for a moment before he produces Sebastian's cleanser, setting it at the threshold of the walk-in shower. Sebastian can't help himself as he peeks out one eye to catch Ren in the act. "Want to help clean my face? I'm drunk."

"Not at all, sir," Ren says swiftly, standing up and going to lean against the sink. Sebastian sighs and begins to smear cleanser on his cheeks dramatically, trying to ignore the nasty sensation of semen which has dried into his face.

"Why d'you hate me, Ren?" Sebastian asks. It doesn't come out as demanding or accusatory as he'd hoped, more pitiful than anything else. He ducks his head under the shower stream, running his fingers up and through his hair. It collects in thick locks of gold against his neck, weighed down by the water.

"I don't hate you," Ren answers immediately. Sebastian pouts.

"Oh fuck off, you *do* hate me. You're always fucking glaring at me, like tonight, in the elevator…" he trails off, finger tracing an errant water droplet as it races down the wall. His voice seems to echo on forever in the marble room, bouncing around insistently. The last word drills into Sebastian's aching head like the ever present pain behind his right eye. He stops studying the water droplet, pressing his cheek to the wall as he looks out at his bodyguard.

Ren is sitting on the closed lid of the toilet, fist propping up his cheek as he watches Sebastian. Sebastian isn't sure if it's the contrast of Ren against the ivory of everything in the bathroom or the lingering buoyancy of tequila, but he notices so much more about him now.

His hair is shaved tight at the back and sides, but long on top, parting effortlessly down the centre of his head and falling into his dark eyes. They glitter (with amusement, Sebastian imagines, because he's never really seen them do that before) beneath the hooded single fold of his eyelids, lashes so long Sebastian can see them through the mist of the shower. Ren's cheekbones are strong and proud, just like his jaw, just like the curve of his thick, glossy eyebrows and his ears are pierced, a silver hoop in each lobe. He's slim but sturdy, broad shouldered with forearms that betray years of meticulous training when he flexes them as he shifts.

Sebastian finds himself leaning forwards as he peels his cheek off the wall. It's suddenly too cold, biting. Perhaps his cheek is too hot? He reaches up to brush his knuckles against it, subtle, discreet, he thinks. Ren raises a brow. Perhaps it wasn't as subtle as he thought.

"Are you feeling sick again? Your cheeks are all red."

Sebastian jerks his head around and dunks it back under the water. It's still cool enough that it provides pleasant relief from the sudden rosiness in his cheeks. He opens his mouth, lets it fill with water, spits it out. His tongue feels raw, still tastes like that other guy's cock. He rinses his mouth again.

He does suddenly feel sick, but not for the reason Ren is thinking.

"... M'fine," Sebastian mutters, barely a sound, but somehow Ren catches it. He drops his hand from his cheek, laces his long fingers together in the space between his spread legs.

"Are you upset? Look, I promise, I really don't hate you. I'm sorry if I made you think that. In the elevator, I was just…" Ren trails away, eyes rolling up to the ceiling as he searches it for his next words. Sebastian doesn't think he'll find them up there. He snorts at the thought, leaning back against the coolness of the tiles. Something wicked stirs in Sebastian's stomach now, as he watches the bob of Ren's throat as he thinks. It's wheelding, bright like the sudden burst of pain after the backs of your knees have been slashed with a riding crop.

"Is it because I brought a guy home to fuck me?" Sebastian hears the words coming from his mouth, but it's as if someone else is saying them. A twist of a knife he didn't know was lodged in his side, testing the sudden hunger igniting his insides at the sight of Ren. Sebastian lets his teeth catch on his bottom lip, dragging the pink flesh taught. Ren's line of sight falls back to consider him, his mouth twisting oddly at the edge. Sebastian takes a deep breath. "Do you hate me because I'm a faggot, Ren?"

"Are you?" Ren doesn't miss a beat, face as blank as ever. Sebastian scoffs, running his fingers below the stream of the shower before flicking water towards Ren. He's too far, it doesn't touch him. Ren watches the drops land on the marble. Stands to retrieve a towel and crouches to wipe them up. He watches Sebastian closely as he rests in a flat-footed squat, barely a metre away now from the walk-in shower's edge. He's not wearing any shoes.

The sudden proximity makes the knife in Sebastian's side slide deeper, determined to reach the thrum of excitement Ren brings with him. Sebastian rolls his eyes, sliding back to lean against the wall.

"As if Ivan hasn't told you," he sneers, shoving his hair back and out of his eyes. "As if when he was giving you the rundown of every shitty thing I've ever done in my life, he didn't mention my… personal *proclivities* and how I just can't seem to help myself!" Sebastian laughs as his drunken tongue trips on the word. A tremor runs through him as he thinks of all the times Ivan caught him and all the times he went running straight to his father to tell him and all the times his head has *ached* since.

Sebastian covers his mouth, trying to stifle the noise, laughter still choking his words.

"I'm not a very *good* faggot, mind you," he amends, his eyes prickling like they're being softly pierced with needles. "I didn't even get off tonight!"

Sebastian dissolves into laughter then, the absurdity of this entire day finally hitting. The anxiety this morning as he prepared to meet his father, knowing that picture of him and Ren was still out there somewhere; the relief when the meeting was cancelled; the panic when the reporters turned up, cameras blinking his vision away to pale nothingness, microphones rammed in his face; sudden calm when he was in the back seat of that car with Ren, amusement when he realised he could finally pull some kind of reaction from him; then he'd been drunk and high and he'd had a dick shoved so far back in his throat that snot had poured out his nose.

He stops laughing, dread suddenly creeping over and settling in. He's certain when he remembers this day as a whole, that will be the one thing that colours the entirety of his memory.

The lukewarm shower has brought new clarity to the lame justifications he'd made to himself in the club, dulled as he'd been by the wicked harshness of tequila.

"You're going to tell Ivan… aren't you?"

He doesn't care that the dread seeps into his words. They're a whisper that catches on the cold planes of the marble. They mock him as they ring out, as Ren blinks slowly, absorbing them.

Ren lets out a long sigh, hoisting himself up from his squat to stand and reach over top of Sebastian to turn the shower off. It hisses to a stop instantaneously.

He drops back down, elbows balanced on his thighs again.

"I have to report everything back to him, sir," Ren says quietly. "The things you do, the company you keep. That's my job."

Sebastian hates that the next noise out of him is more a whimper than anything else. His cheeks burn with embarrassment, pride mingling with frustration and churning up nothing but anger.

"Why? *Why* is this something he needs to know? I know—" his voice catches as he tries to regain some composure, a shiver running across his now cold, damp body.

He can't seem to hold onto the anger for long enough. It leaves behind desperation, and now Sebastian's *sure* he's never been more humiliated. "Look, I know what I just did was wrong, but I didn't *hurt* anyone."

Ren shakes his head then, mouth settling into a decided frown. His brow furrows, his eyes intense but soft at the corners. It's all soft really, his entire expression. Like nothing he's ever shown before, leaning in close to Sebastian and placing an awkward hand on his shoulder.

Ren's fingers squeeze lightly over the bare, wet muscle there. Sebastian wonders if this is what it is to be comforted. He vaguely remembers Rosie, the dog-trainer his dad had groped in their living room and then fired when she'd tried to expose him to the tabloids. Rosie used to give him hugs sometimes.

"It wasn't *wrong*," Ren says tightly. "What you *did* tonight wasn't wrong. But just… look at yourself now, sir. *You're* the one who got hurt."

Sebastian understands what Ren is saying, but strung together as the words are, they don't make any sense. He raises a brow, as if Ren is an idiot.

"I'm not hurt," he says matter-of-factly. "My throat feels a little raw, but it'll be okay in the morning."

Ren studies him for a second longer, lips parting ever so slightly. Sebastian can see the smooth pink of the tip of his tongue. He only just suppresses the urge to reach out and touch it.

"Get out of the shower, you're shivering," Ren says then, standing and fetching a towel for Sebastian to wrap around himself. He hands it over, turning his back. "Take those underpants off too, you'll get sick if you go to sleep with them on."

Sebastian wants the bizarre bloated atmosphere that's inflated the space between them to burst, so he slides the briefs off his legs before standing, wrapping the towel just around his shoulders. He jolts his hip to one side, exposed.

"What's the matter, Ren?" he hums. "Never seen a cock before?"

Ren turns to look at him, gaze plotting a determined course straight down the length of his body, pausing just a breath longer at his groin, before returning to his face. The trail he leaves behind makes Sebastian shiver harder, somehow more naked than he's ever felt in his life.

Ren smiles, and it's slow like syrup, like the look he's just given Sebastian.

"Don't you think it's a little awkward for your employee to see your cock, *sir*?" Ren asks. Sebastian lets the towel slip down his shoulders. He gathers it at his waist, tucks it in carefully. The flush induced by Ren's icy gaze is crawling down his fucking chest and Sebastian can't even bring himself to care because he's never seen him *smile* before.

"Don't answer a question with a question," Sebastian grumbles, stifling himself with feigned aggravation. He grips the front of the towel more firmly to conceal his suddenly half-hard dick.

Ren isn't listening, having already left the bathroom and begun rummaging through Sebastian's drawers. He throws a fresh pair of underwear on the bed, probably leaving a horrendous mess in his wake. Sebastian leans on the precipice of the room, arm pressed up against the doorway which leads to his ensuite.

He stays there a moment, the heavy sway of the dark room more evident now that he's stood up. He's going to be horribly hungover tomorrow, and the thought alone is enough to make him flop over onto his bed, ignoring the clean underwear deposited a moment ago. Ren busies himself with rearranging whatever he's overturned in the wardrobe, vaguely instructing Sebastian to put them on.

He manages to, grateful this time that Ren's back is turned as he's all gangly legs and elbows as he tries to yank the briefs up his body while still balancing on the edge of the bed. His head is swimming, his cheeks still burning. His groin aches with a promise Ren's deliberate gaze didn't even make.

He's too distracted to start touching himself, however, by the slimy press of his own wet hair against his scalp. Sebastian groans.

"I'm too fucking drunk for this," he laments as he fists at the towel and drapes it over his head. He knows he's going to pay for this in the morning as he roughly towel dries his hair, praying it doesn't damage the keratin treatment he just had.

"Let me," Ren says then, suddenly so much closer than when Sebastian had first scrunched his eyes shut. Sebastian doesn't protest, finding the motion is fast making the urge to throw up return. His hands fall limply to his sides as Ren comes to stand between his legs, hands working a much more determined but gentle rhythm across Sebastian's scalp.

The sound of the soft scratching is soothing, a shiver running down Sebastian's spine.

Ignoring the throb in his skull and the sheer effort it takes to lift his arm, Sebastian encases Ren's wrist with insistent fingers, drawing his ministrations to a halt. His head is still covered with the towel, face obscured from view. Sebastian stares at his lap, can't stop the vulnerability he feels peeking out.

"Ren," he says, and the sound cracks in his throat. "Please don't tell Ivan about tonight." He pauses, trying to think of something more. Nothing comes, so he just repeats himself. "Please."

The grip Sebastian has on Ren's wrist is sloppy at best, so he's easily able to slip his hands back to pull the towel off the crown of Sebastian's head. It rests on his shoulders now, freshly dry tufts of gold falling flat against his scalp.

"If Ivan directly asks me what you did this evening, I *will* tell him," Ren says. He lets out a low breath. Sebastian dares to tilt his chin, gazing up to find Ren watching him with that same impossible softness he had before. It sends that familiar knife reaching into his belly, but this time, the pain is dampened somewhat by the blossoming of warmth there too. Ren licks his lips. "But if he doesn't, I don't see any reason to go out of my way to tell him. Not if it would… hurt you."

For the first time in a very long time, Sebastian doesn't know what to say.

He learned at a very young age how to quickly deter-mine exactly what it is people want to hear, and thereby what to say. He also learned at a very young age that nobody really cares about hurting him.

The silence is too long. It balances on a knife's edge, just as Sebastian's mother had when she stood on the precipice of the roof, just above this bedroom.

Sebastian reaches up, just enough to ghost the tips of his fingers along Ren's jaw. It's not smooth like water, like Poppy had been, but it's nice for an entirely different rea-son.

"Thank you," Sebastian says. "I promise I'll stop... try-ing to ditch you as much."

Ren promptly moves Sebastian's searching fingers away from his face, nodding gracefully.

"Let's not make promises we can't keep, sir. Now, you should sleep. I'll see you in the morning."

Sebastian obeys, too drunk and tired to do much else. The bed sheets are cool against his body as he slips easily between them, laying his head down.

"Sorry about all this!" he manages to yell as he shuts his eyes, sleep already encroaching on his spinning brain. "Keeping you here so late... when you have to come back tomorrow."

Ren switches the light in the ensuite off before he goes, and Sebastian thinks that maybe that smile is back on his face. It sounds like it is.

"An apology from Sebastian Clarence. I must be the luckiest guy in the world," Ren says, and then, "... You're the one paying such an impressive overtime rate, sir. Goodnight."

Sebastian hopes, more than he's ever hoped for anything before, that he remembers the way Ren says his name when he wakes up in the morning.

*

Instead, when Sebastian wakes up in the morning, he tries to have Ren fired.

"It's not working, Ivan. It's been a month since my birthday and he's no closer to finding out who tried to shoot me. The Halloween party is in two weeks—what am I supposed to do? Wear a bulletproof vest and go as a member of SWAT?"

"It's probably advisable you wear a bulletproof vest no matter what your costume is, sir," Ivan responds drily, his voice cracking down the line of Sebastian's cellular phone.

"Absolutely not," Sebastian says at once. "I've been planning my costume since this time last year. A bulletproof vest won't match at all."

A sigh on the other end. It makes Sebastian prickle with rage; Ivan talks down to him like he's still the child he was forced to call every week at boarding school.

"With all due respect sir," Ivan says, (and it sounds to Sebastian like he doesn't believe very much respect is in fact due), "I went to a great deal of trouble to hire Ren. We're working hard to chase up the leads on the shooter. If you could just extend your patience to him for a little longer—"

"*A great deal of trouble?*" Sebastian repeats fiercely, the exclamation causing a sharp clap of pain in his already throbbing forehead. He'd had the maid keep the curtains drawn to spare him the light of the new day, but it doesn't seem to be doing much to delay his hangover. "What the fuck are you talking about, *a great deal of trouble*? He's a grunt! A dime a dozen, just find someone else whose brain is made of muscle to follow me around!"

"Now, now, sir," Ivan chastises, and there's that *smug* fucking laugh in his voice, the one he always does when he's about to bring the conversation to a close and rub Sebastian's face in it. "I understand you're upset, but there's no need to be unnecessarily harsh. I apologise, but there's no movement on the matter. The president insisted when I hired Ren that I would ensure he stayed in it for the long haul."

Sebastian takes a deep breath and then another, tries to control the fury which makes his belly roar red hot, but it's soon spilling out whether he wants it to or not.

"I'm not *upset*, Ivan, don't—don't talk to me like I'm a *child*. I swear to fucking God, old man, the second I take over this company—"

"I'm sure a blissful retirement awaits me, yes sir, despite the fact that you and I both know you couldn't cope without me. Until then, I'm afraid I have to go. The president is due to fly back this evening. We'll see you on Monday."

The line goes dead. Sebastian throws his phone across the room with as much vigour as he can spare. It smashes off the entrance to his ensuite, sending bits of plastic spiralling out and into the room. The noise snags right on the edge of his headache, and his forehead feels like it splits open from the pain. Sebastian shoves the heels of his palms into his eye sockets, wills the pain to dampen, but the more he tries to stifle the agony, the more the thrum of panic throughout his limbs distracts him.

He can't stop thinking about Ren.

Since the second he awoke three hours ago, every time he tries to shut the world out, all he can see is Ren's soft expression. It's like it's been seared into the backs of his eyelids, *mocking* him. When he forces his eyes open, staring at the ceiling, determined to put his mind elsewhere, the hairs all over his body stand on end, recalling the magnetic tug of Ren's eyes as he swept his gaze across Sebastian's naked form. Languid, deliberate, just like he would be if he took Sebastian's face between his strong hands and kissed him.

Sebastian barely has time to make it to the toilet before he vomits.

He leans his forehead along the porcelain rim, willing the cool ceramic to drain some of the heat from his body, but it just makes him vomit harder. His nose burns, his eyes stream as the sear of his own stomach acid only serves to further irritate his already painful throat. He's shivering again as he collapses in a heap to wait out the bout of sickness. He thinks of Ren's solid hand on his shoulder last night, the gentle squeeze of comfort. He thinks Ivan had done something similar at his mother's funeral, a light squeeze of his shoulder—a show of condolence.

That's all it was, Sebastian thinks, as he spits more bile into the frothy contents of his stomach lining the toilet bowl. Condolence.

I don't see any reason to go out of my way to tell him, Ren had said. *Not if it would hurt you.*

Sebastian rubs away the blear from his eye with a knuckle, so hard he thinks it might bruise. His throat feels tight, an unfamiliar lump making it difficult to breathe. He shuts his eyes. The memory of Ren's soft expression is still there, taunting him.

Sebastian lets it.

Six

If Sebastian had been distracted by being constantly watched prior to his realisation that he was attracted to his bodyguard, it is nothing compared to the paranoia he now feels.

"*Must* you breathe down my neck at all hours of the day?" he snaps, a week on from the worst hangover of his life (and the sickening recognition that, euphemism aside, he would very much enjoy Ren's warm breath on his neck). "Go and take a break or something."

Instead of a smooth protest like Sebastian is expecting, Ren hesitates. He glances away from where Sebastian is perched, on the green iron bench of a coffee shop patio. Ren's wrapped up for the blustery October air, long leather jacket turned up at the collar, hands shoved deep in his pockets. Sebastian flicks ash off his cigarette, aggravated by how relaxed Ren seems at all times—it only serves to highlight his own waspish demeanour.

"I actually do need to go to the bank," Ren says, casting his eye over the coffee shop behind Sebastian. "You'll be okay if you stay here, right? I'll only be a half hour."

Sebastian takes a drag on his cigarette, heart leaping to his throat at the prospect of having a moment to himself.

"Believe it or not, I went to this college for two whole years before you showed up. Campus is crawling with security. I'm sure my coffee won't be shot out of my hand," he says off-handedly, balancing his cigarette carefully in the ashtray before taking a sip of his espresso. It tastes burnt. Sebastian wrinkles his nose, chokes it down anyway.

Ren tilts his head, his shoulders falling a little as he lets out a ghost of a sigh.

"You shouldn't joke about things like that, sir," Ren says seriously, almost resigned. Sebastian rolls his eyes, wraps his cashmere scarf once more around his neck to combat the brisk breeze. Dried leaves catch on the pavement as the wind pushes them about.

"You can't let *the bastards* think they're winning," Sebastian drops the tone of his voice, imitating the nicotine rattled scratch that is his father's voice. Unexpectedly, Ren looks as if he's trying very hard to contain a smile.

"Was that supposed to be the president?" he asks. Sebastian doesn't try at all to contain his smile, nodding gleefully. Ren shakes his head, looks the other way. This time, there's definitely a smile there. "Very good, sir."

When he looks back, all traces of emotion are wiped from his fine features and he just nods.

"Half an hour then. Less, if there's no line. I'll see you soon."

With that, he gives an awkward little bob of his head and sets off in the direction of the wind. It catches in his inky dark hair, carrying it up and around his head as he pulls his jacket tighter to his body. Sebastian watches him get further and further away, the sudden buzz of caffeine and nicotine not helping to stifle the quickness of his heart.

He downs the rest of his coffee, then wonders what he's supposed to do for half an hour.

Another coffee, another cigarette. He stands to go back inside and order another burnt espresso, but is caught halfway by a sudden onslaught of excitable paws.

"Jesus Christ!" Sebastian yelps, as the dog, up on its hind legs, paws at his side, tongue lolling out the side of its mouth. He instinctively puts his back to it, just as he'd been taught to do when Poppy and Nuca jumped on him, but the dog isn't discouraged. It pivots on its hind legs, bouncing around so it's facing him again, its front legs pressed playfully to the leaf strewn patio. He realises it's a doberman pinscher.

"Donnie! Stop! Sit! Come here!"

Sebastian looks up from where the dog has bounced up to leap on him again, trying its best to cover the tan expanse of his trenchcoat with mud. Its eyes are bright, the feeling of its coat under his fingers slippery like water. Even the curve of its back is so utterly reminiscent of Poppy and Nuca it almost distracts Sebastian entirely from the owner of the voice calling out to the dog.

Pip, whose name Ren had drilled into the side of Sebastian's skull, is slowing to a halt at his side, dog leash dangling from her red fingertips. Her whole face is a little red, huffing for air in the cold as she is. She takes a moment to study him before her brilliant green eyes widen and then narrow. Her auburn curls are piled atop her head haphazardly, a pair of sunglasses barely holding them out of her face. Sebastian silently bemoans the sheer apathy he feels for her DD-cup breasts. She's a pretty little thing, if somewhat on the fat side.

He raises a brow at her.

"Are you trying to confuse the poor animal? If you just yell different words at him, he's never going to learn how to do anything," Sebastian tells her, as she steps into his space to grab the dog by its purple collar and roughly clip its leash back on. She gently tugs the dog over to her side, but it seems far more interested in Sebastian, sniffing eagerly where he offers his fingers. Pip lets out a disgusted sigh.

"What, you can't remember my name, but you're an expert in training dogs?" she asks, watching as the dog calms somewhat and allows Sebastian to run his hand over its head. Sebastian offers her a glimmering smile.

"I told you, I was just so overwhelmed in the moment I couldn't think," he says, before adding, with a wink: "Pip."

It has the desired effect immediately. Pip's mouth falls open in shock before she catches herself and straightens her spine in indignation. Those same angry red spots that had appeared on her face in the mirror are back, betraying her annoyance. Sebastian feels a strange sense of elation—this must be the least he's thought about Ren since he met him.

"What's his name?" he asks, gesturing to the dog, who is licking gently at his fingertips. Pip doesn't answer right away, her glossy pink mouth pressed in an angry line. The dog tries to jump on Sebastian again and he swivels away as he'd done before. This time, the dog doesn't follow, settling back down onto its rear. Sebastian scratches behind his ears, the way Nuca had liked all those years ago. The dog responds with a grumble of delight.

"Donatello," Pip says then, seemingly intrigued by Sebastian's affinity for the dog. "Donnie for short."

"Like Pip," Sebastian remarks, and then, "Donatello? As in the Renaissance artist?"

Pip screws her mouth up to one side, almost a smile. She's looking at Sebastian like she thinks he's an idiot.

"As in the Teenage Mutant Ninja Turtle."

Sebastian continues caressing Donatello's head, raising his eyebrows.

"Hence the collar," he says, the garish purple which looks entirely out of place around the dog's fine neck now more understandable, if still unsightly.

Pip does smile then, but it's reluctant. She seems pleased Sebastian knows what she's talking about. He wonders if she thinks he's lived inside a castle on the side of a mountain his entire life with no access to the outside world.

"Exactly. There were three others in the litter and my sister is a nerd who got to name them," Pip explains, as

Donatello is momentarily distracted from Sebastian's well placed pets by a squirrel scampering across the green on the opposite side of the road. He nearly yanks Pip off her feet—she only just manages to keep him at heel, letting out an exasperated sigh. "He belongs to her really, I'm just walking him while she's away on work. Hence why he doesn't give a fuck what I tell him to do, right Donnie?"

She hunches down to scratch under his chin, earning a pleased little huff from the doberman. She's not looking at Sebastian, and he hesitates for a moment as he tries to think of a smooth exit from the conversation. Before he can, Pip is talking again, still staring determinedly at the dog.

"Look… I'm sorry about what happened at the party," she says tightly, as if it's causing her physical pain to say it. Sebastian frowns, intrigued despite himself.

"Why are you sorry?"

Pip continues to scratch Donatello, her wind chilled fingers sliding across his shiny fur. She sighs again. Sebastian wonders if she's always this incensed.

"I yelled at you and stormed off for forgetting my name, but I guess… you did know it after all? I don't know, I feel kind of bad. I talked a lot of shit about you after," she adds the last part as almost an afterthought, casting him a rueful glance up from her hunched position.

Sebastian gives her a long look, as if he's carefully considering her apology. He reaches out to stroke Donatello, mimicking Pip's movements so their hands almost touch. He offers her a shy smile.

"Don't worry about it," he says graciously. "It's not that big of a deal. I know I don't seem like it, but I can get a little nervous in those types of situations. Makes my brain like a sieve."

It's not a total lie. Sebastian does occasionally get nervous in those types of situations. Most notably when he feels the insistent press of gloss slick lips against his mouth, and he becomes nervous his boner will shrivel away into nothing.

Women like it when you play a little vulnerable for them, so occasionally he allows a measure of 'unguarded emotion' to slip into his demeanour. All shy sideways glances, the lot.

Pip stands up from where she's been crouching by the dog, her eyes a little pinched. Sebastian stares back at her evenly. She tilts her head, considering him. Closely. Too closely.

"Nervous, huh? I suppose that explains it. If I'm honest, you didn't seem that into it," she shrugs, throwing him a bashful smile. "The name thing just kind of pissed me off even more."

Sebastian blinks at her, suddenly unable to focus on the blustery weather or the sounds of spoons clinking off the edges of porcelain in the coffee shop. He wonders when the last time he had an actual conversation with a woman was—one in which he was fully present, able to scrutinise what exactly she was saying.

He finds he can't recall. Perhaps that's why Pip is proving to be so much of an irritating conversational partner?

"What do you mean I didn't seem that into it?" he asks. He watches Pip's eyebrows raise gently in surprise, knows that means she heard the edge in his voice. He tries his best to soften his expression, push through the irritation he feels unfurling in his stomach. The corner of Pip's mouth quirks, a half smile—like she's amused. Like she's caught him out in something. Sebastian squeezes his hand into a fist where it's lodged in his pocket.

"You didn't kiss me once. You barely touched me at all, just wanted to get straight down to it, which I guess some guys do, but I don't know you just seemed like… out of it."

Sebastian searches for a deflection, despite the unease creeping up his throat and attempting to choke him out. Pip hasn't let up on her scrutiny either, edging a step closer into his personal space and considering him closely. Sebastian can feel the unease quickly transforming into panic, and is careful not to let it reach his face. What the fuck is the matter with him? No, he thinks urgently, what the fuck is the matter with *her*?

"I've just had a lot on my mind lately," he says, aiming for gentle evasion, like he's too sensitive to even discuss it all like this. Pip nods.

"I'll bet," she acknowledges quietly. She's not wearing that same half smile anymore, but Sebastian finds he can't discern what she's thinking at all when he properly studies her face. Her bright green eyes are an unsettling contradiction; so open and honest yet clouded with suspicion, like she's already starting to unravel him. "My whole sorority got an invite to your family's Halloween party. Is it okay if I go?"

Sebastian blinks, unable to stop his face from screwing up in confusion.

"Of course," he says automatically. "Why wouldn't it be?"

Pip stares back at him like *he's* the bizarre one, but before she can answer, Donatello is yipping excitedly. He nearly yanks her arm out of its socket as he aims for something approaching Sebastian from behind.

"Donnie, down!" Pip hisses, managing to pull the dog back when he jumps up on his hind legs. Sebastian reaches out instinctively to calm the dog, managing to stop him from strangling himself with his own collar as he turns his back again. Donatello sits.

Ren arrives right in front of Sebastian, all dark hair and leather. His sudden apparition causes Sebastian to swallow a gasp of surprise, uncomfortably reminded of just how attractive he is. Ren tilts to the left slightly to take in the sight of Pip and the dog, eyes flicking over to Sebastian in concern. He searches Sebastian's face quickly. Sebastian *hates* when he brushes past him then, satisfied that all is well just with a ten second survey. He's like an open fucking book to this man, and it's infuriating.

"Hello," Ren says pleasantly, pointing at Donatello. "Is he friendly? Can I pet him?"

Pip blinks, also a little dazzled by Ren's sudden appearance. She glances at Sebastian curiously. Immediately grateful for the distraction, Sebastian smiles.

"This is Ren. He... does a little bit of security work for me," he says brightly, hoping the minor speckle of mystery in his statement is enough to distract Pip from the previous direction their conversation had been taking. Ren is hunkered down now in front of Donatello, large hands on either side of his slim head. He's rubbing the dog's cheeks eagerly, offering Pip a flicker of a smile as he glances up at her.

"Nice to meet you. Oh. You were at the frat party—Philippa right? Pip for short?"

He says it just as Ren says anything else. Unassuming, direct. Sebastian can feel the tide of the conversation begin to pull back towards danger.

Pip appears startled, tucks a loose curl back from her face. The highpoints of her cheeks are pink, all the way out to her little ears. It's chilly enough, but the redness appears to have dramatically worsened in the moment Ren's been talking. Sebastian studies Pip as she huffs out an awkward chuckle.

"Uh yeah, I was. ...Sorry, but I don't recognise you. Have we met?"

Ren shakes his head, still patting the dog, almost aggressively. Donatello is panting with excitement, enjoying every moment of it.

"No, no, I'm good at staying in the background. I just thought you had an interesting name, so I remembered it when you told Mr Clarence."

The tingle of warning Sebastian has sensed throughout the entirety of this interaction dwindles to a dull inkling as he hears Ren speak. He wrinkles his nose in distaste. *Mr Clarence*? What the fuck is that? He supposes Ren's never called him anything but 'sir,' to his face (with the exception of the way he'd teasingly uttered his *full name* after putting him to bed last week). *Mr Clarence* seems so alien coming from him. Foreign, like he *should* be calling his first name with the same care he'd taken to tousle his hair dry that same night.

Pip's eyes narrow. Sebastian's stomach drops, and suddenly, he can't bring himself to give a shit what Ren calls him. In a split second, the tingle of warning has now somehow imploded.

"Oh, you did?" she asks, voice holding that dangerous lilt, straddling innocence and imminent peril that only women seem to be capable of. "That's funny. He seemed to have trouble with it."

Ren shrugs good-naturedly, standing up straight and brushing himself off.

"Yes, well… to his credit, he did remember it as soon as I reminded him."

The way Pip's smile lights up her face despite its inherent repugnance says a lot about how pretty she actually is, Sebastian thinks.

"You're a real piece of shit, *Sebastian*, do you know that?" she asks sweetly, directing the full force of her ire towards him. He doesn't shrink back, just continues to study the fascinating convergence of smug satisfaction with total disgust. It's rare he gets to see such a thing up close. She continues. "And you know what? You're not slick. If I were you, I'd drop the bleeding heart act and just lean straight into being the quintessential asshole you so clearly are. Although," she narrows her eyes even further, angry red spots on her cheeks flaring, puffed up with her own sense of self importance as she rambles on and on—"maybe leaning *straight* into anything is too much of a challenge for you. I feel like you'd be much happier *bending over.*"

With that, she gathers Donatello's leash up into her fist, throwing Ren a far brighter grin than she's ever offered Sebastian.

"See you both at Halloween," she simpers, before pushing straight through the two of them, Donatello tugging her off into the wind-rustled autumn day.

It takes Sebastian a moment longer than it should to process what the fuck just happened. It reminds him of the time just after his mother died, when his father seemed particularly infuriated with any little thing he did. He would often have to pause in the moment after one of those bouts of frustration to take stock of exactly what part of his body hurt the most.

As soon as his brain arrives at Pip's final scathing comment and makes sense of it, he grabs Ren by the arm and drags him down the side of the coffee shop. He releases him like he's poison to the touch, bearing down on him with the full force of his height. They're sandwiched between this building and the next, little room to manoeuvre. Ren leans against the wall, undisturbed.

"You did that on purpose," Sebastian hisses. "You made me look like a fucking idiot."

Ren shakes his head, forehead wrinkling marginally in disagreement.

"No sir, I didn't. I apologise if it seemed that way, but I really wasn't trying to—"

"Don't *bullshit* me," Sebastian lashes out, words barely escaping through gritted teeth. He's clenching his jaw so hard it hurts. The pain behind his right eye crackles in protest, travelling all the way up the side of his head and making it throb. He reaches up to cover his eye instinctively as the discomfort hits. Ren lifts his hands as if to remove it, as if to see if Sebastian is okay.

Sebastian jerks back, away from his touch.

"Stop it. Don't touch me. Just… just *stop*, whatever you're doing," he finishes, the sudden pain making it difficult to focus on anything at all as he shuts his eyes and tries to align his thoughts. "You must have—you must have told someone about the other night… how else would she—? Why else would she say—?"

"Sir, please calm down," Ren is saying, but he sounds far away as Sebastian's mind screams a thousand different possibilities for Pip's choice of words and none of them make any sense. He feels his back hit the opposite wall to Ren, as he shields his other eye from the bright afternoon sun, willing the past ten minutes to just be wiped from existence.

"*Everything* is falling apart," Sebastian says, yanking his hands away from his face and levelling an accusatory glare at Ren. "Everything, ever since *you* turned up. I get shot at and you still haven't found who did it. I get photographed in a compromising position, which is *your* fault in the first place, and you still haven't recovered the pictures. You enjoyed watching me suffer the other night, dunked me in a cold shower and listened to me spill my guts because I was fucked up. And now, you do your best to *undermine* me, to make me look like a fucking idiot!"

Ren's face has fallen beyond its usual display of apathy, straight into anger. It makes Sebastian flounder a little, rely further on the wall at his back to stay upright.

"With respect, sir, I think you're being paranoid," Ren says levelly. Despite the obvious frustration in his face, he's a professional, through and through. If Sebastian weren't so irritated now himself, he'd be impressed, he thinks.

"I wish people would stop offering me their feigned respect," Sebastian manages to keep his voice on a level with Ren's, but it trembles with something more. "How can you respect me if you claim I'm just paranoid? Hm? Tell me what I'm paranoid about, Ren! Tell me you're not just scurrying to Ivan and my father and reporting it all back after making me look like a fucking idiot!"

He can't help but explode as he nears the end of the sentence, massaging his temple as his head thumps in protest. Ren takes a deep breath.

"It was never my intention to undermine you. I spoke without thinking—or at least, I didn't consider what *you* might be thinking. We... operate on different wavelengths, sir. I need to work harder to… understand where your head's at when you're making decisions. That way I can do my job better, and we can avoid confrontation like this."

Sebastian wants to lash out again, but he finds Ren's summation of the situation too on the nose and the pain in his head too poignant. This whole afternoon has just served as a waste of his time—an unnecessarily long interaction with a woman he'd scorned and a follow up bout of inconvenience because his bodyguard must quite simply be an idiot. The pain is beginning to recede, and the lack brings with it a sense of clarity.

"In future, just don't make small talk with the women I fuck—or almost fuck or *whatever*," he adds, pushing himself up off the wall and beginning to fish around the pocket of his coat for his cigarettes. "And do me a favour and keep an eye on that girl. I don't know what sort of idea she has in her head about me, but I don't need it getting around. She already told me she's got a big mouth, so if you think she needs shutting up I want it done sooner rather than later," Sebastian pauses with his cigarette on his lip as they emerge back out onto the coffee shop's patio, gesturing to Ren for his lighter. He's already produced it, igniting the tip and watching it glow as Sebastian inhales deeply.

"Understood, sir," Ren says.

Sebastian pauses for a moment, the nicotine flooding his brain, bringing with it calm.

"But don't do anything to the dog. If you need blackmail or something, figure it out, but don't threaten Donatello."

If Ren thinks this is a foolish request, he doesn't voice it. Sebastian thinks that's a positive—he's a fast learner.

Seven

"Do you want us to stay and help you put the toga on, sir?"

The other makeup artists finish dabbing the last of the paint onto Sebastian's bare shoulders. After considering the pale linen toga for a moment, he shakes his head.

"No. I'll need you in the lobby before I head out for any last-minute touch ups, so set yourselves up down there," he instructs, ignoring the babble of affirmations he receives in response from the makeup team he'd hired for the Halloween party. They collect their cases and go, leaving behind nothing but the soft drone of the stereo in the corner and Sebastian, half dressed already in just a pair of compression shorts.

He stands to consider his reflection, smiling as he appreciates the fine work of the makeup artists. The majority of his bone pale skin has now been speckled with bronze and gold paint. It gives the illusion that he is somewhere between a demi-god itself and an attempt by man to cast his likeness for the purposes of worship. There are specks of glitter strewn throughout his already golden hair, a subtle highlight to the highpoints of his cheeks. The aurelian glow of the paint makes the pale grey-blue of his eyes stand out. He adjusts the laurel wreath, also cast in gold, which is affixed to the back of his head, straightening it up ever so slightly.

The space behind him flickers, and he notices Ren has entered his bedroom. He's dressed in a pair of light-washed jeans (which leave very little to Sebastian's already overactive imagination), a skintight white tank top, and a rhinestone armband. It shows off the taught bulge of his bicep. It's honed in a way that can only be attributed to hard work. Whether it's purely for work or for aesthetics, Sebastian isn't sure.

Sebastian grins, the thrill of seeing Ren out of his dreary workwear only bringing further excitement over his own costume.

"Well?" he asks, gesturing grandly at his half-naked, bronzed torso. "What do you think?"

Ren nods, his mouth a thin line.

"Very nice, sir," he says, folding his hands in front of himself and settling back on the wall beside the door. Sebastian frowns.

"Well, obviously it's very nice," he repeats, rolling his eyes. "But what do you think? Can you tell who I am? Oh wait, maybe it's unfair without the props…"

Sebastian lifts the golden bow and quiver of arrows he'd had specially commissioned down from where his toga is hanging, fully facing Ren now, away from the mirror. He slings the quiver across his shoulder, mirrors Ren's own stoic expression, like the statue he's channelling. Ren shakes his head.

"I can't, sir," he replies simply. Sebastian can slowly feel himself deflating. He lets the quiver slide off his shoulder, checks quickly that it hasn't disturbed the paint on his arm. Satisfied, he looks back at Ren.

"You aren't even going to *try* to guess?" he sniffs, petulance creeping into his words. He's not making much of an effort to keep it at bay, really. Ren has been acting strange since their confrontation at the coffee shop and his extreme lack of interest is beginning to get on Sebastian's nerves. Before, his increasing familiarity had caused Sebastian alarm as it served to highlight his attractiveness—but his apathetic professionalism is somehow worse. It makes Sebastian feel stupid, like a schoolboy with a crush on his teacher.

Ren's hollow eyes slip from the quiver back up to Sebastian's face. He takes a long moment to look him up and down, careful, assiduous, not dissimilar to how he had that night in the ensuite. It makes the hairs on Sebastian's arms stand on end, to be scrutinised by him like this again. He feels a prickle of excitement in his dick, finding he enjoys the scrutinisation very much indeed.

"Cupid?" Ren offers. Any arousal Sebastian had felt is doused with the cold tone of Ren's voice, dripping with disinterest.

"No, not Cupid," he snaps. "Isn't Cupid a child? I'm *Eros*."

Eros, the son of Aphrodite, Ancient Greek goddess of love, beauty and desire. In itself a tantalising role to fill for the evening, however, Sebastian had mostly been swayed by the golden bow and arrow he'd get to pose for pictures with all night.

Ren nods, immovable. Sebastian feels the almost overwhelming urge to grab him and shake him, anything to try to pull some kind of response from him.

"Oh," Ren says. Then, "Isn't Eros just the Greek version of Cupid?"

Sebastian latches onto the statement, a smile flooding his face before he can stop it. He waggles his finger knowingly, turning to resume primping in the mirror. He glances at Ren's reflection.

"See, you try to play dumb with me Ren, but I know that secretly you're a fine scholar—you do know your Eros from your Cupid after all," he says smugly. Ren shrugs.

"I don't know if that makes me a fine scholar, sir."

Sebastian rolls his eyes, forgetting his attractive reflection almost altogether and skewering Ren with an accusatory glare.

"What's your problem?" he demands, impatience finally getting the better of his repeated attempts to remain aloof. This is what Sebastian had *wanted,* after all, some space between them to better manage the undeniable attraction he feels. The chasm that Ren's somehow managed to carve in the two weeks since the coffee shop incident, however, is pushing it too far. It feels as if the void now stretches an impossible length. Sebastian tries to reach out and tease him but Ren is so far he doesn't even appear to notice.

"My problem, sir?" Ren repeats, inclining his head a little like he hasn't a clue what Sebastian is talking about. It's annoying. It makes Sebastian's skin itch with irritation. He lifts the toga down for something to do, stepping into the bottom half of the costume and tugging it roughly up so it rests on his hips.

"Yes, *your problem*," he insists. "You've been standoffish with me for at least a week now. Every time I try to engage you in conversation it's half-hearted answers or you just brush me off," he adds, fastening the toga at his hip. Ren's mouth twitches at the edges.

"I apologise if you've felt that way, sir," he says innocently, but there's a gleam to the dark hollows of his eyes that's been absent since that day and it makes Sebastian's heart do a strange leap. He decides to push it further. Let the hook catch deeper in Ren's skin before he reels him in.

"There you go again. Stop trying to avoid talking to me. You've been doing it since we met that girl and her dog on campus. Tell me what's wrong," he says briskly, pausing as he watches that look in Ren's eyes darken. Anticipation ignites in the tips of Sebastian's fingers. He's onto something, angled in the right direction. What the fuck is his issue? They'd had a conversation about Ren's unprofessional attempt to belittle Sebastian in front of that girl; he'd set him straight, and they'd finished up with a cigarette and a discussion about how to proceed. He doesn't see any reason why the event in itself was so special?

Sebastian's been over and over those moments in his head, to little avail. As he matches Ren's suddenly intense gaze, a thought occurs to him.

"Is it something *I've* done?" he asks.

The moment of silence between them stretches too long. Sebastian is faced with a strange amalgamation of emotion. Satisfaction, that he's finally backed Ren into a corner. Then, confusion over what on earth he could have done to elicit this reaction.

"It's really not an issue," Ren says quickly, obviously realising his moment of hesitation has given the game away. "I'm your employee. You don't need to worry about my emotional welfare. If I'm acting differently, I apologise. I'll try to be more professional."

Sebastian sighs, letting the edge of the toga he's been trying to drape across his shoulder fall to the side. It's more difficult to wind over and fasten than he'd thought it would be.

"Can you help me with this?" he asks, flailing the wispy end of the fabric in Ren's direction. He hovers by the door for another minute before crossing over to where Sebastian is standing in front of the mirror. He takes the long length of fabric and begins winding it around Sebastian's torso, from his right hip to drape over his left shoulder. He doesn't meet Sebastian's gaze in the mirror, determined in his task.

"Professionalism isn't the problem," Sebastian continues as Ren works, "You've had a giant stick up your ass for over a week now. It's annoying."

"I'm not sure what you want from me if it isn't professionalism, sir," Ren replies sharply, pausing then in his task to look firmly back at Sebastian in the mirror. His fingers rest idly on the skin of Sebastian's hip, clinging to the fabric a little too tight. Sebastian is suddenly painfully aware of the press of Ren's warm hands there. They send a ripple of heat across his body, surging down his every nerve.

He finds Ren's dark gaze impossible to look away from. It's like looking into the depths of a tunnel with no end in sight; like gazing beyond the edge of the shoreline where the water becomes too deep to stand. Sebastian can feel his heart resting in his throat, determined to choke back any embarrassing sentiments he might let slip. He feels lost, the pull of Ren's warm body so close to his back the only thing tethering him to the moment.

He can't help but let his gaze flicker to consider Ren's mouth, full lips parted and deliciously tempting as he awaits his response.

He looks him in the eye again. Grasps onto the edges of his sanity with the remaining strength he has. Sebastian leans on the only concrete thing he knows when it comes to Ren—brutal transparency when it's needed most.

"I think we went a little beyond the realms of professionalism when you wiped come off my face and put me in the shower. And looked at my cock," Sebastian adds as an afterthought, the words tumbling out in a jumble. He thinks he plays it off just enough. That Ren will interpret the tremble of nervous energy as amusement. Ren looks away from Sebastian and continues fastening the toga, his face falling a little. Maybe he's embarrassed, Sebastian guesses.

The silence sits heavy around them again.

Sebastian takes a deep breath. Vows to himself that this will be the last time he presses the matter (if only to retain the modicum of sanity and self-respect he has left).

"Ren," he says, and it sounds strange. Sincerity is not something Sebastian practices often. It almost seems like a taunt.

Not enough, though. Ren meets his eyes again when he hears his name fall from Sebastian's lips in that way. His face softens a little. Sebastian takes a deep breath. "Please, just tell me what's wrong."

Ren finishes securing the toga at the back of Sebastian's shoulder, studying the knot carefully for a moment before letting out a low sigh. It seems to be as difficult for him to provide this information as it was for Sebastian to ask for it.

"When we were in the alley that day. And you were talking about me, saying how you thought everything in your life had become more difficult and it was my fault. Did you consider how those words would make me feel?"

Sebastian blinks, trying to pick apart Ren's expression. He falters, shakes his head.

"I don't understand," Sebastian says immediately. "Why would they make you feel anything? I was just reflecting on events that had taken place."

Ren is watching him closely, chin nearly meeting Sebastian's shoulder as he leans further forwards. Sebastian clenches the fabric of his costume on one side, forcing himself to stay still.

"You were reflecting on events that had taken place and then implying they were all my fault," Ren points out. "I'm not saying it was all untrue. No, I haven't got any further along with finding the shooter, and I'm very aware of that. But when you implied I *enjoyed* seeing you in the state you were in that night after the club… that it was my *goal* to undermine you in front of Pip… that upset me." Ren pauses, taking a deep breath before he finishes. "I thought we were getting along better than that. That you were starting to feel like you could trust me. Did I really make you think those things?"

Sebastian's tongue has stopped working, limp and useless in his mouth as he tries to absorb what Ren has just said. He tries to sift through the confusion and apprehension he's feeling at the moment to remember what he'd felt in the alley. Panic, over Pip's implication as she'd stormed away. Fear, that perhaps other people suspected the same as she, that his meticulously crafted image and the years of fucking random girls when he *hated* the supple curves of their bodies was for nothing. Anger, that Ren had put his foot in it at the last minute and inspired her vicious final words. Concern, over the idea that any of it might make its way back to his father.

Even if Sebastian could repair his reputation on a surface level amongst the drones at that useless fucking university, the suspicion would always linger there under everything. Once the seed was planted, it would be incredibly hard to root out. Then what? An outcome he couldn't plan for, couldn't control.

"I don't know," Sebastian blurts out, unable to formulate a coherent response amongst the barrage of worst-case scenarios now entering his head. "I don't know I was just... I didn't think it would matter to you. I don't know if anything I say really matters to you, does it? Does it really matter to anyone? It's all just..."

Fake. The best sort of defence a person can utilise. Well crafted, sharpened over the years to protect himself. Since nothing that he says really matters, why would Ren take anything he says to heart? Why would he care?

Sebastian is yanked from his spiralling thoughts by the determined press of Ren's hand on his shoulder. It's the same as it had been that night in the shower, a deliberate squeeze of his fingers and then release. To show he's listening? To show that he cares?

Sebastian feels the familiar unfurling of anxiety in his stomach, sending his gut churning. He wants to throw up, relieve himself of the tempest but he'll ruin his make up. The party is soon. He needs to get a grip.

He thinks of the promise Ren made the night he cleaned him up after the club. That he wouldn't tell Ivan about the guy Sebastian brought home if he didn't directly ask. He'd survived a dinner date with his father in Carlito's after the fact, with no mention of the event. That must mean that Ren kept his promise—otherwise Ivan would have run straight to his father and exposed him. They never would have made it to dinner, if that were the case. His father would have simply called him upstairs, alone.

No, that had never happened. So Ren must have kept his promise.

Sebastian knows his hands have started to shake, but he turns to face Ren, anyway.

"I do trust you," Sebastian says.

It's the closest thing to an apology as he can muster, stone cold sober as he is. He's not even sure it's entirely the truth.

He lifts his hand (and it's like he's watching from outside his own body, divorced from the movement entirely); lets his fingers settle on Ren's shoulder, a mirror of where he'd paused to comfort Sebastian.

Sebastian squeezes, feels a thrill run through him. He wonders if Ren feels it, too.

"I do trust you," he repeats, as if to convince himself. "I think. I've… I don't think I've ever done that before? I'm not entirely sure how it works. You have to tell me if I fuck it up."

He shakes Ren's shoulder, a little too roughly perhaps, to emphasise his point. Ren tilts his head in the direction of the movement, before locking eyes once more with Sebastian. His face is soft again somehow, like the ice has thawed and left behind something new and delicate.

"Okay," he says. "I will."

The moment is shattered by the sudden blare of the phone in the corner of Sebastian's room. Ren doesn't hesitate to slide away from Sebastian's grasp to answer it. Sebastian feels like there's been a hornet's nest set free beneath the surface of his skin, humming with nervous energy. All of it let loose from the spot on his shoulder where Ren touched. Ren places the receiver down, straightens up, and clears his throat.

"The car is downstairs, sir. We should go if we're going to make it on time."

Sebastian nods, collecting his bow and quiver and draping them across his body. He gives one last glance in the mirror, satisfied he's met his own impeccably high standards, and follows Ren from the room. They don't speak again until they're safely in the elevator. Ren has reapplied his mask of polite professionalism, albeit without the harsh edge of rejection this time.

"Do you like my costume, sir?" he asks.

Sebastian pauses to look him up and down, before offering him a frown.

"A pair of jeans and a tank top? Is that supposed to be a costume?" he replies, rolling his shoulders back and preparing himself for the lines of paparazzi now stationed outside his apartment building. Ren offers a dramatic gasp in response, as if highly offended. Sebastian grins.

"I'm hurt, sir. I put a lot of effort into pulling this together. Oh wait," he adds, rummaging around in his pocket for a second before pulling something dark and furry out. "I suppose it's the same as yours—difficult to recognise without the props."

He lifts the item to his upper lip, pressing it down firmly. It's an ugly little fake moustache. Sebastian doesn't bother to hide his wince of disdain.

"Freddie Mercury?"

Ren nods, a smug smile threatening to cross his features. He doesn't allow it to escape, much to Sebastian's disappointment.

"Of course. I used to do his outfit from 'I Want to Break Free,' but I'm working and that skirt is a killer to get around in. Good for taking a piss though," he adds thoughtfully, stroking his fake moustache. Sebastian snorts before the image of Ren in a black leather skirt and comically conical bra assaults every corner of his mind. He rounds on him, watching the inquisitive uplift of Ren's eyebrows.

"What do you mean you 'used to do his outfit from 'I Want to Break Free'? Where would *you* even get a costume like that? Where would you wear it?" he demands, becoming painfully aware the elevator is approaching the ground floor with rapid persistence. Ren shrugs.

"Just bits and pieces I picked up over the years. Used to work security in a club that was big on dressing up."

Sebastian shakes his head.

"What kind of club is big on dressing up?" he asks, quickly running through the myriad of establishments in the city he's familiar with.

"Ever heard of *Rain*?" Ren asks casually, as the elevator begins to slow down.

The name rings a bell, but not because Sebastian's ever been. He realises that the bell actually sounds an awful lot more like an alarm. Sebastian swallows.

"The gay club?" he asks, but it comes out as more of a scandalised whisper. He internally cringes, managing to keep his expression more or less interested but neutral.

Ren nods in the affirmative.

"Yeah."

Sebastian feels as if the elevator has suddenly dropped another forty stories from below him, his stomach left behind somewhere on the eleventh floor. The door buzzes politely to indicate they've reached the ground floor lobby.

"So does that mean…?" Sebastian hears the words rush out of him in a flurry, desperate to have the conclusion he's instantly jumped to confirmed.

The elevator doors slide open.

Ren throws him the easiest smile he's ever offered and Sebastian feels his heart clench painfully in his chest. The paparazzi have spilled into the lobby, the camera flashes going off almost immediately.

Ren brings his arm around Sebastian to shield him from the onslaught, smiling smaller now with a secret laid just between the two of them. His mouth is close to Sebastian's ear as he presses up against him, his breath damp on his neck.

"Does that mean *what*, sir?" he asks.

Eight

This time, no one shoots at the stage when Sebastian's father raises his glass to toast his son's twenty-first year on earth. The costumed masses raise their glasses, lifting up masks and dodging props as they go. Sebastian can hear the fake laughter echo off the crystal champagne flutes and it's soothing. After all the nonsense he's endured in the time between his first official birthday party and this one, the reassurance that no matter what, the aristocracy will remain unruffled is invaluable. It makes him over-confident.

Coupled with the buoyancy keeping him aloft after his revelation concerning Ren, he's entirely too animated in his opening welcomes to his father's guests. He emotes too ardently, leaving them exclaiming their suspicious delight that he certainly seems to be keeping well despite 'all that business the last time.' He even offers a genial wave when he spots Pip in the crowd, dressed admittedly adorably as Dorothy from the Wizard of Oz. Her curly red hair is in two braids on either side of her head, ruby slippers glittering as she tucks her stuffed Toto under her arm and flips him off, smiling insipidly.

Not even that is enough to curtail Sebastian's enthusiasm. He tries to still the race of his heart as he thinks of Ren heading down into the basement club he knows to be *Rain*. Who would he meet there? What would he spend his evening doing? Would he end up going home with one of the patrons?

Sebastian clenches his jaw and tries to curtail some of that nervous energy. He can't. He hopes the guests just think he's high.

Ren is always close, close enough that Sebastian can sense him. He's becoming increasingly aware of him, just as he thinks Ren is always keenly aware of exactly where Sebastian is and what he's doing. It's a gentle presence, hovering by his back and keeping him under a watchful gaze. Sebastian recalls the weeks following their first meeting when the burn of those dark eyes on the back of his neck had sent his spine crawling with discomfort.

Was it ever truly *discomfort*? Sebastian thinks if he cared to examine it any closer, he would be forced to admit it never was. Always some peculiar pull that this strange man has had on him, drawing him closer to keep him safe while also maintaining a ruthless air of professionalism. The professionalism is waning a little.

Sebastian decides that he would very much like to examine that closer.

He finishes speaking with another of his father's guests, allowing himself to glance over his shoulder. Ren is there, a few steps back in the crowd, scanning it for any trace of trouble. Ivan is a few paces away. He's wearing the usual dour suit, but tonight he's added a pair of dark sunglasses. Sebastian wonders if he tried to convince Ren to go as his opposing Man in Black. It's a frighteningly relevant reference for someone like Ivan—it serves as a sufficient reminder not to underestimate him.

Ren catches the edge of Sebastian's eye then, nodding through the crowd. Sebastian notices he's ditched the stick-on moustache and runs his index finger over his own top lip in question. Ren's mouth stays pinned in a straight line, but his eyes are warm as he shakes his head dismissively. He begins to move closer.

Sebastian's pulse quickens. For once, butterflies erupt in his stomach and not a mound of writhing worms, only serving to further amplify his good mood.

"Sebastian."

It's his father's voice. His heart drops so fast he's worried it might fall out his ass. The butterflies are assaulted by a sudden hailstorm, left to die battered and broken in the pit of his guts.

Sebastian spins back around to his father's side. Offers him a quick smile.

"Sorry dad," he says breezily. "I thought I saw an exquisitely accurate Princess Leia over there."

His father provides a tight-lipped smile of approval (it's okay if Sebastian's attention is pulled off into the crowd if he's ogling a woman half-dressed as a slave, but not his fiercely attractive bodyguard). His father is dressed as Zeus, similarly bronzed as Sebastian with his own pale robes. They cover him up considerably more, a far more modest choice than his outlandish son. They're embroidered with fine golden thunderbolts along the hem.

"I know who you're talking about, but unfortunately I think she came with someone!" another voice chirps up.

Sebastian looks away from searching his father's face for any trace of distaste to instead smile at the two guests standing in front of them. One is an older man, in a pathetic get-up that consists of a standard tuxedo and a cape draped over his shoulders (a poor attempt at some kind of vampire, Sebastian guesses). He's not the one who spoke, however.

The voice belongs to a young man about Sebastian's age, dressed in varying stripes of magenta and purple, his nose and cupid's bow painted to look like the muzzle of a Cheshire Cat. The smile he wears is insidious, an uncanny match to the caricature. A pair of fluffy purple cat ears rest amongst a shock of bright red hair.

The last time Sebastian heard that voice, it had been gasping encouragement as its owner orgasmed on his face.

The bolt of terror that runs through Sebastian only paralyses him for a moment. He compartmentalises it appropriately. The malignant presence of his father at his side helps with that.

Sebastian wills his mouth to return the smile, feels his cheeks twitch with the effort.

"Useful information to have. I'm more interested in who she'll be leaving with," Sebastian replies, earning a chuckle from the shit-vampire and a harrumph of feigned disapproval from his own father.

"I suppose it is your birthday after all," the shit-vampire says, raising his glass as if in another toast to Sebastian. "I don't know if you'll remember us, Sebastian, it's been so long. Roberto Godoy, and this is my son, Jerome."

The shit-vampire reaches out to shake Sebastian's hand. He takes it without question, nodding politely.

What little Sebastian remembers of that drunken night spent with Jerome comes flooding back into his brain. He had recalled his face in some manner, but thought they'd perhaps just crossed paths at university before. Now that he's presented with the facts and spared the influence of too much tequila, Sebastian can place him more clearly. A longtime business associate of his father, Roberto Godoy, had frequented their corporate events for many years now. He hadn't always brought Jerome along; once or twice during their teenage years perhaps, to foster goodwill amongst the next generation or some such bullshit.

It had always been the red hair Sebastian had fixated on when he saw the other boy.

Jerome waits with his own hand extended, all shit-eating grin and half-lidded eyes as Sebastian drops Roberto's grasp.

"Sebastian remembers me, papa. We see each other around from time to time," Jerome says, fingers gripping Sebastian's for an instant too long. Sebastian tries not to recoil in disgust when he manages to tug his hand away.

He can feel his father's discerning gaze linger on the contact. He takes a deep breath.

"Yes, our social circles overlap here and there, don't they?" he adds lightly, tucking his hand down at his side and rubbing his palm discreetly along the fabric bunched at his hip. He suddenly feels much too hot. He hopes the golden paint laden across his chest is enough to disguise any flush which might find its way there. Sebastian snatches a flute of champagne from the nearest waiter, hoping the chill of the glass against his fingers will help in some way. It doesn't.

"Your father was just saying there's still no word of who hijacked your last party," Roberto says, chuckling to himself as he belittles the attempt made on Sebastian's life. "I suppose you just can't get good help these days."

"Your bodyguard is new, isn't he, Sebastian?" Jerome asks, eyes flickering over Sebastian's shoulder to try to pick out Ren from the crowd. "I'll bet he didn't expect to be run this ragged when he took the job."

Sebastian supplies a gentle laugh. It's appropriately aloof, laced with contempt. He remembers the way Jerome had held him down in the darkness and fucked his throat until he was choking for air, and finds the contempt comes easily enough.

"And how is it that you know Ren?"

Sebastian's father speaks unexpectedly, his voice acerbic enough to cause even Jerome to flinch a little. He recovers quickly, waving his hand in dismissal. Sebastian feels his father tense incrementally around the edges. His stomach twists tighter. This conversation has derailed entirely out of his control.

"He called me a cab the last time Sebastian and I happened to be haunting the same locale," Jerome says smoothly. "Nice guy—very professional."

"Sounds like the two of you hit it off," Sebastian says, raising a delicate eyebrow in Jerome's direction. "Consider yourself lucky. I can barely get two words out of him."

Roberto chuckles again awkwardly to fill the silence which follows. Sebastian can sense his father directing more of his subtle hostility towards Jerome and thinks he's perhaps managed to spare both him and Ren any grief in the inevitable follow up to this interaction. It makes the uncomfortable heat in his chest begin to marginally subside. He takes a sip of champagne as a reward.

"Yes, well, we won't keep you," Roberto finally says, glancing swiftly over at his son, who hasn't once stopped staring at Sebastian. "Happy birthday, Sebastian."

"Yes, happy birthday," Jerome adds brightly, all thirty of his teeth glinting in his wide smile. He leans in an inch before following Roberto as he wanders away. His voice drops, his gaze rakes across the exposed skin of Sebastian's torso. "I like your costume."

With that, the two of them are gone, the crowd having absorbed them both into its heaving masses.

Sebastian feels the sudden brush of his father's hand on his elbow, intentional and discreet.

He says the words while barely moving his lips.

"Come with me, Sebastian."

Sebastian nods, waiting until his father's back is turned before swallowing the contents of his champagne flute in one go. The buzz from the alcohol will provide a layer of protection no matter his father's intent. If he's angry, it'll take the edge off any pain inflicted. If he's not (yet) it will provide Sebastian's brain with some fuzzy inspiration to talk shit until he's managed to appease him.

As before, Sebastian is all too aware of Ren stalking him through the crowd a few steps back, as he follows his father out of the ballroom and into one of the adjoining conference rooms. He tries to remember if the company owns this hotel. Decides it doesn't matter when his father waits on the inside of the door for Sebastian to enter the room and then promptly shuts it behind him.

He grips him by the shoulder, leads him over towards a large, empty fireplace.

"What the fuck was all that about?" his father says.

Sebastian swallows past the sudden dryness of his mouth. Shakes his head softly.

"I'm not sure what you mean, sir," he replies. He wills the unease which is rapidly pooling in his gut to recede. He can feel the pain in the back of his eye beginning to twinge in warning. His father frowns. His grip doesn't lessen, remaining tightly in place.

"Don't waste my time, Sebastian," he says. "That slimy little cunt with the red hair. Seemed to be enjoying sidling up to you, didn't he? What's it about?"

Sebastian reaches for the foundations of the story, something wrapped up in a transparent film of the truth.

"He's just an asshole. I ran into him while I was out a few weeks ago. We ended up playing drinking games, and he tried to take me for a fool. Ren stepped in, saw him out. He's a sore winner, you know the type."

Sebastian keeps his speech clipped and to the point. His father narrows his eyes, removes his grip from Sebastian's shoulder.

"Is he one of those fucking sissy boys from that school?"

Sebastian's blood turns to ice in his veins. He shakes his head.

"No, sir," he manages to reply. His father lashes forwards, grabs his wrist. It's the same motion he's made for the entirety of Sebastian's life, so he doesn't understand why it still makes his chest feel so heavy. His lungs struggle to expand as Sebastian tries to suck in air past the panic. His father's grip on his wrist pangs, despite the lax hold he has on it. It's the memory of the pain which burns up Sebastian's arm, keeping him rooted to the spot.

"Don't give me that bullshit," his father says. Sebastian wishes he said it with any feeling at all, then he might understand how he wants him to respond. His words are as clipped and cold as when he's addressing any of the faceless drones that work below him. Then he says, "And if he were, what the fuck do you think he'd be thinking looking at you, hm? What the fuck is the matter with you turning up half-dressed like that? What sort of things are people going to say about you?"

Sebastian shakes his head again. He's beginning to feel dizzy.

"I thought it would be a show of force, sir," he says quickly. "I'm not afraid of anyone trying to make a mockery of us; not a shooter, not a nobody like Godoy—"

Sebastian's speech is brought to a sudden halt as his father yanks his wrist up, twists it just enough that real pain licks its way up Sebastian's bone like tongues of fire. He relaxes his grip as suddenly as he'd tightened it, the lingering threat of further retribution all that remains.

"You listen to me," his father says, and this time his words are quieter. Danger makes itself known in every syllable. Sebastian nods his head to show he's following the instruction. "I've been very patient with you since your birthday, Sebastian, very patient. It would make me extremely unhappy to find that my patience is being met with yet another example of your vicious ingratitude."

Sebastian tries to respond in the affirmative, but his throat is too choked up. He tries to clear it, tries to talk past the knot of dread, but it's not working. He feels his wrist burning in protest.

A fresh wave of pain seems to trigger something in his brain, his heart hammering to feed his body with adrenaline.

"I understand, sir," he manages to keep his voice level, but it's breathy. Pathetic. His father nods, releases his wrist.

"I'm glad to hear it. Now, for the love of God, go and put some clothes on. I don't want to see you skipping around like some kind of fucking fairy the rest of the night."

Sebastian nods, resists the urge to cradle his hand. His wrist aches from the pressure inflicted on the same hairline fracture that's been healing on and off for his entire life.

He continues to stand beside the empty fireplace, staring determinedly at the ground. His father leaves the room without another word. He hears him saying something, probably to Ivan, and then he's gone. Sebastian doesn't know what he said. His ears ring incessantly, drowning out the room around him.

Sebastian lets himself sink to the ground, cheeks pressed to the insides of his knees as he folds himself over. It's safer to be closer to the ground like this. He's fainted a few times in the past after particularly unpleasant run-ins with his father. Despite the fact that the one he's just had was harmless, it's still best to be prepared. He squeezes his eyes shut tight and focuses on breathing in and out slowly.

It's not until he feels the steady press of Ren's palm on his shoulder that the shame takes hold.

Sebastian flinches away from the touch.

"Stop it. I'm fine," he says, standing up straight quickly and brushing himself down. He doesn't look at Ren, finds that he can't for fear the knot in his gullet will return in full force. His wrist is aching, so much so that he can't help prodding a few exploratory fingers at the bone there. He should be very sure it's not fractured. Dr Warren has already made it clear his fine motor skills aren't as sharp as they should be. He winces at the pain. Ren moves around to try to force himself into Sebastian's line of sight. The shame of it all, coupled with Ren's silent concern, makes Sebastian's temper flare.

"Well? How much of that charming interaction did you hear? Or see?" he adds, trying to keep his voice detached. It comes out hoarse, like he's been yelling or crying. It makes the shame all the heavier.

"Enough," Ren says quietly. A second passes, the sounds of merriment from the ballroom which are starting to filter through Sebastian's head again, a stark contrast to the melancholy atmosphere left in his father's wake. "Would you like to come outside for a smoke?"

The thought alone is enough to make Sebastian's tense shoulders fall from where they're hunched up by his ears.

"Yes. Please, fuck yes."

Ren nods and leads him out of the room. They turn the opposite direction to the ballroom, heading for the back service elevator to avoid any other guests. Ren jams his finger on the button for the ground floor, avoiding looking directly at Sebastian as he explains.

"I thought we'd go down to the street. Too many of your guests on the terrace. Might draw you into conversation."

Sebastian nods, grateful suddenly for Ren's level head. He leans the back of his skull against the polished brass interior of the elevator, concentrating on the mechanical drone which ricochets through his brain as they travel downward. It jostles the old injury behind his eye, which distracts from the immediate discomfort in his wrist. It's just gently pulsing with pain now.

The elevator reaches the ground floor and Ren leads him further into the back of the hotel, before finding an emergency exit and propping it open for Sebastian.

They emerge into a sidestreet, the front entrance of the hotel which is still accepting visitors on Sebastian's behalf around the corner to the left. It's a clear and therefore chilly October night, but the heat of the party coupled with the stifling panic that had taken hold of Sebastian's body means he's running too warm, anyway. It's a welcome relief, like plunging headfirst into the ocean after lying on a sunny beach for too long. Sebastian feels a shiver run from the tip of his scalp down to the small of his back, chasing a determined bead of sweat.

Ren is pulling his pack of cheap smokes and his trusty Zippo from his pocket. He produces a cigarette, sets it on his lip and lights it. He inhales deeply, blue smoke escaping from his nostrils in thin jets, as he takes the cigarette from his mouth and places it in Sebastian's.

Sebastian hurries to hold it in place with his fingers, his jaw abruptly going slack.

It would be nonsense to think the tip of the cigarette seems sweeter after being held in Ren's mouth. Sebastian knows that's nonsense, and yet when he inhales for the first time, it makes his mouth flood with saliva. He draws the smoke down into his lungs, lets the soothing effects settle into his limbs. His wrist still twinges a little as he lifts the cigarette from his mouth. It's probably just the cold.

"Are we rationing them, or?" he asks coyly, attempting to sound more like himself and slip back into their familiar teasing.

"That was the last one. Your case is upstairs with the coats," Ren responds.

"Really? Hm. Well, we can share this one."

"There's no need, sir."

"*Ren*. Shut up and take the cigarette."

Ren shuts up and takes the cigarette. His skin brushes Sebastian's fingers as he lifts it, and his eyes flutter closed as he takes a grateful drag.

Ren passes the cigarette back.

"Is your wrist alright? You keep poking it," he says, voice soft as the smoke which clouds his words on the exhale.

Sebastian sighs, tries to focus on the calming effects of the nicotine rather than let the fierce barb on his tongue threatening to launch itself at Ren to escape.

"Just drop it," Sebastian says thinly. "It doesn't concern you."

"Your safety concerns me," Ren says quickly, taking a step closer to Sebastian. Instinctively, Sebastian shrinks away. Something flickers in Ren's expression and Sebastian isn't sure exactly what it is. Ren's true personage is still nearly a total mystery to him and it's driving Sebastian insane.

"You work for the *president*, right?" Sebastian uses Ren's words against him yet again, seizing that fierce professionalism he defends so ardently as a stick to beat him with. "Your job is to protect me, but what you're really protecting is the future and image of the company. The president was making sure I didn't do anything to fuck up the future or image of the company. You're both working towards the same goal, so you should just *drop it*."

Sebastian takes a drag on the cigarette, clenching and unclenching his fist. The pain in his wrist is all but gone now, nothing for Ren to be getting so fucking worked up over. It's horrifying to consider he'd watched Sebastian's father reprimand him like that. A grown man, brought to heel for bad behaviour. It makes the shame cling to him closer, bolstered by Ren's insistence that they keep discussing it.

"But *you are* the future of the company," Ren presses again, shaking his head like he doesn't understand. He *doesn't* understand, Sebastian thinks. He could never understand. "What if he'd hurt you? What if these things he's saying to you make you hurt *yourself*?"

"Oh, for fuck's sake," Sebastian snarls, flicking the spent cigarette to the damp ground and rounding on Ren. He draws himself up to his full height so the other man has no choice but to tilt his head back a little to level him with his dark eyes. They're tumultuous; conflicted. Sebastian wishes they'd go back to being hollow. "I can assure you, Ren, that you're not going to have to peel me off the pavement like Ivan had to with my whore mother. I'm afraid of heights and the one time I did try to slit my wrists, I fainted at the sight of my own blood."

"This isn't a joke, sir," Ren spits back, and he looks incensed. Angry, almost like he could snap and let loose all of those pent-up thoughts at any moment. Sebastian chokes out a burst of noise, somewhere between a laugh and a growl. He shakes his hands despairingly between the two of them.

"Who the fuck is laughing? I'm telling you this because I *trust* you," Sebastian grabs Ren by either shoulder then, imploring him to understand. Anything to stop this line of questioning from continuing, anything so Sebastian doesn't have to feel the pity rippling off the one person who's ever got close enough to seeing the truth of his tragic little life. "I trust that you will let me handle my father. I trust that you will have a cigarette on hand when I need to decompress after the fact. I trust that you will stop asking questions about whether I'm *safe* or whether my *wrist hurts* because it's only going to end badly for you."

Sebastian's path has been preordained since birth, laid out for him every step of the way. He knows how it's going to end up eventually, knows that despite whatever threats his father makes or injuries he causes Sebastian, he's going to make him VP and then, he'll take over. It's only been made more difficult because *he's* made it that way. He cried too much as a child, he barely scraped the honour roll in high school, he'd been born with a sick lust for other men.

Ren doesn't need to be any more involved with Sebastian's father than absolutely necessary.

"Alright," Ren says, as Sebastian's hands slip from his shoulders. "Alright. As long as you keep being honest with me and trusting me, I'll do it your way."

Sebastian snorts.

"Am I supposed to thank you for that?" he asks flippantly, wishing he had another cigarette. Ren doesn't respond right away, but it's eerie the way he seems to know exactly what Sebastian is thinking.

"Let's stop by 7-Eleven. I'll buy you a pack of cigs for your birthday," Ren offers. Sebastian doesn't point out they could just return back upstairs to the party and retrieve his cigarette case. He has no interest in returning to that fray just yet, Ren having succeeded in both pissing him off and distracting him. They walk in silence for a moment before Ren shoots Sebastian a careful sideways glance. "So… did you get anything else nice for your birthday? Nicer than a pack of the cheapest cigarettes money can buy?"

Sebastian blinks at him for a moment in confusion.

"Uh…" he begins, ineloquent. He chews on his lip briefly in thought. "Dad invested in that Carlito's restaurant chain on my behalf, I think. Said I could keep the dividends in ten years when it finally turns a profit."

They've reached 7-Eleven now.

Ren has turned to face Sebastian, his mouth hanging open slightly in shock. It's written all over his face, a fully fledged emotion which Sebastian recognises right away. The thought makes his heart trill in delight, and then flop into his stomach. Ren is upset for some reason.

"But it was your twenty-first birthday," Ren says, before Sebastian can make fun of him for being so dramatic. "You didn't get anything special for your twenty-first birthday? You didn't get to *do* anything special?"

Sebastian opens his mouth to offer a quick retort about how he can have whatever the fuck he wants whenever the fuck he wants it, so it hardly matters. He doesn't. Instead, he shuts his mouth and shakes his head.

Says, "Well… he was never very consistent with that sort of thing. He got me a hooker for my eighteenth birthday. She was a nice hooker, actually. She just sat there and smoked when I couldn't get it up."

Ren clenches his jaw carefully, as if trying to contain himself.

"What *do* you want? Everyone deserves something special for their twenty-first birthday. What do you want, and we'll make it happen," he says finally, earnestly, so impossibly earnest it makes Sebastian feel like he's slit him open from belly to jaw and left his insides strewn across the pavement. Like he can see everything inside, everything he's spent his whole life stifling.

As Ren says the words, Sebastian suddenly knows exactly what he wants, so he asks for it.

"I want to ditch this party," Sebastian says clearly. "And I want you to take me to *Rain*."

Nine

Surprisingly, Ren takes very little convincing. Sebastian's unsure if it's because of the interaction he'd witnessed between Sebastian and the president, or the fact he hadn't received anything 'special,' as Ren put it, for his birthday. Perhaps a combination of the two. Perhaps because Sebastian hadn't even thought to consider any of it as something worth being upset about.

"It's Halloween night, so it's going to be packed," Ren says warningly as they walk through the chilly streets smoking the shit cigs he'd purchased in 7-Eleven. "So if you start to feel overwhelmed"

"I've been to a club before," Sebastian retorts, rubbing his free hand up and down his arm. The hairs all over his body are standing on end, but he doesn't really feel the cold. Excitement is buzzing in his every cell, eliciting a tactile response across the expanse of his bare skin. It feels like static transfers to his fingers. Ren shoots him a withering look.

"Yes, I'm well aware," he says dryly, probably thinking of all the nights he's had to stand in the back of a booth while Sebastian plays nice with other wealthy lay-abouts with nothing better to do. "But you've never been to a gay bar before, have you?"

Sebastian shivers again at the bluntness of his voice, the way Ren just says *gay bar* without glancing over his shoulder. He shakes his head.

"No. I haven't," he replies, and it betrays some of the trepidation he feels bundled up amongst all of the excitement and anticipation.

"Right," Ren says, and if his voice sounds smug he keeps his expression purposefully innocent, "So, I'm just saying. If you start to feel overwhelmed, just tell me and we can leave."

Sebastian kills his cigarette, flicking it to the pavement. He cradles his arms, hands finding the sharp bones of his elbows to hang onto. He leans ever so slightly into Ren's side, feels the smooth expanse of his golden skin, running hot like there's sunshine below the surface there. Ren turns his head to look at him. Sebastian takes a slow breath, tilts his chin around to meet his gaze.

"Do you think I'll be overwhelmed?" he asks. Ren shrugs.

"You like things to happen in a certain way."

Sebastian rolls his eyes.

"Don't dodge the question—or remind me how uptight I am." A flash of pain behind Sebastian's eye rings out, as if agreeing with him.

Ren smiles.

"You trust me, don't you?"

The pain is gone as quickly as it had surfaced, the air leaving Sebastian's lungs as he tries not to lean all the way into Ren's smile.

He thinks of the way Ren had come straight to his side to make sure he was alright earlier. He thinks of him towel drying Sebastian's hair in the quiet of his bedroom. He nods.

"Yeah. Yes, I do," he says. It sounds strangely honest. Sebastian's not sure if he likes this feeling of exposing himself enough to trust someone else to shield him.

Ren looks pleased to hear that, however, nodding as he glances away from Sebastian and back at the pavement as they walk.

"Then it'll be okay. You can be overwhelmed, there's nothing wrong with that. Just tell me."

Before long, they reach the entertainment quarter, neon signs fizzing with the promise of liquor and music and men. The main street where *Rain* is located is full of people. They spill out from the bars and clubs mingling in huge crowds, half waiting to enter, half content to spend their night dancing to the faint bass which makes the ground tremble. They're all in costume too, most far more elaborate than the drab getups Sebastian's party guests had arrived in. The shit-vampire would be laughed out of this street if he dared cross it.

The thought alone, coupled with the thrill of the atmosphere in the street, makes an awkward giggle bubble up in Sebastian's throat. Ren throws him a quizzical glance, his mouth hitched at the corner with amusement.

"They all look incredible," Sebastian shouts to be heard over the rumble of mostly male voices, leaning into Ren's ear so he can hear him. Ren nods in agreement.

"Your costume is certainly more in line with these guys," he yells back, as they begin to press through the crowd towards the stairs which lead down to *Rain*. Sebastian's chest flutters at the indirect praise, but he flounders a little as someone dressed in a latex suit with huge purple wings and a forked tail blocks his path.

Ren reaches back and grabs his hand.

"Stay close to me, okay?" he says, pulling Sebastian easily past the purple latex devil. "You're fresh meat and you're pretty, so we should stick together."

Sebastian lets the compliment wash over him. The offhanded way Ren says it makes him feel tender and warm. Like sinking into a bath that's mostly bubbles. He grins.

"You think I'm pretty, Ren?" he asks slyly, leaning in so his breath paints Ren's cheek with heat. Ren rolls his eyes.

"You know you're pretty," he replies bluntly. Sebastian pokes him experimentally in the bicep, feels a tingle all the way down his arm into his groin.

"Yes, but *you* think I'm pretty," Sebastian insists, following Ren down the steps and past the queue of people waiting to enter the club. He's not sure if it's the flicker of pink neon above the door or a genuine twinge of embarrassment which crosses Ren's cheeks. He chooses to believe the latter.

There's a huge man blocking the entrance, his dark hair braided back in tight cornrows, his beefy arms and most of his chest on view thanks to the tiny green tank top he's wearing. He's also sporting a pair of puffy green and black checked sweatpants and a pair of platform shoes. They make him at least four inches taller, so he's towering over even Sebastian.

He spots Sebastian first and so his face begins to twist in protest, but then he catches sight of Ren and it splits into a magnanimous smile.

"You must be here to let me off, huh, Birdie?" he asks warmly, stretching his arms out expectantly. Ren drops Sebastian's hand to give the huge man a hug, but Sebastian doesn't have time to regret the loss of it. He settles back at Sebastian's side almost in one smooth motion, slipping his hand down and interlacing their fingers. Sebastian can feel every crevice on his skin, lined up perfectly with his own.

"You wish. What are you supposed to be?" Ren asks.

The large man feigns outrage, jaw dropping in disbelief.

"Scary Spice, you fuckin' philistine. Ricky already had all the Baby Spice shit, so we just went with it as a group. I did have a wig but a drunk Cat Woman asked real nice for it so I just gave it to her," he explains, offering a good natured wave to a group of patrons squeezing out the door past them. "You guys get home safe now."

"This is Darius," Ren says then, jerking his chin towards the bouncer dressed up like Scary Spice. "We used to work the door together. Darius, this is—"

Ren stops abruptly, hesitation in the way his eyes widen ever so slightly as he looks between Darius and Sebastian. His tongue is poised, Sebastian's name seemingly on the tip of it, but something stops him from using the word. Sebastian supposes Ren has only ever called him 'sir' or a variation of 'Mr Clarence.' Anxious he's going to revert to the same thing, he interjects.

"I'm Sebastian," Sebastian says, nodding politely at Darius. Darius shoots Ren a look like he thinks he's an idiot.

"What did you forget his name or somethin'?" he guffaws, folding his arms across his chest as he chuckles. "I shoulda *known* you were hanging around somewhere when I seen this guy, Birdie!"

Ren does blush this time, Sebastian is certain of it.

He tries not to dwell on what Darius means by his last statement, but it snags in his brain, caught niggling at the back of his mind.

"It's not like that, D," Ren says quickly. "He just turned twenty-one. I just brought him here to show him a good time."

The strange juxtaposition of Ren giving Sebastian's hand a reassuring squeeze and the dismissive words which leave his mouth have Sebastian's stomach twitching with discomfort. What the fuck is he doing here? It had all happened so fast, the encounter with Jerome, the discussion with his father, Ren taking him outside. He can barely even remember requesting that they come to *Rain*, high on the thrill of the suggestion alone, never mind the prospect Ren might actually bring him.

And now he's clutching his hand so tight Sebastian can almost feel the throb of Ren's heartbeat in his palm. It brushes up against his own, nearly in sync, both racing a little too fast as neon pinks and oranges colour the highpoints of their faces and ears. He feels like an idiot, stumbling blindly along and heeding Ren's instructions like some sort of invalid. He's not used to relinquishing control in this way. Its equal parts freeing and terrifying.

He tries to concentrate on the lightheaded feeling that the freedom brings. It's akin to delirious joy rather than the panic which threatens to overshadow his every move (as seems to increasingly be the case—he really should start taking that Xanax again).

Darius makes a knowing hum and slides to one side, gesturing for them to enter.

"Uh huh, sure, and if my grandma had wheels, she'd be a bike. Don't leave without saying g'bye, Birdie!" Darius yells after them as Ren tugs Sebastian alongside him and into the dark of the basement.

"Birdie?" Sebastian asks curiously as they trundle along like cattle through the cloakrooms (there's a guy handing out tickets dressed in an orange wig and a Union Jack dress who gives Ren an excited wave). Ren's expression twists at the edge a little and he allows a sheepish sound to escape, almost like a chuckle. Sebastian is certain he's never heard him laugh.

"A wren is a type of bird," he explains.

"I know that," Sebastian shoots back, recalling the day they'd first met and the fixation he'd had on Ren's name as he'd tried to cling to consciousness.

"Of course you do," Ren says, amusement painting his words. "Well, it's spelt differently, but I guess the guys thought it was cute, so it stuck."

"Should I start calling you Birdie?" Sebastian asks teasingly. Ren squeezes his hand again, dark eyes skewering Sebastian to the spot.

"No, you should not," he says, unamused. "I never said I liked it."

Sebastian shrugs, snickering at Ren's haughty expression.

"I didn't ask if you liked it," he says. He lets Ren ignore him dismissively as he draws on whatever courage he has left after the confrontation with his father, and the excitement every second at Ren's side is drilling up within him. Sebastian takes a deep breath, says it before the fear holds his tongue back. "I'll keep calling you Ren if you start calling me Sebastian."

"Not going to happen," Ren says immediately, looking away pointedly. Sebastian feels the balloon of hope which has been swelling since Ren grabbed his hand pop all at once. He sighs, and doesn't say anything else as they dip through the door and into the club proper.

It's not that different to the other clubs Sebastian has been in, similarly dark, excessive strobe lighting throbbing in tandem with the music, bodies pressed alongside each other everywhere. The main difference is that it's only men, and these men are not shy about being pressed so close; they dance in a sweaty mass, jumping in time with the music; they wrap themselves around each other as they kiss, some pressed up against standing pillars, others straddled in the booths dotted around the walls.

The disappointment Sebastian feels at Ren's snub doesn't dissipate altogether, but something else starts to fill his chest up as he looks around him. It's warm and comfortable, despite some additional nervous jittering. As they approach the bar, he realises he'd left not only his cigarettes in the hotel.

"Fuck, I don't have my wallet," Sebastian yells in Ren's ear to be heard over the pound of the music. Ren brushes him off before he's nearly hauled over the counter by a tiny little bartender dressed in a white mini-dress. Sebastian can't tell if the person is a man or a woman, their features so dainty and slight, as they clasp Ren's cheeks and plant a kiss on each one.

"Long time, no see, Birdie!" the bartender says. Their eyes flicker over to Sebastian, baby pink lips curving up into a wicked smile. Sebastian can see a gold tooth peeking out where one of their canines should be. Their jaw works furiously over a mound of pink bubblegum. "Who's the hottie?"

"I'm Sebastian!" Sebastian yells, saving Ren from the obviously arduous task of using his first name. Ren shoots him a weary glance, as unbothered by his attempts at pettiness as ever.

"Pretty name, honey. I'm Ricky. What are you having?" Ricky says, blowing a bubble as he picks up an empty glass and jolts it from hand to hand. Sebastian hesitates for a moment, unsure of a number of things—what liquor would they actually have on hand in this bar? If he asked for a specific drink, would Ricky be able to make it? Could Ren afford to pay for whatever Sebastian asked for?

"You pick," he decides, is the safest option, which Ricky seems excited by. He grins, nodding at Ren.

"The usual?" he asks, to which Ren nods gratefully, reaching into his back pocket and pulling out a crumpled bill. He slides it across the bar as Ricky dumps a scoopful of ice into two glasses. Sebastian watches in abstract horror as he yanks a bottle of Jack Daniels from behind him and free pours a double in each cup. He lifts up a bar gun and squirts enough coke into each that they're overflowing, fizzy brown running over the rims. Finally, he lifts three shot glasses and a bottle of nondescript green liquor, pouring so efficiently he barely spills a drop.

"This one's on me," Ricky winks at Sebastian as he tucks the money Ren had offered into the front of his dress, and slides their drinks over.

Sebastian lifts his shot, clinking it together with Ricky and Ren's as they throw them back in unison. It burns his throat like he's just drank a can of lighter fluid. It has no flavour, just feels like a chemical peeling all the tastebuds off Sebastian's tongue.

Ricky has already been swept away into conversation by another patron, working double time to make up for the orders he wasn't taking while chatting with Ren and Sebastian.

"You drink Jack and coke at parties, right?" Ren asks Sebastian over the lip of his cup as he takes a long swig, chasing the foul taste of his own shot. Sebastian wrinkles his nose overtop of the foamy liquid, nonetheless nodding in confirmation.

"I certainly do," he replies, screwing his eyes up and trying to contain the displeasure on his face as he takes a gulp. When he opens them again, Ren is watching him with undeniable mirth written all over his face. Sebastian rolls his eyes. "But it's not because I fucking like it, it's just the best of a bad bunch."

Ren grins at that, knowingly, like he's enjoying watching Sebastian squirm. The expression seems to come more easily to him than it usually does. Perhaps the shot has already started to loosen him up.

Ren leads him over to a ledge which lines the walls, drinks of every colour imaginable scattered across it already. They slide themselves between two other groups of people, a couple with their backs to the rest of the room sniffing something out of a little brown bottle, and a cluster of cowboys trying to initiate a line dance along to the pounding music.

Sebastian takes another few deep swallows of his drink, willing the whiskey to get to work and chase away the last of his inhibitions. He's not brave enough to suggest they go and dance, content for now to be folded into the corner with Ren studying the vast array of individuals in the club. The niggling question at the back of his mind persists however, so he pushes his lips down close to Ren's ear so he can hear him. He's close enough he can feel the heat of Ren's skin on his own face.

"What did Darius mean before?" Sebastian begins. "When he said he should have *known* you were hanging around somewhere when he saw me?"

Ren chews on his bottom lip thoughtfully for a moment before offering Sebastian an apologetic look.

"Wasn't sure if you caught that, but I should have known better, huh?"

Sebastian doesn't respond, just raises his eyebrows to show he still expects an explanation. Ren runs a hand over his face, eyes flickering away from Sebastian and then back again. He seems... stressed? Embarrassed? Sebastian isn't sure exactly which, but he feels a certain wave of pride that he's even able to discern this much from Ren's notoriously cagey expressions.

"I guess... I have a type," Ren says finally, and now he definitely looks embarrassed. He's staring determinedly at the floor, scratching at the back of his neck. Sebastian blinks.

"A type?" he repeats dumbly, like he doesn't already *know* what that means.

Ren sighs, gesturing vaguely towards Sebastian. His eyes follow the movement from his exposed torso to the crown of his head.

"Yeah. Tall. Blonde. A type."

"A type of *man*?"

Sebastian hears the way his voice squeaks and wishes he was fucking dead.

Ren stares at him a moment, eyes tightening with disbelief before he starts to laugh. Sebastian can barely hear it past the pound of the music, but he can see it stretched across his strong, fine features. It makes his eyes glitter, shiny like tempered chocolate; it makes his cheeks full and pink; Sebastian can see his tongue, the glint of something silver peeking out from inside his mouth.

"Yes," he says after a moment. "A type of man."

Sebastian feels positively dizzy. Ren's confirmation, coupled with the heat and intensity of the club, is making his brain feel like it's too big for his skull, pressing against the bone to escape. Incredulous, all he can manage to say is:

"Do you have your *tongue* pierced?"

Ren doesn't respond right away, chugging down the remainder of his Jack and coke, rubbing the edge of his thumb along his chin when a drop escapes. Sebastian watches, entranced, as he leans in close.

"Do you want to find out?" Ren asks.

There is a moment of standstill between them. Ren watches Sebastian closely, gaze hot and inquisitive. His lips part a fraction, as if in offering of what more is to come.

The moment passes and Sebastian can't stop his mouth falling open in shock. Ren raises both his hands defensively. He looks suddenly horrified.

"That was a joke. I don't know why I—Jesus Christ," he finishes weakly, visibly ruffled. Sebastian doesn't think he's ever seen Ren like this before. Perhaps it's the booze? Perhaps it's being in the comfort of all of his old friends? Regardless, it seems to have loosened his tongue considerably. Now, though, he just looks completely mortified, gazing into his empty glass like he's going to find the reason why he'd just propositioned Sebastian at the bottom.

Sebastian wonders for a split second if he should tell him the truth—that he would very much like to investigate the supposed tongue piercing for himself.

At that moment, however, one of the cowboys who have been frolicking alongside the two of them taps Sebastian on the shoulder. He has shiny, coiled hair and a dimple when he smiles. He looks up through curly lashes at Sebastian.

"Hey beautiful," he hums. His pupils look huge. "Wanna dance?"

Brain already working on a delay tonight, Sebastian falters for nearly an instant too long. It's Ren who intervenes, and it's only now with the loss of it that Sebastian realises they haven't stopped holding hands this entire time. Despite the heat of the basement club, the dampness of his hand catches the air and feels cool. It feels abandoned without the steadfast clutch of Ren's fingers.

"You should go," Ren says, with no smile of encouragement present. It's more like resignation. Like he's already decided for himself that tonight has gone too far. "Have some fun—enjoy yourself!"

Sebastian tries not to let the torrent of disappointment show on his face, but his chest feels as if several cinder blocks have now taken up residence there. Ren has already made his decision. Sebastian decides to take back control.

"Fine. Let's go," he turns to the curly haired cowboy and follows him out onto the dancefloor. He feels the sudden press of Ren's hollow gaze on the back of his neck, so familiar and simultaneously so horribly distant.

Sebastian lets the cowboy loop his arms around his waist and pull him in close to his hips. Ren's watchful stare follows them across the dancefloor.

Ten

Sebastian doesn't know where he ends and the next person begins.

The cowboy's biceps rest at the dip of his hips; the air is thick with the fust of smoke machines and synthetic sweetness; a thigh brushes up against him in passing, its owner held tight, wrapped around the hips of another; he can taste the remnants of that acidic green shot on the back of his tongue, the contents of his stomach sloshing angrily as he moves in time with the music; the bass thuds up into the soles of his feet, the sound travelling through him as it tries to escape out the tips of his fingers.

Sebastian snakes his arms around the cowboy's neck, forehead coming to rest against curls plastered to another sweaty forehead. The cowboy's hat tips back, held on only with the shitty string clinging onto the jut of an Adam's apple. The crowd swallows them up, pushes them further into the writhing pile of costumed bodies until they've become one with the monster. Sebastian is hidden here, deep in the belly of the beast. He's safe from anyone who might know him, who might know his father, from anyone who might see a man draped over another man like this and raise their fist in response.

The fear isn't gone, it's still there, a thin film stretched across the room like the sweat which leaves the tip of Sebastian's tongue salty when he licks his lips. But here in the dark, it belongs to them. A thrill that they can hug close to their bodies and take control of. Here, they consume the fear, choke it back and repay it with the hard edges of their bodies squeezed tight around each other.

Sebastian has never felt more free.

He thinks of Ren watching him, the intensity of his gaze gone as Sebastian had waded further into the crowd. It makes something like satisfaction curl in his gut, makes him roll his head back on his shoulders when the cowboy dips his face into the hollow of Sebastian's throat. He can feel his hurried breaths there, the promise of more as he mouths wetly over the thin skin which separates him from the desperate thud of Sebastian's heart.

The crowd sways as the music changes, transforms into something else rougher, the screech of the decks mounting to a fever pitch. The strobe lights shiver spectacularly, catching every sequin haphazardly glued on the cowboy's hat, every speck of golden paint smeared over Sebastian's skin. The vast array of costumes, all varying levels of bedazzled and sparkling, throw rainbows on the roof as Sebastian opens his eyes and watches, before he feels the insistent press of the cowboy's lips on his throat.

Fuck it, Sebastian thinks.

He drops his head and kisses the cowboy, all scraping teeth and probing tongue, and it makes him think of his first kiss with that boy from the lacrosse team. Sloppy, unkempt. It makes him want to rip his mouth away and vomit. He can hear his father, (he *understands what's at stake here*, but does he give a fuck?), can feel the sting of warning behind his right eye. Sebastian wonders what would happen if his father could see through the protection of the costumed bodies, see him like this. He wonders what it would feel like to just throw himself off the roof like his mother did.

The kiss is over as suddenly as it had begun, Sebastian's eyes thrown open in shock as the cowboy's arms fall from his waist. He's thrust back into the crowd. Sebastian watches his face contort in anger, before he realises who has stepped between the embrace. The cowboy's mouth moves with heated words that Sebastian can't hear, before he turns and disappears from view.

Ren watches him go for a moment, before he turns back to look at Sebastian.

Ren reaches down, takes both of Sebastian's hands.

The music is impossibly thunderous, so loud it's making Sebastian's ears throb, but he's so close to Ren now he can read every word on his lips.

Do you still want to find out? he asks, as his tongue slips lethargically between his teeth. The glint is there again, light bouncing off the silver and straight into Sebastian's eyes, nearly blinding him. Still, he can't bring himself to look away from Ren's smooth jaw, from Ren's furrowed brow, from the molten *hunger* in his eyes as he slips one hand free of Sebastian's and fixes it on the back of his neck.

There's a magnetic rush like Sebastian's never felt, the anticipation of something he's never wanted so much and could not have.

Ren kisses him suddenly. All at once, then not at all.

His lips are so hot, they leave Sebastian gasping. When he pulls back, Ren searches Sebastian for something, eyes roving over every inch of exposed skin, but Sebastian doesn't know what face he's making. He finds he can't control it either, can't force his cheeks to move to show how his heart swells. His eyes sting a little, sharp and overwhelming like the lump in his throat.

He surges forwards and kisses Ren.

Their noses bump together at first as Sebastian moves his lips urgently. Ren lets go of his other hand, lets it travel up Sebastian's half bare torso and find purchase in the sweat slick strands at the nape of his neck. Ren doesn't seem to care that Sebastian is sweat drenched, fingers twisting in golden locks to pull him back a little, soothing the intensity of his desperate kisses. Sebastian feels like his heart is going to explode out of his chest. Feels like if Ren pulls away from him then the spell will break for real this time and he'll wake up on the floor of the hotel, slurring his words as blood tickles his inner ear.

Instead, he feels the steady stroke of Ren's fingers, firm hands keeping him tied down to the moment, calming the insistence of Sebastian's kiss until he feels his shoulders fall and the urgent tension melt away. Ren rewards this with a delicate sweep of his thumb across Sebastian's ear lobe, finding the pocket of his jaw and pressing tenderly. Sebastian feels the heat of Ren's mouth in a rush of warm air, tastes the same insipid mixture of coke and cheap liquor. His stomach does a bizarre lurch at the cold presence of Ren's tongue piercing, clacking against the back of Sebastian's teeth lightly as Ren licks into his mouth.

Sebastian's jaw aches with a chaotic tingle, the feeling emerging from somewhere deep in his core. He wonders if this is what kissing should be like. Is this what other people feel like when they kiss? Is it normal to feel like you're about to collapse?

He's still gasping for air as Ren pulls away, hand on the small of Sebastian's back suddenly, steadying him. He looks concerned, his forehead scrunching in the middle. He points over Sebastian's shoulder, mouths the word *outside*?

Sebastian is certain now he's going to faint, so he nods.

Hand still pressed reassuringly just above Sebastian's tailbone (like he'd done the first night they'd met, the first time someone had touched Sebastian and made his spine tingle with undiluted desire), Ren leads him out of the club. They pass Darius who is busy with a patron who is puking their guts up into a bowler hat. They make their way up to the pavement, where Ren stops and pulls Sebastian down to the curb.

Sebastian lets the cold autumn air fill his lungs, sucking it in gratefully before replacing it with smoke as Ren sets the end of a lit cigarette on his tongue (perhaps even more gratefully).

His legs feel as if he's just climbed every floor of his apartment building, thighs burning and knees jittering together as he clutches the curb.

He's not sure how long they're quiet, because the street itself is not.

It's almost strange to hear Ren's voice again when he speaks, a tone that Sebastian's never heard him use before.

"Why did you kiss that guy?" Ren asks.

Sebastian stares at him for a second, wondering what exactly Ricky gave them a shot of. That must be why he feels so chock full of adrenaline, like he's going to throw up everything he's ever eaten. He blinks, shakes his head.

"What?" he asks Ren, having heard exactly what he said but requiring more time to formulate a response.

Ren looks away as if in defeat, kicks at a stone on the road. Sebastian's faculties are slowly rebooting themselves, the chill of the pavement through the thin fabric of his toga grounding him significantly. He nudges Ren with the side of his shoulder. Ren looks at him again, his gaze hard.

"You came here with me."

Sebastian studies Ren's face for another moment, searching the square set of his jaw for an answer.

"Are you… jealous?" Sebastian asks bewilderedly. He feels something uncomfortable catch onto the balloon of elation currently swelling inside his chest, tugging him more firmly back into his sore, sweaty body. "Um… you told me to go dance with him? When you *suggested* I go dance, I did. I didn't realise that coming here meant I had to be chained to you all night."

Sebastian loathes the petulance in his tone, but he's genuinely confused as to what the fuck sort of answer Ren expected? Does he think he's some sort of wilting flower now? After one kiss, one demonstration of weakness, Sebastian will lay down and take whatever he wants to give him?

"It didn't," Ren says quickly. Sebastian raises a brow, jaw clenching in frustration.

"Okay. So why start this conversation? Especially after what we just did?"

Ren shakes his head, looks away.

"You're right, it doesn't matter."

"So why bring it up in the first place?" Sebastian demands, his impatience quickly taking over. It seems as if the sweetness of their kiss has only served to set alight his other emotions more furiously—irritation quickly ablaze, that Ren would ruin such a moment with stupid fucking questions. "Don't brush me off like that, Ren, especially if you're going to act all pissy about it."

"I'm not acting pissy," Ren snaps back, facing Sebastian with the full intensity of his dark eyes.

"You are," Sebastian retorts, running a hand distractedly through his clammy hair. "Just because you don't shout and yell like I do doesn't mean you're not pissed off with me, right? Am I understanding you correctly? I'm *trying* to consider your feelings and right now, I have no idea *why* your feelings would be making you try and pick a fight with me?"

Ren wilts a little as Sebastian's voice raises. He glances around like he's embarrassed, like *he* didn't start this fight.

"I didn't want to pick a fight with you, sir—"

Sebastian feels his hand twitch involuntarily, like he could lift it and strike him at any moment.

"Don't call me *'sir'*!" Sebastian says tightly. He takes a deep breath, tries to focus. "You bring me here and parade me around in front of your friends and *kiss* me and now suddenly it's *'sir'* again? I hate that." Sebastian also hates the way his voice cracks. He hates that he feels embarrassment crawling up the fair skin of his face, the aurelian glow of the paint doing little now to disguise the fact. When he breathes again, it rattles, like he's a *child*, like he can't contain his own emotions.

"You need to decide," he continues. "Are you just an employee that calls me *sir*? That brought me here tonight because you felt bad for me?" Sebastian can feel his heart hammering in his throat as he leans in, desperate to hear the truth, but terrified he's just a melodramatic idiot that's interpreted everything tonight all wrong. He swallows, licks his lips past the aching dryness in his mouth. He stares at Ren's lips for a second too long, anger bleeding out of him like ink into paper. "Or… are you someone I can trust?"

Ren doesn't say anything for a long moment. He just watches Sebastian, his face falling with each passing second, harsh facade slipping into nothingness by the time he shakes his head hopelessly.

"I don't get to make that decision, Sebastian."

Sebastian falters. He tries to remember the last time someone said his name like that—like it meant something to them.

"Well, I'm not making it for you," his words are pained, but decisive. "This isn't something I can *make* you do." He takes a deep breath, stares Ren down with all the intensity his cold blue gaze can muster. "I don't want that."

Sebastian has spent his life with his birth dictating what he could make people do. Whether it's maids in the apartment waking up in the middle of the night to cater a drunken afterparty, or teachers being convinced that his pathetic excuse for a term paper deserves a higher grade, or girls agreeing to go on empty, one-sided dates with him just to satisfy his father's pestering. He wants something else now.

"What *do* you want?" Ren asks, as if he can read his mind. It's always seemed like that, somehow. That since Ren met him, he's known him better than anyone; at times seeming to peer beyond what even Sebastian knows about himself. That's why they're here now, isn't it? Because Ren has always been unnervingly attuned to something that, for his entire life, Sebastian has refused to admit about himself.

Sebastian doesn't hesitate.

"I want *you* to want *me*," he tells him. Ren swallows. Hard.

"I do," he says. "I do want you."

"You have a funny way of showing it," Sebastian cuts back quickly, the harshness in his voice an unfortunate symptom of a lifetime spent at arm's length.

Ren's mouth twists at that, a sharp intake of breath through his nostrils as he considers what he's about to do.

This time, when he kisses Sebastian, he doesn't immediately pull away. Ren presses his mouth against Sebastian's, confident and sure, slips his tongue along the moist seam until he opens it, like he's dying for another taste. The wind brushes the tips of Sebastian's shoulder blades so harshly he can't help but shiver, but Ren slides his hand up to pull him closer. He smiles, like the spongy giddiness lining Sebastian's brain is catching. Ren pulls back only to draw breath, to shift to the opposite side of Sebastian's nose and return to the kiss with vigour. A long held sigh of relief escapes Sebastian's nostrils, the tension melting away from his limbs as he succumbs to Ren.

"Get a room!" a gruff voice that sounds vaguely like Darius calls from behind them, but Ren ignores it and so Sebastian follows his lead. He can feel his dick starting to harden, uncomfortable in the restrictive tightness of the compression shorts he'd donned under his toga, fear fluttering down his spine alongside the arousal.

When Ren pulls away and looks at him, *looks* at him in that way Sebastian has never seen *anyone* look at him before, he forgets it. It's as if he's someone else. He decides to let himself be someone else, even if it's just for tonight.

"Do you want to go back downstairs?" Ren asks, his mouth barely a breath from Sebastian's, "Or you know, my apartment isn't far if you want to shower and hang out—"

"I'm fucking freezing," Sebastian responds, his teeth giving an involuntary chatter as if to emphasise the point. "Booze is only so good at masking October wind when you're half dressed. Don't want my wrist to actually seize up."

Ren laughs, and Sebastian hears it this time. It's a smooth chuckle, low in his chest, and Sebastian can feel it in the palm of his hand, where he'd pressed it against Ren's heart at some point. Ren runs a hand through his hair, as sweat drenched as Sebastian's, and nods.

"Yeah, sure. Although I think it's November now."

Sebastian rolls his eyes, his cheeks roaring red. That's why he's cold, he thinks. All the blood in his body is in either his cheeks or his fucking dick.

"What*ever*. I'm cold. Let's… go back to your place," he finishes, unable to withstand the full intensity of Ren's dark brown eyes. He glances at the pavement, patches of it beginning to glisten with frost where people have spilled their drinks. His heart hums in his wrists with the implication of Ren's suggestion. Does he plan to do more than kissing? How far would he be comfortable going tonight? How far would Sebastian be comfortable going tonight?

Ren nods, seemingly ignorant for once to Sebastian's internal babble, planting his palms on either side of his body and hoisting himself up in one smooth movement.

"Okay. I think I have a spare pair of pyjamas which *might* be up to your standards," he says coolly as he offers Sebastian his hand. Sebastian takes it, snorting as he's pulled to his feet.

"I doubt it," he replies, offering Ren a sideways smirk as he intertwines their fingers. Ren watches the movement as if entranced for a moment before he sighs for the show of it, and jerks his head in the opposite direction of the club.

"It's good to see you're still a brat, kiss or no kiss," Ren says lightly, tilting his head as if in contemplation. Now that he's stood up, Sebastian can feel the full effects of whatever the shot was they'd taken earlier. It's making every step he takes feel like he's wading through jelly, seeming too slow as he walks along beside Ren. He thinks Ren is maybe thinking the same thing, the constant colour high in his cheeks perhaps betraying his own loosened inhibitions.

Sebastian doesn't care. He makes a mental note to get Ricky's details and send the guy a fat fucking tip whenever he has access to his wallet again. Maybe they can come back to *Rain* and Sebastian can give it to him in person.

No one watches them duck down the street beside *Rain* and carry on towards a shabby apartment block but the moon. They merge effortlessly with the crowds lining the streets, with the people hailing cabs and holding their friends' hair back as they puke on the pavement.

Sebastian is sure of it then—he's never felt so free.

Eleven

Ren's apartment building is as shabby inside as it is out. It's barely any quieter than the street, people on every floor having Halloween parties with their doors open, spilling between apartments and hanging out on the stairs as they walk up. There's no elevator, Ren explains blankly, as they enter and Sebastian looks expectantly around. He's never been in an apartment block without an elevator, but Sebastian supposes it's nowhere near as tall as the one his father owns.

On floor five, Ren tells him they only have two more to go. Sebastian tries not to snap back at him, truly he does, but something vaguely sarcastic slips out anyway. Two girls smoking in the hallway compliment his toga as they pass. Sebastian thinks they must be very drunk, because at this point the toga is half hanging off him, streaks of gold and bronze paint transferred at its hems.

His boner faded three floors ago, the blood indefinitely being redirected to his exhausted legs as they climb, until finally, they reach Ren's door. It's shabby too, needs repainting. Sebastian tells him as much. Ren says if it bothers him so much, he can be the one to give the 75-year-old superintendent a generous tip at Christmas time.

Ren's entire apartment is about the same size as Sebastian's bedroom, but it's modestly furnished and well kept. He flicks a lamp on when they enter, one of those energy saving ones that seem to spit and hiss as they jolt into life. There's a kitchenette, a door at the back of the living-come-dining room which seems to be Ren's bedroom, and a door off the entranceway which leads to a cramped toilet and shower room.

There's so much *green* though. Sebastian marvels as Ren slips his shoes off and asks him to do the same, at the array of houseplants which line the tiled half wall between the living room and kitchenette. Sebastian's never seen so many all in one enclosed space. He thinks of the half dead palms in the lobby of the Clarence Building, and wonders vaguely what Ren must have thought when he'd seen them.

"I didn't peg you for a gardener," Sebastian says mildly as he sets his shoes carefully alongside Ren's, bare feet cold on the threadbare carpet which lies beyond the entranceway. Ren raises an eyebrow as he walks past the plants and into the kitchen, returning a moment later with two cans of beer.

"You need a garden to be a gardener," he says simply, handing Sebastian a can as he cracks his own open. Sebastian opens his, sipping idly as he runs his fingers along the leaves of the nearest plant.

"Oh, to be as pedantic as you are sometimes, Ren," Sebastian coos in reply, the rubbery smoothness of the plant's leaves pleasant against his drunken fingers.

"Only when in present company," Ren responds, coming to stand at Sebastian's shoulder as he gently caresses the plant. Sebastian shoots him a wary side-eyed glance, to be met with Ren's smile over the lip of his beer can. He looks almost embarrassed when Sebastian catches him, the tips of his ears blooming a wonderful pink colour as he clears his throat and looks determinedly at the plant.

"It's a Chinese money plant," he explains. "Facing south easterly like that, it's supposed to attract wealth and prosperity." Ren offers Sebastian a small smile on the side of his face. "And look, here you are."

Sebastian huffs at that, letting go of the plant's leaf.

"A few drinks and suddenly you're a comedian? I should've plied you with liquor far sooner," Sebastian says, plonking himself on the back of Ren's sofa, facing the rest of the plants. He raises a brow. "So, is that why you have one?"

Ren frowns.

"Is what why I have one?"

Sebastian raises a brow, taking another sip of his beer. It's tangy and bitter and definitely not something he would usually drink, but the fizzy warmth of alcohol is rife in his limbs. It makes it decidedly more palatable.

"You said it was a Chinese money plant," Sebastian says, nodding at the plump, round leaves of the hearty little plant. Ren nods as if he's understood, studying the plant for a second before turning to face Sebastian, realisation colouring his features.

"I did say that… but given I'm Korean and Japanese, I'm still struggling to see the connection."

Sebastian feels his stomach lurch in discomfort, eyes darting anxiously away from the plant to Ren. He's not smiling, but his eyes dance with amusement. Sebastian balks for a moment, rejuvenated from his climb up the stairs enough that blood is able to rush freely back to his face.

"Right. Of course. I didn't mean to assume…" Sebastian takes a deep breath, tries to claw the conversation back onto more even terrain. "So what are they like? Korea and Japan?"

Ren shrugs.

"I don't know," he says, smile twitching at the edges of his mouth before he even finishes his sentence, "I've never been."

Ren dissolves into laughter, his nose scrunching up and his eyes shutting as he lets himself fully surrender to the moment. Sebastian knows he should be more embarrassed, should start trying to apologise for his faux pas, but he can't help but be swept up by the pure childish innocence in Ren's laughter. He's never heard anything like it from him before, so relaxed, so free, and it makes Sebastian start to laugh too.

"What the fuck are you laughing about?" Ren asks between giggles. "You just insulted me!"

Sebastian covers his mouth with his hand, his brain overwhelmed with the absurdity of the entire situation, forbidding him from forming any kind of sensible sentence.

"I know," he manages between laughs, "I know, I really didn't mean—I didn't think, I've never even thought about it before, what the fuck is wrong with me?" he manages, running a hand haphazardly through his hair. "I'm sorry, that was so bad, I didn't mean to be such an idiot."

He stops laughing as he finishes, and Ren soon tails off too, taking a sip of his beer as he watches Sebastian through glassy eyes, wet at the edges with mirth.

"That's two apologies from you now," he lifts his index and middle finger lazily, one eye shut as he stares at Sebastian with the other through the gap. "I'm racking them up."

Sebastian slurps on his drink thoughtfully, struggling to recall the other.

"When did I apologise to you the first time?" he asks, mind too giddy to recall. Ren sets his beer down on the counter next to the money plant, and moves in closer to Sebastian.

"That night I put you in the shower and took care of you," Ren says. His voice seems to have dropped an octave somehow, a low timbre that shudders through Sebastian's chest and straight to his dick. Ren lifts his hand to Sebastian's temple, brushes a stray hair back from his face. "Do you remember?"

Sebastian swallows, nods his head. He suddenly finds himself unable to speak, like Ren has sucked all of the air out of the room. Ren leans in a little closer, taller than Sebastian for once as he stands over him still perched on the edge of the sofa.

"Do you remember asking me if I'd never seen a cock before?" Ren asks, words thick and deliberate like warm molasses as he lets his thumb work smooth strokes against the side of Sebastian's face. Sebastian almost winces in embarrassment at the memory, brow furrowing in annoyance immediately at Ren trying to make a fool of him like this when he's laid so vulnerable before him. This only seems to make Ren happier. He looks pleased as he smiles, that glint of silver on his tongue through his teeth now unmistakable.

"Yes," he adds thoughtfully, when Sebastian doesn't say anything. "You made that face that night, too. When I looked you up and down. Petulant, even though I was just giving you exactly what you wanted. Petulant and thrilled despite yourself. Right?"

Ren leans in, lets his lips ghost easily over the hollow of Sebastian's cheek until he reaches his ear. Sebastian can't contain the shiver of arousal which overtakes him, breath caught in his throat. He can feel Ren's smile there now, pressed into his skin.

"I felt like that was the first time I *saw* you," he breathes. He pauses, pulling back enough that he can look at Sebastian again. Sebastian's breath hitches, almost a whimper escaping at the loss of him, and Ren doesn't smile quite as broadly as he had while laughing. It's gentler, probing. Once again, Sebastian feels exposed. "What do you want, Sebastian?"

His own name curled around Ren's tongue is nearly enough to send him reeling, but Sebastian manages to reach up and grab Ren's hand, keeping it firmly pressed to his cheek. He licks his lips, watches him carefully through his lashes.

"I want you to fuck me," Sebastian says, and if his voice breaks in the middle, he pretends that it doesn't, because he's never felt like this before in his entire life—

Ren raises a brow ever so slightly, offering Sebastian a soft laugh as he's taken aback by the bluntness of the response.

"Impatient as always," he hums, leaning down and pressing his lips carefully to Sebastian's. He pulls back languidly, lips plucking satisfyingly at Sebastian's as he watches him. "Let me make you feel good first."

Ren kisses him again, his other hand finding Sebastian's shoulder and pulling him to his feet. Sebastian tries not to succumb to his impatience, annoyed that Ren would point it out so plainly, so he matches the pace of the kisses. Slow, easy, like they have all the time in the world, like they've done this a million times before. Ren leads him over to the bathroom, reaching out at some point to tug at a pull cord which jerks a dim light and fan into life. He breaks away from the kiss, beginning to work at the knot on Sebastian's shoulder which he'd fastened earlier on tonight.

"Shower's standing room only, I'm afraid," Ren tells him, leaning away to turn it on as he gets the knot undone and leaves Sebastian to unwind the toga. He does, fingers twitching as he tries to bunch up the fabric tidily as he goes. Ren yanks his tank top over his head then, exposing the sharp, sculpted edges of his torso, a trail of dark hair disappearing temptingly into his jeans. Sebastian immediately loses interest in the integrity of his Halloween costume. He hooks his thumbs on either side of the toga, yanking it down around his ankles and stepping free of it, left only in his compression shorts. He hesitates.

Ren, as painfully observant as ever, notices right away. One hand in the water, checking the temperature, he extends the other to Sebastian, beckoning him closer. Sebastian knows the outline of his hard dick is pressing painfully against the edge of the shorts, uncomfortably held down against his thigh. Ren can see it, can see how much he wants this.

"Need a hand?" he asks carefully. Sebastian nods, the jolt of his Adam's apple in his throat pronounced as he swallows. Ren pulls him in close, the cold buckle of his belt pressing into Sebastian's belly as he kisses him again. One hand wet from the shower, one dry, Ren lays them at the jut of Sebastian's hips, thumbs sliding along the elastic band of the shorts and pulling them back from his skin. Sebastian almost sighs in relief as the pressure is released from the tip of his dick, leans into the kiss with a satisfied grunt. He licks into Ren's mouth as he slips the compression shorts over the curve of his ass, his dick hanging heavy and now free between his legs. Ren doesn't stop the kiss to pull back, to look. He slides the shorts down until Sebastian can step free of them, then uses his palm to press against Sebastian's heart and back him into the shower.

When the kiss breaks, Sebastian gulps in several lung-fuls of air, the spray of the water hitting the back of his neck and shoulders first. He shuts his eyes and lets his head tilt into it, enjoying the steam which has quickly filled the small bathroom, dragging his hands up his chest to try to wash away some of the paint.

His skin prickles with the telltale intensity of Ren watching him, but he can't bear to look. No one has ever seen him like this, stripped naked and painfully aroused—every other sexual encounter he's had up until this moment has been half-dressed and fumbled.

Sebastian finds he can't stand it another second, turning into the stream of the shower so his back is to Ren. He can hear him rustling around, no doubt removing the rest of his clothes, and the desire to peek over his shoulder at the other man is dizzying. Just as he's about to drum up enough courage to do it, he feels Ren step into the shower behind him, shutting the door and enclosing them both in the compact space.

He feels the smooth skin of Ren's torso meet with the expanse of his back, the press of soft lips at the nape of his neck. He feels the warm slap of Ren's fully hard cock against the cleft of his ass as his hands encircle Sebastian's waist and he holds him tightly in place. Ren continues to litter kisses along the back of Sebastian's neck and shoulders, hands coming up to caress the sides of his ribs, to drum a sense of serenity into his tense limbs.

"Relax, Sebastian," Ren murmurs, mouth wet and skin wet and dick wet as the shower continues to shelter the two of them.

Sebastian takes a deep breath and tries to concentrate on the intense tingles of pleasure chasing Ren's every contact with his skin. He feels light-headed, the buzz of alcohol coupled with the harsh waves of arousal overwhelming his every synapse. He steadies himself with his palms against the cool tile of the wall, lets himself lean back into Ren's embrace.

A gasp for air transforms into a low moan, and he almost smacks his hand across his mouth to shut himself up. Ren responds by running his hand up Sebastian's throat, thumb stopping to pluck at his bottom lip.

"That's good," he offers encouragingly. "Don't stop. I want to hear you."

Sebastian shivers at the praise, finding it sends another throb of intrigue straight to his cock and he leans forwards the slight distance to rest his forehead against the tile too. It's refreshing, the contrast of cold, slick ceramic making him feel more present in his body; less heady sensation, more grounded reality.

Ren slips his hand down then, taking Sebastian's dick firmly in his grasp.

"Fuck," Sebastian hisses, the sudden relief of Ren's fingers closing around him and stroking him slowly, utterly maddening. He feels any remaining tension ease from his shoulders, slumps down a little so he's leaning more of his weight against the wall. He can still feel Ren's dick resting firmly against his ass, shuddering with pleasure as he positions it more firmly between his buttocks.

Ren kisses his shoulder again.

"Does that feel good?" he hums, stroking carefully as he grinds his hips in time against Sebastian. Sebastian can barely speak, an affirmation emerging as a whimper as he presses his hips back carefully, affording Ren a tighter space in which to chase his own pleasure. Ren rewards him with a low groan of his own, the sound reverberating off the steamed up glass of the shower.

"We need to talk about a few things," Ren says then, reducing the movement of his wrist so he's pumping Sebastian carefully every few words. Sebastian lets out a needy whine, attempting to jerk his hips up into Ren's grasp to chase a quick rhythm, but Ren's grip on him loosens a little when he does.

"Listen to me, Sebastian," Ren chides, drawing all of his focus in as he lets go of Sebastian's dick altogether.

The commanding tone of his voice doesn't help with Sebastian's distracting arousal, but he shifts his forehead a little to feel more of the chilly tiles, before nodding against them.

"I'm listening," he says, words hoarse as he licks his lips. Ren kisses his shoulder again, strokes his dick once, twice in reward.

"Have you ever done anything like this with a guy before?" he asks carefully. Sebastian shakes his head.

"No," he answers honestly, the word trembling. He can feel the pink of his own embarrassment making his ears flush. He feels Ren nod.

"Have you ever done anything like this to yourself?"

As Ren asks, he lets his other hand slide down the contour of Sebastian's spine, dragging on the water droplets which litter his skin, until Sebastian can feel a finger circle his hole. Sebastian shivers.

"Yes," he croaks, eyes fluttering shut as he takes a deep breath. "I usually… when I'm with girls, I usually have to finish… like that. Otherwise I pretty much can't…"

He doesn't finish the sentence, the familiar cold claws of shame which surround the action finding their home in the pits of his stomach. It draws him harshly into the reality of this moment, reminds him of what the fuck he's about to do, what he so intensely *wants* to happen.

"I see," Ren replies gently, hand coming to settle over the curve of Sebastian's ass.

Sebastian finds the lack of his probing fingers to be altogether more panic inducing than the shame which threatens to ruin the moment. He takes a deep breath.

"So I'm clean," he adds hurriedly, willing the cold tiles to sap the embarrassment from his body. "I thought I might have to… you know… after the party, so I made sure I was clean before…"

Ren has reached back around him, taking his throbbing cock back in his hand and beginning to gently stroke him again. Sebastian's breath hitches at the end of his sentence.

"Okay," Ren says easily, like this is the most natural thing in the world. Maybe to him it is. "Okay. We don't have to do anything you don't want to. We can stop anytime."

Sebastian shakes his head firmly.

"I don't want to stop," he replies, and for the first time since they'd begun kissing in Ren's living room, his voice is free of a telltale waver. He takes a deep breath, turns to face Ren, rests his forearms over Ren's shoulders.

Sebastian kisses Ren full on the mouth, not desperate as he had before, but determined, certain. He doesn't let the glimpse he catches of Ren's own erect cock induce panic; he refuses to. Tonight, he's someone else. He'd decided to be someone else. He's someone Ren calls by his first name, invites back to his apartment. He could be anyone that Ren encountered at *Rain* and took a liking to. He could be someone who's done this a thousand times before.

Ren kisses him back fervently, reaches up to cradle his face. It makes Sebastian's chest flutter with delight.

Ren pulls away, forces Sebastian to meet his gaze with his hands still planted firmly on his cheeks.

"You tell me to stop at any point," he instructs. "If you want to stop, if you change your mind, tell me. Okay?"

Sebastian nods, feels his mouth turning up at the edges involuntarily.

"Okay," he says as he smiles, and Ren smiles back.

Ren proceeds to reach for a bar of soap hanging from the end of the shower hose, lathering it up between his hands and beginning to work the lather across Sebastian's chest. Sebastian relaxes into it, letting Ren scrub the paint from his skin diligently, before cupping his hands below the stream of the shower and using them to ladle the water over him.

"Turn around," he instructs again, before reaching for more soap and proceeding to do the same along Sebastian's back. It's incredibly soothing, the deliberate but gentle way Ren works, letting the spray from the shower carry the suds down the slope of Sebastian's spine. Eventually, his hands arrive at the dip of his back, fingers reaching back down to his hole to continue washing him. Sebastian's breath catches at the movement. He remembers what Ren had said earlier, moans into his touch. He feels Ren press the length of his torso against Sebastian's back again, urging him to lean against the wall once more, before two hands part his ass cheeks and expose his hole to the warmth of the shower.

He opens his mouth to tell Ren it feels good, but the words die on his tongue as he senses Ren drop down into a squat.

Sebastian jerks forward as he feels the tip of Ren's tongue slide around the circumference of his hole. There's a pause as Ren seems to be waiting for Sebastian's reaction. He gathers what little sanity he has remaining and nods against the tile.

"I like that, Ren," he says shyly, breath catching in a choked whimper again as Ren repeats the motion.

Sebastian's fingers clench at the slippery tiles to no avail as he tries to keep himself up. Ren begins teasing the edges of his rim with delicate kitten licks, just close enough to his hole to conjure deep bolts of pleasure aching through Sebastian's groin. He catches the meat of Sebastian's ass with both hands, spreading him apart and nosing at his core as if he's desperately holding himself back, before changing up the pace, drawing the flat of his tongue across Sebastian's hole.

Sebastian can't stop the embarrassingly lewd noises which escape him now, desperate moans of pleasure among aborted gasps for air, as he reaches down and begins to jerk himself off. Ren seems to enjoy this, letting out his own moan of satisfaction against Sebastian's rim, which he feels shudder up through his entire body. Without warning, Ren thrusts his tongue forwards, breaching the tense ring of muscle there. He works his tongue in and out at a voracious speed, each exploratory jolt sending Sebastian reeling closer to the edge.

Suddenly, Sebastian feels the sharp twinge of warning in his balls, unable to stop the inevitable. He cries out helplessly as he comes all over the tiled wall of the shower, knees trembling as he tries to stay standing. All the blood in his body seems to have relocated to his cock, his forearms tingling like they've gone numb. Ren offers one last stroke of his tongue along Sebastian's hole before moving his mouth up to suck a bruise into Sebastian's hip.

As Sebastian catches his breath, leaning his full weight on the wall, Ren stands up behind him and rinses his mouth. Sebastian tries to angle his body out of the way so that the shower will hit the ejaculate he's left all over the wall. His heart is racing, thrumming with the intensity of his orgasm and the reality of the situation.

Sebastian turns to Ren, who is watching him carefully. His own cock is still hard against his smooth stomach, the tip shiny and enticing with pre-come.

Sebastian wants it in his mouth.

Ren seems to sense this is coming, because he reaches up and shuts the shower off quickly, one palm on Sebastian's chest as he smiles.

"I think you're all clean now, right?" he asks smoothly. Sebastian nods, wondering if the power of speech has left him for good. Ren nods too.

"I can put you to bed again if you like," he adds, a tease to his words but an offer there too. He wants Sebastian to feel in control. The realisation makes Sebastian's stomach stir warmly. He kisses Ren gently on the mouth, shakes his head.

"I want you to come with me," Sebastian says, kissing his way down Ren's neck and leaving the words at the curve of his throat.

Ren's smile is warm enough it chases away the sudden chill of the room as he opens the shower doors, gathering up a towel for them each.

Sebastian follows him from the bathroom, into the dark comfort of Ren's bedroom.

Twelve

Ren seems different as they kiss now. His tongue is messier, the cold steel of his piercing searching as he and Sebastian fall onto his bed in a tangle of limbs. The bed squeaks under their weight, the only other sounds in the room the wet mash of lips and the desperate gasps of breath between each kiss.

Sebastian is overwhelmed by Ren. He pushes him down against the rough cotton of his sheets, the smell of him all encompassing. It's that familiar musk of cigarette smoke, the tang of something else earthy and sweet in the back of Sebastian's throat as he breathes it all in. Sebastian reaches down to grasp Ren's dick, to pump it leisurely as Ren had him in the shower, and he relishes the way it makes Ren halt in his determined kisses. He leans back a little, his eyes fluttering shut as his teeth scrape across his bottom lip. They drag across the plump flesh, leaving it pale for a moment before it blooms once again with the redness of their frantic kisses.

Ren reaches over to his bedside table then, rummaging around in the top drawer for a second before he returns to pepper kisses on Sebastian's neck. He pulls back further, resting on his heels over Sebastian, letting his eyes slide open. He surveys him through those long, dark lashes, eyes hot with lust as he watches Sebastian lazily jerk him off. His chest is rising and falling with every rapid breath, the tempo of his heart matching Sebastian's beat for beat.

He runs his index finger over Sebastian's hole again, watches Sebastian shiver beneath him. Ren lifts a bottle of lube procured from the table and retracts his finger to smear it with the clear gel. Sebastian reclines further back into the pillows, takes a deep breath as his wrist slows at Ren's cock. Ren licks his lips.

"Ready?" he checks quickly, a little more impatience bleeding into his careful words. Sebastian nods, running his hands up Ren's chest to lock his hands behind his head as Ren presses his lube slick finger against Sebastian's hole. He's never done this with another person before, but he's intimately familiar with the mechanics.

The intrusion is not unfamiliar, Sebastian having frequently fingered himself to completion over the years, but the fact it belongs to someone else—to *Ren*—is enough to make the sensation feel entirely new. Sebastian moans slowly as Ren sinks his finger in, hisses gently as he retracts it. Ren uses his thumb to massage Sebastian's rim as he works his index finger back and forth, pressing a little further each time to open Sebastian up.

He leans in to press a kiss to Sebastian's collarbone once his finger begins to shift more freely, and Sebastian can't help but arch his back up into the motion, already desperate for more. Ren is careful, however, despite the obvious angry throb of his own erection. He thrusts distractedly back and forth over Sebastian's softened cock, the friction both inside and out causing intrigue to rapidly pool once more in his gut.

"More," Sebastian gasps into the space between their mouths, arching further into Ren's touch. Ren reaches down to shakily deposit more lube on his middle finger, easing his index finger all the way out before slowly working Sebastian open with the second. He takes his time pressing past the initial tightness and leans down to kiss Sebastian deeply as he sinks both fingers past his first knuckle. Ren swallows the whimper he elicits from Sebastian, the sound lost where their mouths are still joined, and Sebastian rocks instinctively into the touch. This time, when Ren begins to move his fingers a little faster, he makes a beckoning motion with the tips of them. Each curl of his fingers sends a tremor of pleasure racing through Sebastian's core, close to something that he's suddenly desperate to feel.

Sebastian whines outwardly when Ren's fingers finally brush something internal that makes his dick jerk suddenly against his stomach, quickly beginning to harden again. Sebastian hurriedly grabs Ren's wrist, gasping for breath and uncertain what just happened. Ren presses butterfly kisses to his face, holds his hand still for a moment.

"Did it feel good?" he asks, a low rumble which Sebastian feels more than hears. Sebastian swallows, lets his tense neck relax again and his skull settle against the pillow.

"Yes," he murmurs, voice choked. "Yes, but just… different." He feels Ren nod his head, moving his fingers again devoid of the beckoning motion, returning to stretching.

"It's okay," he whispers, continuing to press kisses to Sebastian's chest and torso. "It's supposed to feel good. Just relax, okay? I promise I won't hurt you."

Sebastian feels relief flood his senses for some bizarre reason—it's as if Ren's reassurance is all he needs. Is this what trust is? Is this what it feels like to *want* to surrender yourself entirely to someone?

Sebastian finds himself unable to speak again, some strange emotion he hasn't got a name for blocking the capacity of his brain to form sentences, but he nods and hurriedly kisses whatever inch of Ren he can reach.

Ren continues scissoring his fingers intently before pausing to add a third. Sebastian has to concentrate on relaxing this time, the tight walls of muscle releasing with each pass of Ren's fingers. He pauses again to sweep them forward in that same beckoning motion, and this time, Sebastian surrenders to it. Pleasure tears through him like that first heady wave of allure that a rip from a bong hits you with, and he feels wetness forming in the corners of his eyes.

"Ren," he manages to gasp his name, and it comes out helpless and strangled with pleasure. "… Feels good."

Ren nods at the encouragement, continues to pump his fingers in and out of Sebastian evenly, changing the movement every few thrusts to brush against that same sweet spot.

By the time he pauses to add a fourth finger, Sebastian is begging for more, desperate to just *feel* him.

"Ren, *please*," he pants, and it doesn't sound like him at all. His voice is barren of all alternative intent, all calculation. It's undiluted desire which has swallowed him up, brought him to the cusp of something else at the end of Ren's fingers and he wants *all* of him. "Please, I want you to fuck me."

Ren eases the fourth finger in with a little more urgency than the previous ones, stretching Sebastian out as delicately as the act will allow. Sebastian can see a bead of sweat run the length of his face, disappearing in the hollow of Ren's collarbone. Sebastian sits up, leaning forwards to lap it free with his tongue and Ren groans. He lets his fingers slide free of Sebastian, leaving his hole pink and fluttering.

"Okay," Ren agrees, leaning in to kiss Sebastian quickly as he fumbles with a condom. His fingers are slick with lube, trembling with his own palpable want, so Sebastian reaches up and plucks it from his hand. He rips it open, eases the condom over the leaking tip of Ren's cock, and rolls it down securely. Ren exudes a hiss then, stomach muscles clenched hard as he tries to exercise restraint, before Sebastian falls back onto the pillows once again.

Ren takes his dick in hand, poised at Sebastian's hole. He glances up, watches him carefully for another second.

"Ready?"

"Yes, yes, I'm ready," Sebastian tries to stifle the snappish tone of his voice, but he feels so empty now without Ren's fingers, and his dick has stiffened once more, every part of him throbbing with arousal. Ren grins, the blunt head of his cock lined up to press past Sebastian's rim.

"What did I say about being a brat, Sebastian?" he mutters through his smile, and Sebastian can't help but choke back a protest as he feels Ren push himself inside. Sebastian feels a sudden dizzying burst of pain as his entire body protests at the intrusion, but Ren strokes a hand up and down his ribcage, murmuring sweet praise.

"Just relax, you're doing so well," he urges, pausing where he is. His jaw is locked with determination, like it's taking an incredible amount of willpower to resist pushing in further. Sebastian tries to listen to him, palming softly at his cock to distract himself from the discomfort, before he feels his body get used to the sensation.

"Keep going," Sebastian tells him then, the need to have Ren deeper inside him overwhelming. Ren continues to move slowly, pausing every few centimetres to stroke Sebastian's skin gently, to lean forwards and drop soft kisses on his forehead as Sebastian stretches and takes him, until eventually he bottoms out. Ren stays still again, letting out a rough groan as the fronts of his thighs reach the back of Sebastian's ass. He grasps Sebastian by the hips and pulls him up a little, adjusting him so it's more comfortable to take him.

The sensation is alien, but entirely welcome. Sebastian feels his cock throb as Ren shifts a little, bracing himself carefully above Sebastian but still trying to give him time to adjust. Sebastian can't think of anything else in this moment but Ren, Ren all over him, Ren *inside* him, Ren's smell enveloping his entire body and suddenly the lack of movement is stifling.

"Ren, *move*," Sebastian says, intending to sound authoritative but instead coming out desperate and breathy. Ren lets out a huff of a laugh, tight in the back of his throat as he continues to grasp Sebastian's hips on either side. Ren slowly drags his hips back a little, his cock sliding easily into Sebastian's slick hole. Ren rocks gently back in at first, little by little watching his cock disappear inside Sebastian until eventually he's able to slide out nearly completely and thrust his way back in. His eyelids fall closed, he bites his lip.

"Fuck," he all he manages to gasp as he plunges his hips forward, flesh meeting slick flesh as Sebastian lets his legs fall open wider on either side of Ren, pulling him in deeper. Ren takes a shallow, wobbly breath, fucks into Sebastian again. "Fuck, you're so tight," he finally manages to say, clenched in his teeth as he sets a steady rhythm.

Sebastian feels almost delirious, the thickness of Ren's cock filling him up as he thrusts in and out of him repeatedly, coupled with the jolt of electrifying pleasure he feels when the tip of each thrust brushes against that same sweet spot. Ren folds forwards, unable to hold himself up on trembling arms, curving his torso in atop Sebastian and catching his mouth in a sloppy kiss. He pulls back almost immediately, nearly unable to breathe as he rides him harder.

Sebastian is only vaguely aware of the cries of delight which escape him each time Ren buries his cock in his ass, unable to focus on anything but the euphoric feeling of fullness each time he bottoms out. Bent overtop of him as he is now, Ren's taut abdomen catches on Sebastian's dick as he fucks him, trapped between their sweaty bodies. He looks so *good* fucking him, Sebastian thinks, as he struggles not to clench his eyes shut against the blinding pleasure, focusing on those dark brown eyes which had enraptured him since the first moment he'd seen Ren. Strands of onyx dark hair hang in Sebastian's face as Ren pants with exertion, adjusting his grip on Sebastian's thigh and pushing it back and up so he can fuck him deeper.

"You're so pretty like this," Ren blurts out then, one hand cupping Sebastian's skull as he tips his head back ever so slightly to study the redness which flushes his entire face and chest. "You've always been pretty. Do you know what it's like trying to stay professional when you pout at me? When you look at me with those pretty eyes and bat those pretty lashes? And the worst part is, you don't even know you're doing it. You *know* you're pretty, but you don't know how much it drives me *crazy*."

Sebastian feels like he's just been hit upside the head, the sudden onslaught of praise rushing straight through him and making the pleasure wrack his body anew. He's never heard Ren say more than two sentences strung together, the pleasure they're both partaking in inspiring him to babble.

The strangled mewl that escapes him in response would, at any other time, render Sebastian useless with embarrassment, but here, beneath Ren, he doesn't care. He wants him to have it all, to see it all, to take all of him for himself and do whatever he wants.

"Ren," Sebastian whimpers, and it's all he can say, his name, a frantic cry falling from his lips as he hurtles towards a second orgasm. Ren growls roughly, fucking into him harder, reaching down between them to grasp Sebastian's cock and stroke him hard and fast.

"Yes, Seb," Ren whispers. "Let go for me, Seb. Come again for me."

Sebastian comes again, so hard he can see stars explode on the backs of his eyelids, arching up into Ren's touch in desperation. It's all over his stomach, all over Ren's, but it only seems to spur Ren on. His hips begin to stutter, his own broken cries released unbound from his mouth as he chases his own end. Ren lasts another few seconds before his hips jerk with finality, and he clenches the meat of Sebastian's ass for dear life, emptying into the condom.

There's a few moments of stillness as both of them adjust to the sudden quiet in the room. Ren runs a hand through his hair, brushing it out of his eyes as he watches Sebastian.

"Was that okay?" Ren asks gently then, so gently, his voice, his eyes, the concerned slant of his brows. Sebastian finds he can read every inch of the expression on his face without difficulty, joined still as they are. Sebastian wonders if this is it now—if now he'll be able to see Ren as easily as he sees Sebastian.

Instead of answering, Sebastian leans up to kiss Ren, long and slow and still trembling at the edges despite the high of his orgasm wearing off with each passing breath. When he pulls away, Ren is smiling, a small upturn of his lips at the edges, but still a smile. It feels secret; just for Sebastian.

Ren slides out of Sebastian, wincing apologetically when Sebastian cringes in discomfort, the haze of sex lifted and the brutality of the act left in its wake. Ren removes the condom, ties it off and throws it away, before standing off the bed.

"Stay there, I'll get something to clean you up," he says, disappearing into the apartment once more. Sebastian gazes up at the ceiling, unable to feel anything in this moment but the warm satisfaction purring in his chest like a fat, happy cat. He feels sated, finally, after twenty-one years of being alive. He finally understands how a kiss should set your skin alight. He finally understands how sex can be an altogether pleasant experience.

Ren returns with a damp towel, sits on the side of the bed and rubs come off Sebastian's stomach and chest delicately. It's different than the night he'd found Sebastian left used and abandoned by Jerome in his own bedroom. That night, Ren had seemed almost disgusted. Sebastian is beginning to think it wasn't just the fact he had another man's ejaculate coating his cheeks, but rather the pathetic state he'd been left in. Ren paws at him cautiously, like he might break if he scrubs too hard, and finally, tosses the used towel into a laundry hamper at the end of his bed. He takes a deep breath.

"So… Do you want to stay here? Because if you'd rather sleep at home, I can call you a cab, it's no problem," Ren says quickly, picking at a loose thread on the bedsheets as he says it. Sebastian frowns, anxiety suddenly making his blood run cold.

"Do you want me to leave?" he asks, hating the nervous trill in his words.

Ren shakes his head immediately.

"No, of course not," he says surely. "I want you to stay. I just wanted to make sure… that you…"

The anxiety quickly disperses from Sebastian's body again, and he relaxes back into the pillows.

"Ren, I don't think I could move right now even if I wanted to," Sebastian says dryly, before peeking one eye open to look up at Ren. "Not that I want to. I want to stay. Please."

Ren smiles, that same all-encompassing warm one, and pulls back the duvet on the bed, quickly sliding below it. He beckons Sebastian to follow, offering the crook of his neck for Sebastian to settle into. He does, without hesitation, seeking out the warmth of Ren's body between the cool sheets. The rise and fall of his chest is hypnotic, quickly lulling him down towards sleep.

"Goodnight, Ren," Sebastian manages to say, already having lost the battle to stay awake. He feels the steady pressure of a kiss atop his head, a breath which ruffles his hair.

"Night, Sebastian," Ren replies.

*

When Sebastian wakes up the next morning, the bed is empty beside him. He knows it's not his own bed—the way the fabric irritates the skin of his cheek is the obvious give-away that it's not his Egyptian cotton sheets. The smell is different too. Sweet and intoxicating, like a fire that's just been set. It smells muskier too, like the warmth of two grown men and the slickness of bodies coming together.

Sebastian opens his eyes and blinks, gazing around at the inside of Ren's room in the cold light of day.

He hadn't seen much of it last night, as preoccupied as he'd been. Sebastian sits up, suddenly more aware that Ren isn't there. He's still completely naked, his head only slightly heavy from the alcohol he'd consumed the night before. The pale November sun shines in through thin wooden slats, one small window taking up half of the wall beside the bed.

Sebastian hears rustling beyond the bedroom door, looks around for something to wear. Deciding there's nothing else for it, he throws the duvet back and pokes around in Ren's drawer for a moment, looking for a pair of underwear at the very least. He finds the frigid air of the apartment to be too much to withstand, however, and soon also recovers a huge grey sweatshirt from amongst the neatly stacked clothes.

He tries to place how he's feeling throughout the entirety of his mission to secure clothing. Sore is the first thing he notes, his ass twinging sharply every time he tries to make too definitive a movement. This only further reminds him of what transpired between him and his bodyguard the night before, sending his mind reeling to a place it's difficult to come back from.

What the fuck are they supposed to do now? It's not like they can skip hand in hand back to his father's office and proclaim themselves lovers. *Fuck*, if anyone saw them last night—Sebastian forces that thought to the back of his head, determined not to spiral before he knows where Ren is, knows what his thoughts on it all are. Sebastian recalls the bustling streets beyond the gay clubs, the throngs of people milling around and anonymising them amongst the other variously extravagant costumes.

What are they supposed to do now? Sebastian thinks again, more urgently, as his fingers grasp the tarnished brass doorknob of the bedroom. Perhaps they could have come back from the kiss, recovered some semblance of professionalism after that one drunken slip up. The real problem was, neither of them had been particularly drunk when they'd got back to the apartment. Neither of them had been particularly drunk when Ren pushed himself up against Sebastian in the shower and Sebastian had moaned into the tile as he'd given him a fucking *rim job*.

Sebastian squints as he steps into the apartment, the sunlight brighter here. It's shining directly in, falling on the row of houseplants which take up the counter space separating the kitchenette from the living room. Sebastian sees the money plant, leaves turned proudly towards the bright morning light, green and shiny and exuberant.

Ren is standing in the kitchen, back to Sebastian as he fusses with an appliance. He senses Sebastian at once, turning to see him standing there clad in Ren's own clothes. His dark hair is pushed back from his face with a thin Alice band, and he's wearing a pair of shorts and a sweatshirt. He stares at him for a second, the only sound in the apartment the electric kettle spluttering into life on the countertop behind him.

Sebastian thinks it would be simpler if all he felt was regret. If, when he looked at Ren here and now in the cold light of day, he felt the sinking lead weight of shame settle heavy in his stomach. Then he could forget it ever happened, return to his life as it was before Ren.

Instead, Ren smiles and Sebastian smiles back.

"I only have instant coffee," Ren says, jerking his thumb towards a jar of off brand instant granules on the counter beside two chipped mugs. Sebastian wrinkles his nose in distaste.

"I don't know what would be worse," Sebastian acknowledges. "The lack of any caffeine at all, or the damage to my colon when I inevitably shit myself."

Ren rolls his eyes, mouth now set in a firm line.

"Charming," he replies, turning back to the cups and spooning instant coffee into both, regardless of Sebastian's prim comment.

Sebastian takes this as an invitation to make himself at home, so he crosses to the single sofa in the living room and sits down on it. It sags under him, the leather worn away in the seat where Ren must sit every day. Sebastian scoots over and adjusts himself appropriately.

A moment passes before the kettle finishes boiling, and Sebastian hears the satisfying bubble of instant coffee as Ren pours water over the granules. He brings Sebastian's cup over, sitting down on the sofa. He blows steam away from the edge of his cup, eyes meeting Sebastian's carefully over the top.

He isn't smiling anymore, but his eyes are soft, crinkled at the corners.

"Did you sleep okay?" he asks. Sebastian nods, leaning forwards to pluck his own coffee up from the table.

"Surprisingly, yes. Those sheets feel like they were woven from stalks of grass or something," he says, rubbing at the delicate skin of his cheek with his knuckles for good measure. Ren offers him a flat look before taking a sip of his still scalding coffee. He winces a bit, leaning over to deposit it on the table. He studies Sebastian for another moment.

"And how do you feel this morning?"

Sebastian tenses ever so slightly, the elephant in the room making quick work of interrupting their usual easy banter with the memories of last night. Sebastian squirms in his seat, his ass twinging a little in response. He looks away from Ren into the still swirling darkness of his coffee.

"I feel fine. A little… sore, but I'm quite good with pain, so."

This doesn't seem to amuse Ren in the way Sebastian meant it to. His brow furrows ever so slightly before relaxing again.

"I'll bet," is all he says quietly. Then, "Want a smoke?"

Sebastian nods. Ren stands and goes to the bathroom, presumably where his jeans still lie from the night before. He comes back with a cigarette lit in his mouth, and another which he offers to Sebastian, along with his lighter.

Sebastian frowns as he puts the cigarette in his mouth, looking between the lighter and Ren's face. Ren raises a brow.

"I like it when you light it for me," Sebastian says reluctantly. Ren smirks at that, flipping the Zippo open easily and holding it poised at the tip of Sebastian's cigarette.

"See how easy things can be when you use your words?" Ren says smoothly. Sebastian takes a drag of his cigarette, plucking it from his mouth quickly.

"As if you're one to talk," he retorts at once, thin jets of smoke leaving his nostrils. He chews on his next words for a moment before deciding just to come out with it. "Although last night you were quite willing to use your words."

Ren glances away at once, suddenly finding the tips of his fingers exceptionally interesting. Sebastian watches him lace them together and apart as his cigarette burns away to ash on his lip. Sebastian wonders if he isn't flushing a little.

Devoid of the influence of alcohol, however, Ren has reverted quite definitively back to his usual stoic demeanour, and he quickly regains his composure enough to look at Sebastian again.

"I suppose I was. You seemed to enjoy it," he adds pointedly. Sebastian nods his head, taking another drag on his cigarette.

"I did enjoy it," he says honestly. He finds himself unable to stop, now that the dam has been opened. "So what does it mean? Last night. For the two of us and... and everything?"

Ren reaches over to the coffee table and grabs a small round ashtray, tapping the end of his cigarette against it. He offers it to Sebastian, who does the same. He sighs.

"I don't know," he answers quietly.

All at once, Sebastian realises that isn't what he wanted to hear. Ren's face is carefully expressionless as he takes a deep breath and continues.

"I mean, you're technically my boss. And you have so much going on, I don't want to get in the way of that. And anything we did... it couldn't be public, for obvious reasons."

Sebastian thinks this is a rather creative way of referring to his frankly abysmal love life up until this moment. He can see it now, for what it is, having spent last night wrapped around Ren. As he stares at him, he recalls the tender way Ren kissed him; the way he had checked in with him at every possible step; took care to offer him as much pleasure as he could. No one else has ever done that for Sebastian. If he's honest, he's never really *wanted* it from anyone else before. It seems clear to him now, when faced with the option of either having that with Ren again or not, what he wants.

Sebastian sighs.

"Well, why can't we just keep it between us?" he asks innocently. "We're together all the time, anyway. It can be our secret." Ren shoots him a blank look.

"Don't be naïve, Sebastian."

It's strange to hear him say his name in the morning time, lost the thrum of lust that held it aloft last night. Now it sounds decidedly pleasant rolling off his tongue, innocent and thoughtless.

Sebastian tosses his head dismissively, taking a last drag of his cigarette. He stubs it out.

"Don't talk to me like I'm a child, Ren. How old are you anyway?" he asks, the thought only just now occurring to him. Ren quirks a brow.

"Oh, now you're worried about how old I am?" he says, a coy undertone to his question. "And what if I said thirty-two?"

Sebastian rolls his eyes.

"I'd say you may be Asian, but even that would be pretty impressive."

Ren gives him an odd look.

"A vaguely racist way to put it, but okay. I'm twenty-seven."

Sebastian snorts at that, trying his best to conceal his amusement and ultimately failing.

"Cradle-snatcher, are you?"

"Be serious," Ren insists then, sitting forwards so the distance between them on the sofa closes. Sebastian sobers immediately, the intensity of Ren's gaze so reminiscent of the way he'd looked at him last night as he fucked him that it makes his dick twitch with interest. He chews on his lip, tries to do as Ren asks.

"I *am* serious. All I know is that I really enjoyed last night, and I would like it to be an option that it happens again. If you don't want that, then we can forget it ever happened. I'll understand if you want to keep things… strictly professional."

As Sebastian says it, he leans in too, lashes falling heavily over his eyes as he studies the outline of Ren's lips. They're so full and pink, gone the plump kiss-bruised redness. The air between them is heady now, thick with want and promise, both of them knowing full well what they can offer the other.

Ren swallows thickly, licks his bottom lip.

"There would need to be ground rules," he says, voice a hoarse crackle as he tries to speak past the undeniable attraction that tugs the two of them closer. Sebastian nods, the tips of their noses almost touching.

"As many as you want," Sebastian agrees, certain he'd agree to fucking anything right now if it means Ren will touch him again.

They don't manage to lay out any such ground rules, choosing instead to succumb to temptation as the sun continues to rise.

Thirteen

They settle on two main ground rules, in the end:

No funny business during Ren's working hours

If, at any point, it becomes apparent that furthering their relationship will cause more harm to either party than good, their hook-ups come to a firm halt

The second point, Sebastian thinks, is moot anyway, because by definition the actions they're engaging in would bring irreparable harm to them both if they were found out. Ren would lose his job, and Sebastian would be subjected to whatever punishment his father saw fit. Ren seems to think they can stay ahead of those problems ever arising if they stick to the first point. The first point is, however, far more difficult to maintain than the second.

Ren is scheduled to be off work the two days following the Halloween party. By the time he returns at 8am on the third day, Sebastian is practically gasping for his touch.

Ren slides the curtains open in Sebastian's bedroom, weak November light barely illuminating the lavish space.

"You have a 9am class, sir," he says plainly, taking the silver tray a maid brings with a cup of coffee on it and depositing it on Sebastian's bedside table. The second his door shuts behind the maid, Sebastian's hand snakes out from below the sheets, grasps Ren's wrist with insistence.

"I don't feel well," he mutters, his voice thick with sleep. "I think we should stay here today."

Ren jerks his wrist free of Sebastian's grip.

"I don't think so, sir. You're already behind on your credits for this class, what with that time you took off after your birthday. What's wrong with you? I can call the doctor, see if she can prescribe anything to help you get through the day?" he says, folding his hands behind his back and watching Sebastian carefully. Sebastian groans.

"I'm fucking *horny* is what's wrong with me," he hisses, falling dramatically back on his pillows and peering up at Ren through one eye. Ren appears unimpressed.

"I don't think the doctor can help with that," he says stiffly. "Why don't you go shower and relieve yourself of that problem? Two birds with one stone."

"Why don't you join me?" Sebastian tries, but he's met with a flash of annoyance in Ren's otherwise immovable face.

"I can't imagine that would be appropriate sir," Ren tells him sharply. Sebastian sits up in bed, his duvet collecting around his hips and barely exposing his lower abdomen. He doesn't miss the way Ren's eyes jolt down momentarily as the fabric moves. He clenches his jaw tighter.

"You were very serious about those ground rules, weren't you?" Sebastian observes quietly, running a hand through his hair before reaching up above his head in a stretch. His spine pops pleasantly as the duvet slips down a little further. Ren doesn't shift.

"As a heart attack," he replies, crossing to the door. "I'm going to make sure the car is ready. When I come back in fifteen minutes I expect *you* to be ready."

Sebastian throws his legs over the side of the bed, rolls his head on his shoulders as he stands up. He's completely naked, hairs on the backs of his arms rising a little in the gentle chill of the morning air.

"Such a professional. I thought I was supposed to be the one in charge," Sebastian says playfully, throwing Ren a pointed look over his shoulder as he makes his way over to the ensuite. Ren hesitates for an instant with his hand on the doorknob, before turning to cast his gaze decadently over Sebastian's body. He nods.

"Between the hours of 8am and 8pm, you are," he says. A pause. "I'm not free for overtime this week either, so please be aware I'll be clocking off promptly at 8."

Sebastian gives him a luxurious grin then, the thrill of Ren's words making his dick stir with interest.

"What, you have a hot date lined up every night this week?" he asks, relishing in the hunger left in the dark hollows of Ren's eyes when he finally tears his gaze away from Sebastian's body. Ren nods.

"Something like that."

He does leave the room then, and diligently returns in fifteen minutes to find Sebastian clean and ready to go.

When the two of them fall through the door into a hotel room Sebastian procures for them that evening, the hunger hasn't left Ren's expression.

"You were on your worst behaviour this morning," Ren says against the curve of Sebastian's jaw, fingers working quickly to remove his belt and jacket. Sebastian lets out a burst of laughter, which rapidly transforms into a gasp.

"You loved it," he manages to retort weakly, back pressed against the wood of the door. Ren hurriedly undoes the buttons on Sebastian's shirt, tongue laving at the flushed skin of his torso as he goes. He takes Sebastian's jaw between his thumb and forefinger, holding him steady.

"That's neither here nor there," he growls, disallowing Sebastian to dip his head forwards and seize his mouth in a kiss. He reaches down with his other hand to cup Sebastian's hard dick, standing proud between them and already begging for Ren's attention. He doesn't exercise any friction on it at all, simply squeezing until Sebastian grunts at the sudden discomfort. Ren relaxes his hold, lets a smile escape as he leans forwards and kisses Sebastian softly. It sends a warm shudder of pleasure through his centre, the sudden pain cauterised with Ren's gentle kisses exhilarating. "If you can't follow the rules, then I won't let this happen again," Ren finishes as he pulls back, still holding Sebastian's face in position.

"Liar," Sebastian berates him, sliding his tongue out of his mouth to run the edge along Ren's fingers. "You want this just as much as I do."

Ren responds by jerking Sebastian away from the door, stripping him of his final items of clothing and leading him over to the bed.

"I know it's potentially a foreign concept for you, Sebastian," he says delicately, as he reaches up and undoes the buttons of his own shirt. "But these rules have to be followed. Now, because you tried to cause me trouble this morning, you have to get yourself ready for me."

Sebastian watches as Ren produces a small bottle of lube from his pocket, throwing it on the bed alongside him. It's nearly embarrassing how quickly he moves to snatch it up, to uncap it and deposit some of the thick, clear gel onto the length of his index finger.

Sebastian positions himself so he's sitting up on his elbows against the plush pillows of the bed, legs spread, one hand on his hole, one already reaching for his leaking cock.

Ren climbs atop him, slapping away the hand Sebastian has already palming at his dick. He shakes his head.

"I said get yourself ready for me. You don't come until I say you can," Ren says slowly, laying one last kiss on Sebastian's mouth before he leans back entirely to watch.

Sebastian opens his mouth to protest, but finds a whimper escape instead, the ripple of pleasure throbbing through his body and straight to his hole nearly overwhelming. He does as he's told, circles his rim for a moment before dipping the first finger inside himself as Ren watches.

"Good boy," Ren whispers softly, earning another broken whimper from Sebastian's parted lips. "See? You can follow instructions after all."

The next full day is spent in the university library cramming for a mock-exam Sebastian forgot that he had; that evening he attends a gala dinner in place of his father, away on an extended business trip somewhere in Europe. By the time Ren drops him off at his apartment building, he's already four hours overtime despite the coy arrangement he'd made with Sebastian at the beginning of the week, and so must return home to get some rest. They've sort of wordlessly agreed not to hook up at Sebastian's place; Ivan sometimes returns sooner than the president post business trip and he's been known to just fucking let himself into Sebastian's room when he feels like it, so it's decidedly too much of a risk. The day after that is spent flitting between class and committee meetings for committees Sebastian doesn't even fucking know how he ended up on, and that evening he has a conference call with his father. Ren returns home at 8pm as his schedule dictates.

Thursday is a similar story, full of study and fruitless social engagements that leave Sebastian's patience run horribly thin.

By the time 8pm on Friday rolls around, Sebastian calls at the last minute to cancel a trip to the theatre planned with the company directors, claiming he has too much studying to do. He leaves his apartment building through the side entrance, calls a cab to the dive bar around the corner from Ren's place.

When Ren answers the door, Sebastian has barely got his shoes off in the entranceway before he's being swept up by Ren's arms, held tightly to his body as he kisses him deeply.

"I need a shower," Sebastian complains when he pulls away for air, but Ren's hardly listening, lips messily catching Sebastian's again and tongue roving hungrily inside his mouth.

Sebastian's vaguely aware they're moving towards the shower as Ren tries his best not to stretch the fine woollen weave of Sebastian's sweater as he pulls it over his head, uncaring as he turns the shower on and the stream immediately soaks the sleeve of his shirt.

They help each other get undressed, kissing languidly as they go, before Ren sets about rubbing the tension from Sebastian's shoulders in the steamy enclosure of his little stand up shower.

"This week has gone on forever," Sebastian mutters as Ren massages shampoo through the golden strands of his hair, running the tips of his fingers from the crown of his head to the stiff tendons in Sebastian's neck.

"But you learned your lesson after Monday," Ren hums approvingly, as he rinses the suds from Sebastian's head. "You were almost too well behaved. I was worried you'd gone off me."

Concern jolts through Sebastian then, and he quickly turns on the spot so he's facing Ren, eyes wide and searching.

"What—? Ren, I'm trying really hard to do what you want, I can't be on my best behaviour *and* give you fuck me eyes every morning," he says, but no sooner have the words left his mouth than Ren is kissing them away, brows furrowed.

"I know, I was just kidding," he says gently, running his hands across Sebastian's now tense features to try to alleviate his concern. "I'm sorry, I didn't mean to give you mixed signals. You did just what I wanted. I wasn't really worried."

Sebastian softens again, lulled into the warm safety of Ren's arms as he reaches up and pulls him into a hug. Sebastian winds his hands around Ren's waist, lets his fingers slide over the sharp lines of Ren's hips and come to rest at the curve of his ass. Ren turns the shower off, pushes the door open to let some of the steam escape.

"You want your reward?" Ren teases carefully, mouth quirking at the edge in a playful smile. Sebastian answers by leaning in and kissing him deeply, slowly, like he's been thinking about since they parted early on Tuesday morning.

Ren leads him into his bedroom, sinks down onto the bed with Sebastian still wrapped around him.

"Let me eat you out, baby," he murmurs against Sebastian's lips, earning a sigh of pleasure from Sebastian at the soft purr of the pet name. Ren crawls further onto the bed, lies down on his back and instructs Sebastian to get on top of him, facing the opposite wall.

Sebastian can't help but feel exceptionally vulnerable in this position, but the way Ren's fingers clutch the firm flesh of his thighs is reassuring. He soon loses the ability to demonstrate self-consciousness at all, when Ren runs the tip of his tongue around his rim before latching greedily onto his asshole. Sebastian tries to keep himself steady, to subdue the embarrassing gasps and groans that leave him, all vaguely sounding like Ren's name. Ren slides one hand off his thigh, reaches up to begin stroking Sebastian's painfully hard cock. Ren's tongue dives hungrily inside him, fucking in and out of his hole as he works Sebastian in a steady rhythm. He pauses to catch his breath every now and again, maintaining the agonisingly controlled movement as he murmurs praise against his skin.

"You did so well," Ren coos before continuing to eat him out. "You were so good for me all week, so now I want to make you feel good."

It's the praise more than anything else, Sebastian realises, which sends him hurtling towards completion, as his gasps turn to all out cries of pleasure as he grinds his asshole on Ren's willing mouth and tongue. Heady pleasure overwhelms him as he comes over his own stomach, some of it dripping from the tip of his cock to spill onto Ren's fingers. He eases himself off Ren's face, realising he's probably crushing him, and watches as Ren lifts his hand to his mouth and sucks Sebastian's spend off his fingers.

"So do you have a little bit of a praise kink, or what?" Ren asks blithely, mouth still around his own fingers as he gazes up at Sebastian. Sebastian feels his cheeks roar red, slumping down immediately into Ren's side on the bed and hiding his face. Ren chuckles fondly at him, reaches over onto his bedside table to retrieve a baby wipe. Sebastian watches him through the cage of his own fingers, finding the courage to speak as Ren works to tenderly clean him.

"If it makes any difference, I've only just realised how bad it is thanks to you," he says through his teeth and Ren laughs properly at that, pressing a kiss to the top of Sebastian's head.

"It's cute," he says easily. Then, "Where do you think it comes from?"

Sebastian frowns a little, weaving his arms around Ren's waist as he settles deeper into the soft warmth of the bedspread. The sheets may be rough and the tog on the duvet may be low, but Ren's soothing scent envelops his every sense.

"Does it have to *come* from something?" Sebastian asks, a yawn swallowing the end of his sentence. Perhaps it's the post-orgasm bliss, perhaps it's the incomparable comfort he feels bundled up, surrounded by Ren, but he considers the question a moment longer. "I don't know. I used to have dogs. Two Dobermans, Poppy and Nuca. One time, Poppy had an accident on the carpet. She was only a baby, but I was worried my father would be angry if he saw it, so I lifted my hand to hit her across the nose. Their trainer caught me in the act, stopped me before I could."

He pauses thoughtfully, remembering the way he had flinched back from Rosie when she'd caught him by the wrist. She'd pulled her fingers away like she'd been burned, concern written all across her pretty features. Ren is silent, combing his fingers slowly through Sebastian's hair as he talks.

"Rosie said having a pet is all about mutual respect. If I expected the dogs to act a certain way, I had to afford them the same respect. She said praise is the best motivator. I would reward the dogs when they did something I wanted them to, and she praised me for working hard. It was… fairly alien to me, I think." Sebastian pauses, the conversation having veered into uncomfortable territory, his defences left abandoned at Ren's bedroom door. He clears his throat. "You've seen the sort of relationship I have with my father. I think I could count on one hand the number of times he's praised me in my life."

Ren doesn't answer immediately, just continuing to stroke Sebastian's hair. The silence makes Sebastian squirm a little, the feeling of exposure suddenly too much as Ren ponders on the right words to meet him with.

Instead of suffering the pity that's inevitably coming, Sebastian sits up in bed, leaning down to catch Ren's mouth in a slow kiss. He pulls away grinning, fingers sliding curiously down Ren's stomach.

"Sorry to kill the mood. Forget I said anything and let me repay your attentiveness," Sebastian purrs, fingertips ghosting over Ren's collarbone in the way he knows he likes. He continues his ministrations, managing to silence any response Ren might have provided with hot kisses and a wandering hand.

Sebastian spends the weekend on a bullshit frat team-building residential trip at someone's lakeside manor. It's fucking freezing because it's November, and Sebastian finds it increasingly difficult to maintain posi-tive team relationships when all he can think about is Ren. The following week is a flurry of activity too, his father's business trip meaning Sebastian has to appear at far more company meetings and social events than usual, which in turn affords no time to sneak away to be with Ren.

By the end of the third week of November, Sebastian doesn't seem to be the only one suffering the conse-quences of his packed calendar.

"Do you have anything planned this weekend?" Ren asks him suddenly that Friday morning, careful to ensure his voice is kept low and the door to Sebastian's bedroom is shut tight. Sebastian shakes his head.

"I should probably be studying for my final exams, but realistically there's no fucking way I'm going to be able to focus," he admits, straightening his tie in the mirror of his wardrobe. The damned thing doesn't want to sit still, and he very nearly tears it from around his neck to fashion a noose. Ren comes to his side at once, gesturing for him to turn so he can adjust it.

"If you wanted to, you could go upstate or something," Ren offers quietly. "Lock yourself away to study. Somewhere unwanted parties wouldn't be able to bother you."

Ren finishes tightening the tie, his fingers catching a moment too long on the lapel of Sebastian's suit jacket. Sebastian reaches up and ghosts the tips of his own fingers along the back of Ren's hand, the contact alone sending a torrent of attraction spilling through his veins. It takes every ounce of self-control he has not to undress Ren and suck him off right there, busy-body maids be damned.

"I could definitely do that," Sebastian says. He studies Ren carefully, the brief skin on skin contact rewarding him with a sense of serenity as well as arousal. "Go ahead and arrange something. I need somewhere quiet, secluded, where I won't be interrupted. And of course, you'll be off the clock, but if you wanted to come and relax and simultaneously make sure I'm taken care of...?"

Ren grins, pulls his fingers away from Sebastian slowly.

"I could definitely do that," he agrees. "Make sure you're taken care of, that is."

He lets out a deep breath, considering his words more carefully. "And if I'm honest, I still have no leads about the shooter from your birthday. If he didn't show up again at the Halloween party, it could mean he's planning to strike on a more personal level." Ren's mouth is a thin line as he gazes meaningfully up at Sebastian. "It's my job to make sure you're safe. I want to keep you safe."

Sebastian brushes him off with a smile, shutting the wardrobe and concealing his reflection from view. He turns to Ren, gives his elbow the barest of squeezes.

His good sense tells him it's entirely irrational, but with Ren at his side, he feels safer than he's probably ever done in his entire life. Even with the prospect of an unknown shooter lurking at the back of his mind, he's certain there's no one better placed to look after him than Ren.

The act of sincerity is still not something Sebastian wears comfortably, but he hopes Ren can feel it in the way his fingers curl around his arm and stay there.

"You make me feel very safe," he says.

Fourteen

While Sebastian attends class on Friday morning, Ren arranges for the trip upstate. He picks him up from classes with the car already packed up, insists on driving for the majority of Friday afternoon into the evening to allow Sebastian to 'make the most' of the entire weekend free of distraction.

They have to drive for ten minutes down a dirt track before they come upon the log cabin, the key under the welcome mat to let themselves in. Sebastian raises a discerning eyebrow.

"Where the fuck did you find this place?" he asks as he steps over the threshold and takes in the slightly stale smell of the room. "Are you actually planning on executing my grisly murder up here?"

Ren rolls his eyes.

"It came very highly recommended, actually. My old boss uses it for the lake in the summer, but he's not interested in how cold it gets in winter. I called and asked if I could use it if I cleaned it up a little," he tells Sebastian, setting their bags down and immediately going to set a fire in the old stone fireplace.

Sebastian supposes the place is quaint enough. It has handsome wooden beams which crisscross the high roof, the walls made up of slats of maple coloured wood. There's a small kitchen, a bathroom off to the back of the cabin and a set of narrow wooden stairs which lead up to a loft and what Sebastian soon sees to be the only bed. It's low to the ground, covered in animal pelts and colourful woollen blankets.

"Sebastian?"

Ren calls his name so easily here. It makes Sebastian's chest swell with happiness.

"Mmhm?" Sebastian calls back, dumping their bags at the foot of the bed.

"I need to go out back and get some wood for the fire. Do you want to start cooking dinner? I bought groceries."

Sebastian arrives back in the living area of the cabin, watching the tight muscles of Ren's forearms as they move distractingly below his golden skin as he sets the fire. When Sebastian doesn't respond, Ren throws him a quizzical glance over his shoulder. Sebastian frowns.

"Can't we just order food?"

Ren stands up straight, dusts off his hands free of wood shavings.

"Were you in the car when we drove here? It's an hour to the nearest town. I thought you wanted to go somewhere you wouldn't be interrupted?" Ren grins, knowingly. "You know. From your studying."

Sebastian lets out a deep sigh, crosses his arms.

"Would you be shocked if I told you I've never cooked a thing in my life, Ren?" Sebastian asks snidely, batting his eyelashes antagonistically across the room. Ren gives him a puzzled look.

"Nothing? Okay, well… you can chop vegetables, right? And then I can do the actual cooking?"

Sebastian reaches up to the back of the door where they'd stowed their outdoor clothing, pulling his coat back on.

"Tell you what," he answers. "Rather than go through and highlight all of my culinary ineptitude, why don't *you* just start dinner and tell *me* where to find the firewood?"

Ren agrees this is probably a more efficient way to handle things and provides Sebastian with instructions for retrieving the wood. When he's back, something meaty is already browning in a pan on the stove. Ren is wearing a stripy apron, chopping an onion on a thick wooden board, a bottle of wine already popped open and left to aerate. It's revoltingly domestic; it makes Sebastian feel stupid, how easily it brings a smile to his face.

"Full disclosure," Ren says as Sebastian stacks up the wood by the fire. "I'm not exactly a chef and my mother only ever taught me to cook Korean food. Beyond that I can make this one kind of pasta. So that's what we're having."

Sebastian slides in to sit at one of the barstools on the other side of the counter to where Ren is diligently chopping. He reaches over to pour them both a glass of wine, raising a discerning brow at the label.

"Why aren't we having Korean food?" Sebastian asks, swilling the wine around his glass carefully before taking a sip. It's lush and fruity, and leaves a delectable tang on the back of his tongue. Ren finishes chopping onions and moves onto carrots. He raises a brow.

"Have you ever had Korean food?" he asks. Sebastian shrugs.

"No, but I've had Chinese food," he says. Ren shuts his eyes, pausing his knife gently on the board, before offering Sebastian a blank look.

"I think you need to come to terms with the fact Korea and China are different countries," he settles on saying as he continues to chop the carrots. Sebastian shuts his mouth then, worried he's offended him. He supposes he isn't very knowledgeable at all when it comes to Asian countries or their cuisines. He makes a mental note to get some books out from the library when he gets back to college.

He takes another sip of his wine, watching as Ren finishes chopping his vegetables and turns to lift chunks of beef from where they've been browning in the pan behind him. He deposits the vegetables in then, a pleasant hiss following as they land in the fat left behind from the beef. It already smells incredible. Sebastian can't remember if he's ever sat like this and watched as someone prepared him a meal.

"So is your mother your Korean side, then?" Sebastian asks, as Ren lifts his own wine and takes a sip. He nods, throwing a kitchen towel over one shoulder as he watches his vegetables cook.

"Yep. Dad was Japanese."

"Why did he come here?"

Ren hesitates.

"I don't know. I never met him."

"Why not?" Sebastian asks. Ren's mouth does a funny twitch. He doesn't answer immediately, choosing instead to move the vegetables around in the pan with a wooden spoon. Sebastian waits, watching his every move carefully.

"Uh…" Ren finally makes some noise, opening two cans of tomatoes and adding them into the vegetables. "He owed a bunch of money to the wrong guys. Made himself scarce before I was born. It was rough for *eomma* those first couple of years. We moved a lot. She's never been able to come back to the city."

As Ren speaks, Sebastian finds himself feeling simultaneously fascinated and foolish. He realises he's never asked Ren *anything* about himself, except for those first few moments spent in his bedroom following his failed birthday party. In fairness, Ren has never voluntarily disclosed anything, bar the fact he worked in *Rain*, and the brief summary of his heritage. Sebastian watches the way Ren stumbles awkwardly through the words, gone his usually slick demeanour. No matter what persona he's embodying, that of the aloof bodyguard or the attentive lover, he's always confident in everything he says. Now, he seems uncertain. Uncomfortable.

Sebastian wonders if perhaps he doesn't want to talk about it.

"We… don't have to talk about it anymore if you don't want to," Sebastian says as soon as the thought enters his head. Ren glances up from the pot then, and he looks overwhelmingly grateful. He lets out a low breath, takes a sip of his wine. He gives Sebastian a quick smile.

"I don't mean to act so weird about it, it's just… yeah. I'd rather not talk about myself, if that's cool."

Sebastian aches to probe him further on the matter, but restrains himself with practised ease. He's very good at not looking into things too deeply; sometimes it's better that way (although he's not entirely convinced this is one of those times). He's suddenly very aware that Ren probably knows almost everything about him.

They chat easily back and forth as Ren finishes cooking dinner, eventually presenting Sebastian with a rich, red ragu atop thick sheathes of pappardelle. It's utterly delicious, and Sebastian makes sure to tell Ren every other bite. Ren tells him there's no need to sound *quite* so surprised, but also not to expect anything else. This is honestly the only thing he knows how to make taste this good.

After dinner, they curl up below one of the many thick woollen throw blankets in front of the fire. It's taken surprisingly well in the time they've been eating, and the little log cabin has soaked up the heat.

"Thanks for dinner," Sebastian says quietly as they watch the flames dance inside the fireplace. He's sitting between Ren's legs, his back pressed up against Ren's stomach and chest. Ren plays absently with his hair, drawing his fingers through the strands of gold.

"That's alright," Ren tells him, pressing a gentle kiss to his cheek for good measure.

Sebastian can feel uncertainty unwinding in his gut, however, amid the comfort Ren's tenderness and domesticity brings. It's familiar, a longtime companion of Sebastian's, and its cold, unfeeling claws peel back the layers of solace and embed them with shame and guilt.

"This… was more of a date than a hook-up, wasn't it?" Sebastian asks slowly.

He thinks he feels Ren tense a little behind him, but his fingers don't stop winding through his hair.

"I guess you could see it like that," Ren says finally.

Sebastian's stomach continues to churn with what little conciliation Ren's statement brings.

"Do you see it like that?" Sebastian asks. Ren stops moving his fingers, leans his chin forwards and sets his cheek on Sebastian's shoulder. He looks up at him with careful dark eyes, watching Sebastian's face for his every emotion playing across it.

"Sebastian, are you okay?" he asks.

Sebastian opens his mouth to tell him that everything is fine. He opens his mouth to make a flirtatious comment about how he'd be better if Ren stopped cooking him dinner and weaving his fingers through his hair and just fucked him. He opens his mouth to shut Ren out in the way he knows best.

Instead, he says,

"I'm not sure."

His voice wobbles with unease as emotion makes his throat dry. Suddenly, he feels impossibly overwhelmed. Ren readjusts himself, sliding one leg around a little more so he's sitting at Sebastian's side now rather than directly behind him. He raises a brow, takes his hands back and keeps them to himself.

"Okay. Tell me why," Ren says. Sebastian shakes his head.

"I don't know," he tells him honestly. "Dinner was nice. The drive up here was nice. The fact you thought of a way we could be together all weekend was nice. It's just what I wanted. But now I'm here and it... I feel like this, and I don't know why."

"Well, try and describe it," Ren says, practicality taking over as ever. Sebastian squeezes the soft wool of the blanket between his fists and sighs.

"It's not that simple," he snaps back, and he hates the waspish tone his voice takes on and he *hates* that he doesn't understand what's making him feel like this. He takes a deep breath and tries to pinpoint what it is that's making him panic all of a sudden. Sebastian covers his face and talks to the palms of his hands. Maybe if Ren can't see him, it'll be easier to sort through his feelings. "I'm not... I've never... I don't *know*. It's *bad enough* I want guys to fuck me, but like, I can just put it down to how good it feels, right? Guys know how dicks work, so naturally they'd be better at giving handjobs, wouldn't they? But then… having dinner together and talking and… and just being together like this. That's different. That's something else."

Ren doesn't say anything for a long time. So long, Sebastian has to peer from between his fingers at him. Finally, after a deep breath, Ren shakes his head.

"It doesn't have to be something else," he says gently. It's so gentle, so *forgiving* that Sebastian can't help the way his heart clenches in agony. It's as if Ren's soft acceptance is a hundred times worse than any blow his father could have dealt him; the twinges of pain behind his right eye are nothing but far away memories every time he's safe with Ren.

"But it is," Sebastian says brokenly. He tears his hands away from his face, looks at Ren full on, his cheeks burning with embarrassment. "It *is* something else, isn't it? That's why I feel like this—" he cuts himself off before he can babble any further, running a tense hand through his hair. "I can't do this, Ren. I can't… I can't *like* you, I'm only supposed to *want* you—"

Ren cuts him off abruptly with a kiss. It's not forceful or wanting, nor is it delicate and chaste. It's just that, a kiss, a firm press of his lips to meet Sebastian's.

When he pulls away, he rests a reassuring hand on Sebastian's shoulder.

"You're new to this," he says matter-of-factly. "You've spent your life dating girls who you have no interest in, romantically or otherwise. It's understandable that this is a lot. Maybe… I shouldn't have gone quite so deep into the cabin getaway idea."

Sebastian shrugs his shoulders. He really doesn't know if that would have helped or not; perhaps even without the time to themselves this panic would have cropped up, eventually. When he doesn't respond, Ren draws a tight breath and continues.

"I got excited, I guess, to have some time with you. There's… just… something about you, Sebastian," he finishes, apparently unable to find anything else in his own vocabulary to accurately describe his feelings. Still, his words make Sebastian's chest hum with that warm feeling again, his heart thrumming ten times faster at the thought that Ren, handsome, intelligent, brave *Ren* would be sitting opposite him saying all of this.

Why the fuck *is* he sitting opposite him saying this? Why would someone like Ren waste his time with someone like him? He doesn't know anything about… this.

The words are spilling out of him before he can stop them.

"Whatever it is, you're the only one who sees it," he says quickly, and then, as his brain attempts to sabotage the sincerity of Ren's words, "Besides. Didn't Darius say you have a type? The *something about me* is I'm tall and blonde."

He doesn't miss the flicker of hurt which passes over Ren's well-placed features. It almost makes some sick kind of satisfaction settle inside him, pleased that he's succeeded in twisting Ren's heartfelt words into something negative. Sebastian grins, trying to play it off like he doesn't care. Like it doesn't matter how Ren sees him, whether it's just as a tall blonde distraction or otherwise.

Infuriatingly perceptive as always, Ren sees the flicker of doubt in Sebastian's nonchalant grin and leans in closer.

"Do you remember that night I put you in the shower?" Ren asks, as if he can *hear* Sebastian spiralling, as if he wants to bring him reassurance. "You asked me if I hated you. I said I didn't, and you told me to fuck off, I was always glaring at you, like in the elevator?"

Sebastian nods, barely recalling the entirety of the interaction he'd been in such a state, but remembering the hollow look Ren had given him as Jerome's hands roved his body in the elevator. It had made him angry. He thought it was because Ren thought it was disgusting that he had another man all over him, but he knows now that couldn't rightly be the case.

"I was so jealous," Ren admits, fingers picking a thread loose from the blanket between them just for something else to look at. "Even then. I'd been working for you a month at most, and I was so stupidly jealous." Ren pauses for a moment, and it looks like he's taking a deep breath, steadying himself to be this honest. It makes Sebastian feel warm inside, full. Like he could be… a little less alone? That the brutality of coming clean about the panic he's feeling wrapped up around the undeniable pull Ren has on him could be reciprocated in some way.

"I wanted you to look at *me* like that," Ren finishes.

The fire spits as it licks along a wet piece of wood. The cold wind beyond the cabin whistles through the cracks in the door. The thud of Sebastian's heart is deafening in his ears. He thinks he can hear Ren's too.

He remembers Ren's fierce expression in the elevator—how he'd wished at that moment that it was jealousy which made up the distaste in the curl of his lip.

"I don't know how to do this either," Sebastian admits quickly. "Talking about things. Figuring shit out. I'll just fuck it up." Ren gives him a small smile, devoid of pity. There's just patience there, raw and abrasive against the wounds on Sebastian's heart that he didn't think were still open.

"It's all part of the trust thing," Ren says. "I told you I'd tell you if you fuck it up. You're doing just fine."

The physical urge to touch Ren overwhelms the doubt clouding Sebastian's mind, swallowing it whole and leaving nothing but sheer want in its wake. Unable to withstand the intensity of Ren's gaze for a moment longer, Sebastian lunges forwards and captures his mouth in a kiss. Ren returns it enthusiastically, fingers dropping the loose thread forgotten in favour of holding Sebastian's jaw. He rubs the pad of his thumb soothingly below Sebastian's ear as he does sometimes when they kiss like this, and it makes Sebastian want to melt into him.

They kiss slowly for another moment, noses crushed against each other's faces, hands reaching out to hold the other.

"Ren," Sebastian whispers, desire suddenly outweighing concern.

"What do you want, Seb?" Ren murmurs against his mouth, words hot and wet as Sebastian feels them tremble across his tongue. "Tell me what you want."

"You," Sebastian practically moans the word, the sound getting trapped, wrapped around a groan of pleasure as Ren reaches between them to run his fingers over Sebastian's semi-hard dick.

"Go upstairs and get everything," Ren instructs him calmly. Sebastian tries not to vault over the back of the sofa, but the excitement in his bones has entirely replaced the apprehension that had cowered there before. He makes it up the stairs to the loft in four strides, hands fumbling as he unzips Ren's overnight bag. Something falls out onto the floor as the bag slumps over in the wake of his searching, but he's already back downstairs, goods in hand.

Ren has thrown one of the thick blankets out over the top of the animal skin rug directly in front of the fire. He's wrestling his shirt off when Sebastian reaches him again, planting a firm kiss on his chest while his head is still trapped in the confines of the fabric.

"Jesus Christ," Ren's voice is muffled by the fabric, his face bright with amusement when Sebastian helps him finally remove it. "What, did you teleport back down here?"

"Shut up," Sebastian grumbles, throwing his arms around Ren's neck and returning to kissing him.

"I thought it would be warmest here by the fire," Ren says suggestively, nosing at the skin of Sebastian's collarbone as he peels his sweater off. "What do you think?"

Sebastian hums as if he's considering it carefully, undoing his belt and dropping to the floor to wriggle out of his slacks. He doesn't stand back up, shivering a little at the sudden lack of clothes and fanning his fingers out experimentally on the uncannily soft fur.

"Think it's still too cold down here on my own," he replies, blinking up innocently at Ren as he reclines on his elbows. Ren throws him a devilish grin before stripping off his own jeans, crawling across the blanket until he's between Sebastian's legs. Sebastian drops from where he's propped to lie prone, Ren caging him in with his arms as he kisses him again. It's slow and deep and accompanied by the comforting roar of the fire, impossibly warm. Sebastian feels like his very skin is going to catch alight, spared from the fire only by the incessant press of Ren's hands across every inch of him.

Ren is mouthing across the expanse of Sebastian's chest and stomach now, nipping as he goes and quickly flicking his tongue across the reddened flesh to soothe it. It makes Sebastian's heart race, all the disquiet he'd felt in the aftermath of dinner abandoned in favour of this. Ren slides his fingers along the waistband of Sebastian's briefs, teasing the edge instead of peeling them back to reveal his stiff cock, and Sebastian moans low in the back of his throat.

"Please, Ren," he manages to say, brain lagging behind as he tries to focus on all the points of pleasure left littered across his body. "*Please*, I need this… need you."

"I hear you," Ren responds slowly, ceasing his coy movements and pulling Sebastian's briefs off in one swoop. He runs the length of his tongue up the underside of Sebastian's cock, swirling it around the glistening pink head. The chill of his tongue piercing causes Sebastion to jolt in surprise, and he moves to pause Ren by taking his shoulders.

"Prep me," he begs, his hole twitching in response to the thought of Ren's careful fingers working to diligently stretch him open. Ren raises his eyebrows, reaching up onto the sofa to retrieve the lube Sebastian had brought.

"You really are impatient today," he hums as he runs his slicked finger across Sebastian's hole, only pausing to momentarily torture him before sliding the length of his index finger in. Sebastian had purchased an entire menagerie of sex toys since their first time, taking to stretching himself out as he jerks off in the shower to thoughts of Ren. He's become far more used to the feeling and better equipped to work himself up faster.

Tonight, as Ren works two then three fingers into his hole, Sebastian keens with want, only pausing to wrap his own hand around his dick and gently stroke himself as each new finger enters him. Ren murmurs praise throughout the act, curling his fingers up just so every few pumps to brush against Sebastian's prostate and make him shiver with pleasure.

By the time Ren is rolling the condom onto his own fully erect cock, Sebastian is a panting mess, barely able to pull himself up onto his knees as Ren coaxes him into his lap.

"Come on, baby," Ren says softly, as he positions Sebastian's knees on either side of his thighs, his hole positioned carefully over Ren's dick. "This way feels really good, but it can be a lot more intense the first time. Just tell me if you need to stop, okay?"

Sebastian nods, his forehead resting on Ren's shoulder, his hands gripping the wiry muscles of his traps as he pushes the head of his cock past Sebastian's rim.

"You're doing so well," Ren whispers the praise, reaching up to stroke Sebastian's spine haphazardly as he tenses to stop himself plunging straight in. "Just relax for me, Seb… relax."

Sebastian lets out a shuddering breath, letting his body become used to the intrusion before he lowers himself a little more onto Ren's cock. Sebastian taking control of the motion like this seems to please Ren, as he lets out a strangled moan in the back of his own throat. He rocks his hips gently up into Sebastian, pulling back when Sebastian tenses up again a little.

Sebastian presses a kiss to Ren's shoulder, lifts his head up to watch him as he works himself down further onto his cock. Ren's eyes are heavy lidded, his lips parted as he relinquishes control to Sebastian, hands grasping onto Sebastian's hips so hard he's certain there's going to be bruises. Sebastian finally closes the remaining distance between his ass and Ren's thighs, letting himself rock gently back and forwards.

He would like it if the bruises on his skin were left by Ren. At least Ren leaves them out of affection; bites and kisses, fingers carving into flesh so he can stop himself from fucking into Sebastian too soon and hurting him. Sebastian's never had any bruises left in the wake of pleasure, never associated them with anything gratifying before.

"Do you feel okay?" Ren asks, as Sebastian continues to rock. Sebastian nods, makes a soft noise of affirmation, as he lifts himself up a little and sinks back down onto Ren's cock. Ren lets out a long groan, one which rumbles through his entire chest and into Sebastian's where they're pressed together. He does it again, sliding off a little further this time, each time rocking his hips softly when Ren bottoms out again. Soon, Sebastian's moving quicker, the slick sounds of his wet asshole swallowing up Ren's cock merging with the aborted pants of his own pleasure. He continues to move like that for a while until his thighs are exhausted, after which time Ren readjusts himself a little so he's better positioned to thrust his own hips back and forth and his cock up into Sebastian's ass.

"Fuck, you look so good on my cock like this, Seb," Ren mutters between movements, good sense quickly careening off the edge as he surrenders to the sensation. "You take it so well, baby, just like that. Take it like that for me."

Sebastian can barely speak, only whimpering in response to the praise, the gentle words of encouragement and the accompanying stroke of Ren's fingers along his hips dizzying. Sebastian's cock bobs between the two of them, red and heavy as Ren thrusts up into him harder this time, the tip of his cock meeting with Sebastian's prostate.

"*Yes*, Ren," Sebastian manages to pant. "Yes, right there, please—!"

Ren continues to thump a brutal rhythm up into Sebastian's ass at the same angle, brushing the same spot with each thrust, as he takes Sebastian's cock in hand and starts to stroke.

"Fuck, Ren, I'm going to come," Sebastian whines, eyes squeezed shut in delirium as he gasps for air.

"Me too, Seb. Come for me, Seb. With me, do it with me, baby."

The instruction is well timed, Ren's hips stuttering in time with Sebastian's as they both race to meet their end. Sebastian collapses over Ren as he comes all over his chest, feeling the tense shiver inside him as Ren finishes.

There's a moment of stillness as they catch their breath, still intertwined with one another. Eventually, Ren softens enough that he slips out of Sebastian, trying to ensure he doesn't let the soiled condom touch the blanket below them. He slips his boxers on, tying the condom off and disposing of it.

"Up you get," Ren then eases Sebastian onto wobbly legs, supporting most of his weight as he helps him over to the bathroom. He sets Sebastian down on the toilet seat and begins to draw a bath. He leaves Sebastian in the bathroom while he tidies up in the main room, returning some time later with fresh towels and Sebastian's pyjamas. He lays them out carefully, before reaching over to a jar on the edge of the bath and emptying the Epsom salts inside into the water.

When the bath is finished running he jerks his chin towards it.

"In you go, Seb," he instructs. When Sebastian doesn't move Ren tilts his head, studying him carefully. "It'll help with the pain. Come on, I'm sure your legs still work. Mine do."

"You weren't the one getting railed," Sebastian grumbles, acquiescing to Ren's request and hobbling over to the bath to slip in. Ren's run the water just lukewarm, so it's actually a relief against Sebastian's searingly hot skin. He wonders if it's possible to get third-degree burns just from being in front of a fire for too long. He settles down into the bath, the gentle sting of the water on his asshole strangely comforting. Ren sits on the opposite edge of the bath to where Sebastian is, letting his fingers trail idly through the water.

"Ren...?" Sebastian asks quietly, after too long has passed. Ren sighs, almost as if he knew it was coming.

"Yes?"

Sebastian takes a shuddering breath.

"Am I... gay?"

Ren doesn't miss a beat.

"I don't know," he says, not unkindly. "Are you?"

It's the same thing he'd said to Sebastian that night he'd declared himself a faggot. It's different now, the word is different, the feeling altogether different. It's not just self-loathing reaching around Sebastian's neck to strangle the life out of him. There's the patience and forgiveness Ren exudes in his every word, the reverent way he holds him when they have sex, the care and attention he provides to make sure Sebastian feels good, too.

And he feels so very *good* when he's with Ren.

"Can't you just tell me?" Sebastian asks hopefully. Ren laughs, carefully, and stops just before Sebastian starts to feel self-conscious again.

"Wouldn't that be nice?" Ren asks.

He scoots up the edge of the bath, trails a finger along the length of Sebastian's face. Ren leans down to press a kiss on Sebastian's forehead.

"But you know," Ren adds, running his fingers absent-mindedly through soft water. He fixes his dark gaze with Sebastian's bright one. "You don't have to figure everything out all at once. There's no rush. I'm not going anywhere."

Sebastian pouts as he says,

"I'd like to hope so. I don't think I can stand up on my own."

Fifteen

They make it back to Sebastian's apartment late on Sunday evening.

"Just leave the bags," Sebastian insists, as Ren climbs out of the car and hands his keys off to the valet. "I can carry them to the elevator, I'm not an invalid."

Ren hauls the bags out, giving Sebastian a raised brow.

"It's fine," he says easily, "I'll bring them up to your room. So we can say goodbye."

Sebastian doesn't need to be told twice, a slow grin finding its way onto his face. He rolls his eyes in mock-frustration.

"If you insist," he says, following Ren through the lobby and into the elevator. As soon as the doors slide shut, Sebastian is all over him, crowding Ren up against the shiny interior and pressing a hard kiss to his smiling mouth. Ren breaks away, doing his best attempt at appearing annoyed.

"We're in your apartment building, *sir*," Ren mutters. "You need to contain yourself."

Sebastian ignores him, catching his lips in a sloppy kiss again and running his fingers up the side of Ren's sharp jaw.

Over the weekend he'd learned Ren shaves every day; that he never takes his tongue piercing out, he doesn't need to; that, despite the popular myth, shoe size has nothing to do with how well endowed a man is. Ren has been trying to quit smoking for a year now, and Sebastian's forced him to regress; he doesn't like white wine, just red; he hates the feeling of suede against his skin.

The elevator doors slide open and Sebastian expertly removes himself from Ren, lips popping free with a loud smack for dramatic effect. He takes one of his bags despite Ren's attempt to snatch them both up at once again and makes his way through the apartment's dark hallway to his bedroom.

Sebastian feels Ren hesitate behind him. He turns to see him looking at the family portrait they have hung on the wall, the only thing that's hung on the wall. Sebastian's father had hated it after it was completed, so instead of taking pride of place in the lounge, he'd downgraded it to the dark hallway that only Sebastian would ever really see.

Sebastian walks back to Ren's side, studying the portrait along with him. Ren points.

"That's your mother, right?" he asks quietly. Sebastian nods.

"Yes," he says. When he doesn't add anything else, Ren glances at him uncomfortably.

"I'm sorry about what happened to her," he says, and his voice sounds strange. Sebastian doesn't quite know how to place it, so he just shrugs.

"Why are you sorry? I've kind of always found that phrasing redundant," Sebastian says stiffly. There's quiet for a moment until Ren releases a gentle snort.

"Yeah, I guess you're right," he agrees. A moment passes and then, "What was her name?"

It almost takes Sebastian too long to reach around in the crevices of his memory for the woman in the portrait's name; his father had rarely called her anything that wasn't a slur.

"Lydia," he answers finally. It feels strange to say it after all these years. He wonders if he's ever even said it aloud before now.

"Lydia," Ren repeats thoughtfully. "That's pretty. You look just like her."

Sebastian blinks at him curiously before searching the painting more closely.

He was about five or six when it was painted. In the still image, Sebastian sits on his mother's lap, while his father stands austerely behind the chair she's stiffly seated in, his hand gripping her shoulder. He looks back and forth between the soft smile on the child's face and the sadness on his mother's. While their expressions are incomparable, the shiny golden hair is the same. It falls in loose waves around his mother's shoulders, just as it does across his forehead. They have the same bright eyes, although his mother's are slightly bluer than Sebastian's. The shape of their faces are the same though, the way their noses curve down a little at the tip, a mirror image. Now that he thinks about it, Sebastian sees little resemblance between his dark eyed, dark-haired father and the golden boy reclining in his mother's lap.

Sebastian nods his head finally, aware Ren is studying him cautiously.

"I suppose I do," he says. Then he grins. "Maybe that's why my father's always hated me."

Rather than belabour the point, or suffer any of Ren's earnest protests, Sebastian continues down the hallway, immediately changing the subject.

"Where should we go on our next adventure?" he says brightly as they walk, hoping to distract Ren with talk of more activities that aren't purely related to fucking. "This place is so fucking dreary, it's nice to have something to look forward to. What about the beach?" Ren makes a face. Sebastian frowns. "What's wrong with the beach?"

"I hate the beach," Ren says immediately, pausing as Sebastian fiddles with the knob on his bedroom door. "I hate sand in my shoes, I hate salty water, I hate seaweed. Please, never the beach."

"I don't think I've ever heard you act so *dramatically* about something," Sebastian tells him, enjoying Ren's sudden turn to the melodramatic. Ren raises a brow, an air of good-natured disbelief in his careful expression.

"I thought I'd take a page out of your book," he agrees. Sebastian opens the door, turning back to grin brightly at Ren, whose eyes have fixed over Sebastian's shoulder, staring into the room. The blood drains from his face, causing Sebastian to look back in alarm.

Ivan is sitting in the armchair by the window, legs crossed as he reads some kind of tabloid newspaper. It's not one of the especially trashy ones, as reputable as tabloids go. The reading light illuminates the front page, the pictures splashed across in colour. Easily distinguishable—Ren and Sebastian, emerging from the alley next to the coffee shop on campus. Ren and Sebastian, sharing a cigarette at the side of the hotel, dressed for Halloween. Ren and Sebastian, leaving *Rain*, shoulder to shoulder but not hand in hand.

Sebastian feels as if his heart has fallen into his stomach.

He can't move, frozen in place as Ivan shifts the newspaper and meets his eyes. Pale and sinister and shark-like, they're a familiar sight. They've been there his whole life, watching every horrible thing that's ever happened to Sebastian from the sidelines. Ivan folds the paper closed, glances down at the front page. He's sporting an amused sort of smile as ever, shaking his head back and forth as though in deep disappointment.

"Tomorrow morning's issue," Ivan says lightly. "We know a guy down at the paper, you see. He was able to get an advance copy. Lucky us."

Sebastian can't bring himself to answer. He feels his bag slip from his grasp, land on the floor with a soft thud.

"What the fuck is this?"

It's Ren's voice, dark with fury as he shoves past Sebastian into the room, closer to Ivan and the paper. Ivan folds the tabloid over once again, setting it on the end of his knee where his legs are crossed. He looks relaxed, almost disinterested in Ren's outburst. Sebastian remains rooted to the spot.

"It's exactly what it looks like. You have eyes, don't you? The headline begs the question, 'SPOTTED: Mystery man on the arm of Sebastian Clarence—could the rumours be true?'" Ivan reads the text breathily, as if trying to drum up intrigue. It doesn't work particularly well, his dry tone of voice coming out bland and detached.

Ren shakes his head, fists clenching at his sides. Sebastian manages to shut the door behind him, watching as Ivan's eyes twitch up from the paper to survey Ren with raised eyebrows.

"You said I had the only copies," Ren says.

Ivan nods, tucks the newspaper under his arm.

"Of the frat party pictures? I did say that, didn't I? And you do. I didn't lie," Ivan responds quickly, pausing to tilt his head with measured condescension. "Unfortunately, you provided me with ample opportunities to generate insurance. You're the one who forced my hand with this, Ren. I have to say, I'm disappointed in you. I thought I'd made our arrangement clear."

Sebastian's nervous system suddenly seems to jolt back into life. The words being said around him don't just feed listlessly into his ears now, he's really hearing them. They settle like stones in his belly, fit to drag him down to the seabed with them as they fail to make any sense.

"What?" he asks no one in particular.

There's silence for a moment. Ivan sighs deeply, his smile gone now. The scar which splits his thin mouth too wide when he grins twitches with impatience.

"Will you tell him or shall I?" he asks Ren, lifting his wrist to glance at his watch.

When Ren doesn't respond, Sebastian's panic flares.

"Tell me what?" he demands, attempting to sound austere but coming across desperate instead. "Ren? Tell me what? What does he mean by *arrangement*?"

Sebastian almost lets out a growl of frustration when Ren continues to stare maliciously at Ivan, face cold and devoid of all other emotion. He looks like he had that first morning he'd come to Sebastian's room. Aloof. Professional.

Finally, he turns to face Sebastian. He seems to forget Ivan is even there, as he steps forwards a little, his eyes taking on an air of desperation. Sebastian steps back warily, pressing into the door of his room. Ren takes a deep breath.

"The pictures of us on the porch at that frat party," Ren says. "Ivan had me set them up. I had to make sure you went out onto the porch, and I had to make it look like there was something between us. Ivan said they were materials to keep you in check but would never actually make it to the tabloids. You just had to think they might."

Sebastian stares back at Ren. He can understand the words, but there's something in the back of his head screaming so loudly it almost drowns them out—a desperate protest; *no, no, no, no—please let it all be lies*, he thinks.

Ren doesn't lie. Or at least, Sebastian had thought he didn't.

He takes another step towards Sebastian, imploring him to understand. He looks so different than he had done not five minutes ago in the elevator. There he had been straightforward and kind, so confident in himself and so willing to extend that same grace to Sebastian as he tried to figure himself out. Now Ren's eyes are pleading and desperate; he looks pathetic, scrabbling to piece together something that won't make him look so bad.

"I swear I didn't think he would publish them," Ren continues, running a hand through his hair. "They were never supposed to be anything more than to keep you in line. A threat, that was it. And he gave them to me, so I thought it would all be okay."

"Is that what all of this has been, too?" Sebastian says, his voice so tight in the back of his throat, barely holding back the tidal wave of emotion which is threatening to spill out of him. He jerks his hand between the two of them abstractly, shakes his head. "You trying to 'keep me in line'? Under..." he swallows, the rest of his sentence escaping in a choked whisper. "Under your control?"

"No," Ren raises his voice, and Sebastian can't help it when he flinches back against the wall, away from him.

Every instinct in his body is screaming at him to make himself smaller, to find some way he can escape this situation. He's trapped, backed into a corner, and for all he knows, everything Ren is saying now is a lie too. Ren's face contorts with pain as he watches Sebastian inch further and further away.

"No, Sebastian. The pictures were supposed to be a one-time thing. Ivan said that was all he would *need*, I had no idea he had arranged for others to be taken. I—" Ren grasps at his neck with his hand, as if the words are stuck in his gullet. His eyes are bloodshot, wet at the edges like he's in pain. "It started out one way, but you have to *believe me* Sebastian, none of this was fake, none of it—"

"You're a fucking liar," Sebastian says breathlessly. He can't yell, not in moments like this. Not when he's been caught in a trap like this, left to bleed out in front of them both or gnaw his own leg off to escape. Either way, he's been hurt, irreparably, *as usual*, and he fucking deserves it, he deserves everything he gets because he's always been a *fucking sissy, a fucking baby, a whiny little bitch* his whole miserable life.

"You're a liar and you used me and you've been doing it all for Ivan and my father the whole time." Sebastian pauses, horror clouding his chest with its frigid malice. "Are you even really—do you even—?"

"Sebastian, please," Ren is practically begging now, edging closer to Sebastian every second like he's a wounded animal he needs to clobber over the head and put out of its misery. "You have to understand I took this job because I really needed the money—I told you, didn't I? About my dad and the debts—and Ivan told me he had no use for me if I wouldn't stage these pictures. I thought I had the only copies. I thought we were safe."

"I don't give a fuck why you did it," Sebastian says coldly. "You *lied to me*. You *used* me. You're just—you're just like the rest of them."

"I didn't mean to lie! I thought that you would… do something irrational if you thought Ivan had any hand in those pictures. After we started… after we… I wanted to tell you, but I thought you'd be in more danger if I did," Ren says finally, pathetically.

Suddenly, Ivan stands up from where he's been observing the conversation, expression relaxed.

"Oh, Sebastian's in quite a bit of danger anyway if the president does find out about the two of you," Ivan remarks calmly, shifting his weight easily forwards and backwards as he contemplates it. "Pictures in tabloids are one thing. They can easily be explained away as a bodyguard just doing his job. A first hand account from a hotel maid cleaning up your mess or a neighbour who's watched the two of you falling through an apartment door. That's dangerous." He turns to watch Sebastian, lip curling in distaste.

"Does that mean you haven't told him?" Sebastian asks quickly. The tone of his voice is almost pleading—it's embarrassing the way it slips out of him, childish and desperate. He remembers sounding similar, the day Ivan came to the boarding school in place of his father for parent's evening. The faculty member who had found him with the boy from the lacrosse team, on his hands and knees in the locker room, had told Ivan as much. Sebastian had begged him to keep it to himself—just let this be between the two of them and he promised to never do it again. In the end, after his father had landed him in the ICU, he'd addressed the issue as merely a kiss. For whatever reason, Ivan had chosen to water the story down somewhat, perhaps to spare him a killing blow.

Now, as Sebastian stands at the mercy of his father's most trusted hound once again, he realises that it was probably all part of whatever power play Ivan's making to force Sebastian under his thumb. Years of dulling the blow, of staying one step ahead in whatever Sebastian is planning to ensure Ivan is the one in place of all the power.

"The president has been busy lately," Ivan states plainly. "An opportunity hasn't presented itself yet to discuss the matter."

Sebastian can feel his hands beginning to shake, the pain behind his eye having snuck up on him all at once. It's very nearly blinding, sending bolts of agony shooting down through his right arm and chest, his fingers trembling incessantly as the pain reaches them and has nowhere else to go. His stomach churns with the heaviness of Ren's admission, leaving the back of his tongue watering warningly as nausea begins to take hold. He tries to remain on his feet, but finds that his knees have started to shake now, too.

Sebastian slides down the wall, tucking his chin in against his chest as he shuts his eyes and tries to block it all out.

Ren betrayed him. Ren posed for those pictures, he watched as Sebastian agonised over them, he took advantage of him when he knew he was at his weakest and made him think that he *cared*. Sebastian wonders if this is why the tightness in his chest is so much worse than usual. It's more than a physical reaction to the fear his father induces, of the pain which is inevitable. His father has never *cared* about him and therefore Sebastian has never felt anything other than the need for self-preservation. He can't name the feelings which gnaw at his chest now. He knows that's what they must be, a psychosomatic reaction to the betrayal, but it *hurts*. It hurts like Ren has reached inside him and plucked his heart out of his body, left a cavernous rift where it should be. Cold and empty.

"Sebastian."

He can hear Ren's voice, close, pleading, a warm hand grasping his upper arm. He shoves the feeling away, loathing the way that his skin burns icy cold at the once soothing touch.

"Get away from me!"

He doesn't think the words come out properly. His lips feel so heavy, and he can taste the salt of his own sweat. It's better than the taste which proceeds, acidic bile as the nausea gets the better of him and he heaves violently. His body's instinctive tactic to cast out whatever is inside him that's making him feel this way.

He's barely able to hold on to consciousness, the room fading in and out of blackness as time seems to slow to a standstill. Sebastian can't think of anything but *Ren*. His kind eyes, the way he combs his fingers through Sebastian's hair; the way his kisses feel, slow and tender and like they *mean* something; dark hair falling in his face as he runs the tip of his tongue up the inside of Sebastian's thigh; his patience, his attentiveness. All of it, *all of it*, all of it, Sebastian *believed* all of it.

The next thing he feels is the freezing spray of water over the top of his head. It shocks his body back into awareness, his eyes blinking back the assault of the shower to see the inside of the bathroom. This time he hasn't been stripped carefully and laid down gently. There's no one watching him attentively from the other side of the bathroom, no one who cares if he's alright.

Ivan stands there instead, studying Sebastian with unfeeling eyes. He perks up a little when Sebastian blinks up at him.

"Good—I thought you were going to end up catatonic and then all of this would have been for nothing," he says. He flips the light switch on in the bathroom, the sudden intense brightness of the overhead lights making Sebastian's head throb with pain. "I've suggested Ren take a leave of absence. He needs to reassess his priorities. Hopefully it won't be too long before he can return to his duties."

Ivan leans down, in closer to the shower where Sebastian is sprawled, blood in the water to Ivan's sharklike gleam. He smiles, and it's cold and grey and so very familiar.

"But you understand now, don't you, sir? You understand what's at stake here?"

Sebastian nods.

Ivan smiles wider.

"Lovely. The president will be away for the remainder of this week and next, so you have some time to prepare for his return and the discussion that will follow. I'm flying out to meet him again on the next red-eye, so stay out of trouble until then, won't you?"

With that, Ivan sweeps from the room, the soft click of Sebastian's bedroom door behind him indicating he's alone.

Sebastian's clothes are glued to his skin, soaked in the freezing water. The way his teeth chatter in protest and the ripple of chill across his body is less painful however than the thoughts of Ren every time he shuts his eyes.

Sebastian thinks, if he were still able to cry, now would be a good time to do so. It might be cathartic. Help expel some of the torrent of emotions he can't quite name.

The tears don't come. He thinks that's one thing about him that his father could be proud of.

Sixteen

Sebastian spends the next four days in bed with the curtains drawn, smoking cigarettes and drinking whiskey until he is able to slip into dreamless bouts of sleep. On day five, a maid appears without the fresh bottle he'd requested, in its place, a cellular phone. Ivan is on the other end, telling him in no uncertain terms that he is to return to classes as usual. Sebastian's hissy fit has been poorly timed with the release of those pictures in the newspaper. Ivan is worried people might be more inclined to believe the gossip is accurate if Sebastian appears to be in hiding.

He makes his argument to leave the apartment a convincing one, when he vaguely threatens to divulge more intimate details of Sebastian and Ren's relationship to the president.

Just hearing Ren's name makes Sebastian want to curl up under the blankets in his room and drink himself to death. If he does that before his father can get back from his business trip, then it doesn't really matter what Ivan told him. Unfortunately, Sebastian knows he's too much of a coward to take his own life, so instead he asks the maid to bring him more cigarettes, a Bloody Mary, and a box of Advil, and peels himself out of his squalor.

He manages to shave (nicking his skin twice in doing so), wash, and get dressed despite his limbs feeling like lead weights and his head aching with each move he makes. He swallows what is probably too much Advil in conjunction with his Bloody Mary and has the maid call his car around.

He feels painfully alone in the elevator as he heads down into the lobby, the past few months spent in the constant company of Ren. He hates that. Even in his own home, he feels the sting of loss without the other man there. It doesn't matter how Ren betrayed him—it doesn't matter that he probably just used Sebastian for sex, a compliant bottom who just so perfectly embodied his *type*—he still aches with the loss of him. Would he accept Ren back, just to be free of the sheer *want* that accompanies his every action?

His pride says no. Sebastian wonders how long that would stand if he were faced with Ren right now.

He makes it to class and falls asleep in the back. When he wakes up, the hangover is finally starting to creep in. Sebastian doesn't think he's ever felt this bad in his life. Even lying in the ICU he'd felt better than this. At least the painkillers had actually been effective there.

Around lunchtime, he ventures to his favourite coffee shop on campus. The alleyway beside it is like a lingering spectre, an unsuspecting accomplice to Sebastian's humiliation. He sits at his favourite table, orders an espresso and places a cigarette on his lip.

Sebastian realises he no longer carries a lighter.

He slams his head down onto the table, sending his espresso cup clinking against the saucer. Some of the coffee spills, seeping into the white cuff of his shirt. The urge to flip the table is nearly overwhelming.

"*Fuck* me," he says out loud. It sounds pathetic, which is fitting, given how utterly pathetic he feels.

He keeps his forehead pressed to the filigree iron of the table, staring through the gaps in the metal at his shoes and the stony patio below.

All at once, a pink tongue is lapping at the hand resting on his knee, a pair of bright, excitable eyes looking up at him. The same gaudy purple collar hangs loosely from the dog's fine throat. Sebastian's chest throbs uncomfortably.

"Hi Donatello," he says weakly.

He lifts his fingers for the dog to lick excitedly, before reaching over to scratch behind his ears. His fur is soft and slippery, an almost perfect match with Poppy's. Sebastian feels the familiar tightness in his throat that once might have been accompanied by the relief of tears. Donatello whines in response to the tremble of Sebastian's fingers.

The arrival of the dog, however, indicates someone else will soon be along. Sebastian is proven correct when he sees a pair of chunky brown loafers appear on the opposite side of the table, their owner tapping her foot impatiently. He sighs as he lifts his head, squints as the pale winter sunlight frames the halo of Pip's curly head.

"Hello, Pip," he says bleakly.

The girl's face is twisted into a look of disgust, but it falls a little as she takes in the sight of his face. She raises a brow.

"Hello, Sebastian," she says. The disgust is gone now, made room for snide amusement. "You look like shit."

Sebastian offers her an equally acidic smile.

"Thank you," he says, still scratching distractedly at Donatello's head. "I feel like shit." A moment passes in which Donatello makes a happy sort of squeak, planting his rear on the ground and leaning further into Sebastian's hand. A thought suddenly occurs to him. "Do you have a light?"

He gestures to the cigarette which has fallen out of his mouth at some point during his moment of self-pity. Pip glances between his face and the cigarette, before shrugging.

"Maybe. If you watch Donatello while I get a coffee, I'll tell you," she says, already beginning to lean away from the table and towards the coffee shop. Sebastian nods weakly, deciding he really has nothing better to do, and he's enjoying the soothing effect the dog's warm head is having on his still aching chest. He thinks the relief from the nicotine will be worth it too, even if it means he has to talk to Pip some more. She's probably the last person in the world he wants to talk to right now.

No, the sad little voice in the back of his head corrects him. *That's Ren.*

Sebastian knows however, that if Ren were to stroll up to him right now, he'd probably dive into his arms and talk non-stop. How low can he possibly stoop? Sebastian wonders. Desperate for the reassurance of the very person who'd caused this pain in the first place. What the fuck is the *matter* with him?

Pip returns a moment later with a takeout cup and plonks herself down in the seat beside Sebastian. She lifts his cigarette case from where it's lying abandoned on the table, helps herself to one and produces a disposable lighter from her pocket. She throws both the case and the lighter down on the table as she takes a long drag, releasing a plume of green-grey smoke into the air around them.

"So, where's *your* guard dog? He was pretty easy on the eyes," she remarks, as Sebastian lights his own cigarette. His fingers stutter over the crappy release of the disposable lighter, irritating him every second he's not breathing in tar. Finally, he takes a draw on his own cigarette, finally able to enjoy a sip of his espresso. It's nearly cold. He leans his forehead on the heel of his palm, watching Donatello lie down comfortably at his feet.

"He's on sabbatical," Sebastian says tonelessly. Then, "Don't you read the tabloids?"

Pip shakes her head, flicking ash off her cigarette over her shoulder.

"Nah," she sniffs. "My family had a nasty spread in one of those gossip rags when I was a kid. I have no idea what about mind you, but it was pretty bad, apparently. That's why I picked journalism as my major—to introduce a new generation of integrity into the profession and all the rest of it. That tabloid stuff is all bullshit, right?"

"Right," Sebastian agrees, choosing to take another long drag on his cigarette instead of saying anything else. Pip watches him for a moment, before curiosity seems to get the better of her.

"The girls in my sorority were buzzing about something yesterday, now you mention it," she adds thoughtfully. "Something about a sordid love affair between some high-profile heir and his bodyguard. Was that about the two of you?"

Sebastian winces, finishes off the dregs of his coffee. This seems to be answer enough for Pip, whose eyebrows shoot up so far they almost reach her hairline.

"Damn, okay. Guess I maybe struck a little close to home last time we saw each other, huh?" she pauses, before scrunching her face up again in a frown. "Not that you didn't deserve it, mind you."

Sebastian opens his mouth to level a sour retort at her, but nothing comes. He shakes his head, silently smokes his cigarette. Pip shrugs.

"So, what? You got outed?" she asks. Sebastian sighs, annoyed by her constant commentary.

"You have to be gay to get outed," he responds quickly. Pip stares at him like he's an idiot.

"So you're not gay?" she probes. Sebastian stubs his cigarette out aggressively, throwing the butt into the ashtray. His hangover is starting to creep back into his limbs with a vengeance. Donatello lifts his head at Sebastian's feet, nosing at his knee as he can sense the tension in his limbs. Sebastian strokes the dog's wet nose, lets the rhythm soothe him.

"I'm fucking exhausted is what I am," he snaps finally, retrieving another cigarette. He doubts very much chain smoking and drinking coffee is going to do much to actively help his hangover, but at the very least, he needs to keep it at bay. Being seen with Pip on campus like this is a good thing. Perhaps it will lessen the scrutiny levelled at him come the next big frat party.

Pip leans back in her chair, finishes her own cigarette.

"*Jesus*, whatever, man. Tell it to your therapist," she says coldly, reaching over to take a sip of her coffee.

Sebastian takes a drag on his cigarette, the gaping emptiness in his chest now accompanied by an annoying niggling feeling. It's like he can *hear* what Ren would say in this moment, somehow managing to reach out and gently scold him from only his memories. Sebastian takes a deep breath, turns in his seat a little to look at Pip.

"Look," he says awkwardly. "I'm sorry for trying to have sex with you at that party and for forgetting your name. That must have made you feel… bad," he finishes brokenly, hoping that his extremely lacking empathetic ability doesn't come across too callous. Not that he particularly cares if Pip sees him as callous overall; but it wouldn't do for an apology to be viewed as such. Sebastian's fairly sure that's what Ren would say, if he were here.

He wishes he gave less of a fuck about what Ren would say. He *betrayed* him, for fuck's sake.

"It's whatever," Pip says finally, shrugging the matter off. "I kind of got that you weren't into it when there was no kissing and minimal touching above the waist," she glances at him pointedly over her coffee, but then grins. "Honestly, I just really wanted to get laid. But then that fucking *smug* look on your face when you couldn't remember my name just pissed me off so much." She shakes her head, gazing out at the campus lawn in front of them. "Frat-boys are all the same. Egotistical pieces of shit."

Sebastian is surprised to find himself smiling at that, the blunt and aggressive way she puts it sounding out of place amongst her curly red hair and sweet round face.

"You're funny," he says, killing his second cigarette of the sitting. Pip shoots him a dirty look.

"If you'd spent any of that party actually listening to what I was saying, you'd know that already," she tells him haughtily, but there's a reluctant smile in her voice. They're interrupted by a sudden obnoxious ringing noise. Pip taps around her coat pockets for a second before producing a cellular phone, flicking the aerial up on it as she indicates to Sebastian she has to take a call.

"Hello?... yeah, we're at the coffee place on the campus lawn. You can come pick him up now if you want, I can hang out here a little longer. Mmhm...Okay. See you in five."

Pip hangs up the phone, stowing it away in her pocket.

"Sorry Sebastian, but your favourite doggie pal has to go home. My sister is coming to pick him up."

Sebastian feels a sudden panic grip him at the thought of both Pip and Donatello leaving at once. He flounders a little—he knows he has to stay out of the house, or else his maids will no doubt report him back to Ivan.

"Are you busy this afternoon?" he finds himself asking. Pip gives him a curious glance, like she finds it both un-believable and impossibly amusing that he's trying to ask her to spend time with him. Sebastian falters, wondering if Ren has permanently destroyed his ability to interact with other humans. "I could really use some more of your caustic honesty."

Pip laughs brightly at that, before sobering and looking at him with wide eyes.

"Oh, you're being serious," she says, before her mouth twists into a frown. "I'm not trying to be mean or anything, but I feel like we wouldn't have much to talk about."

Sebastian wilts a little, but supposes he can't rightly blame her. The sting of rejection doesn't even really linger, lost to the gaping pit of self-pity, which has already worn a hole through his core. They sit there in silence for another minute, Pip seemingly waiting for some kind of response, Sebastian trying to decide how to convince her without coming across as desperate. As he opens his mouth, Pip seems to let out a simultaneous sigh of relief.

"Oh look, it's my sister. I guess I'll just head home with her. Thanks for the cigarette, Sebastian. You should go home and get some sleep or something."

Pip moves to push her chair back and stand from the table, as Donatello perks up at once and dashes from his spot below the table towards a woman making her way towards them. She stops dead in her tracks when she's ten paces from the table, catching the end of Donatello's leash and staring at the pair of them like she's seen a ghost.

As Sebastian meets her eyes, he's certain he's seeing one. The last time he'd laid eyes on her, he'd been a child, standing at her side in the long field they rented for training exercises, watching Poppy and Nuca sprint obediently back to his side.

"Sebastian Clarence?" Rosie asks breathlessly. "What are you doing with my sister?"

Pip looks between her sister and Sebastian in confusion, before sitting slowly back down in her chair. Rosie walks the ten or so paces so she's standing at the table, Donatello gazing obediently up at her with his deep dark eyes.

"Wait," Pip says, her head swivelling between the pair of them. "How do you know each other?"

Rosie sinks into the seat opposite the pair of them, taking a deep breath as she goes. She looks older than she does in Sebastian's memories, but he supposes it's been over ten years since they last saw each other. Her hair is the same chestnut frizz, her face the same friendly, heart shape it had always been. She has a few fine lines worn into her smiling eyes, but the same spatter of orange freckles across her turned up little nose. Now that he sees them side by side, he can see the resemblance between Rosie and Pip. There must be twelve or so years separating them in age, but still, they have the same sharpness about them. In Rosie's case, Sebastian had always attributed that to her fine sense when it came to the dogs. In Pip's he attributes it to her brusque way of phrasing things.

"I used to work for Sebastian's family," Rosie explains. Sebastian recalls the way her employment with the family had been severed. A story in the tabloids about an affair with his father. His mother had cried and cried when she found out, which Sebastian had always thought bizarre. He didn't think his mother liked his father that much.

"She trained my dogs," Sebastian adds unhelpfully. Suddenly, Rosie is standing again, reaching over the table to where Sebastian is sitting and pulling him into a tight hug. She had hugged him a lot when he was a child; anytime he successfully got the dogs to heel; anytime he taught them a new trick; at the end of long walks when they'd returned to his apartment, and she'd dropped him off with Ivan.

She hugs differently than Ren, but Sebastian can't help but lean into it. She smells different than she did back then too, more grown up than when she'd been fresh out of university and working for his family. Still, it's warm and it's worryingly comforting, so much so that he slumps a little into her touch and almost forgets to lift his hands and pat her awkwardly on the back.

Rosie pulls away and gives him a bright grin.

"You're all grown up," she says fondly, settling back into her seat. "I can't believe you're tiny Sebastian all grown up. And you're friends with my little sister? What a small world!"

"I think 'friends' is probably pushing it," Pip says tightly from her seat, but Rosie ignores her in favour of calling a waitress over and ordering a coffee. Obviously irritated, Pip grabs Sebastian's cigarette case from the table and procures another for herself, lighting it up and taking a deep breath. Rosie frowns.

"That's a disgusting habit, Philippa," she says, wrinkling her nose. Pip scrunches up her own nose in a mirror of her sister, smiling around her cigarette.

"Nobody asked you, Rosalind," she fires back sweetly, blowing smoke in her sister's face. Sebastian looks dumbly between the pair of them, trying to find something else to say. Just as he had been finding his feet in his new-found truce with Pip, the afternoon has been upended once more.

Rosie makes an excited squeal all of a sudden, patting her thigh so Donatello jumps up and rests his front paws on her.

"Good boy, Donnie," she tells him, before grinning widely at Sebastian. "How exciting—so you've already met the runt of Poppy and Nuca's litter?"

Sebastian just blinks at her dumbly. When he doesn't say anything, Pip casts him a curious sideways glance, and Rosie's brows knit together in concern. Sebastian licks his lips, trying to spur his mouth on to move.

"The… what?" he asks, looking from Rosie to Donatello's happy face. His tongue is lolling out of his mouth at the side, just like Nuca's used to do. No matter how much the tilt of Donatello's head looks just like Nuca's, no matter how his shiny fur slides beneath Sebastian's fingers like Poppy's, he *knows* what happened to his beloved pets. He *knows* what Ivan did to them. They'd never been bred before their demise—there was no possibility Donatello was of any relation to them.

He shakes his head, forcing down the glimmer of hope now glowing deep in his chest.

"Poppy and Nuca," he says weakly. "Ivan had them killed, Rosie."

Rosie frowns at him deeply, slowly beginning to shake her head from side to side.

"No," she says. "No, Ivan gave them to me. He said you were..." she pauses, looking a bit paler as she continues, "he said you were too sick to look after them. That you'd been in the hospital for a while and probably wouldn't be able to take care of them when you got out. So he gave them to me. And I'll admit I was a little too scared of him to refuse."

Sebastian doesn't know how to react. On one hand, his heart feels like it's beating again for the first time in five days—dragged up from the pit of his stomach and re-energised by the knowledge that his beloved dogs hadn't met the grim fate he'd always imagined for them. On the other, it only serves to further highlight Ivan's underhanded dealings throughout the entirety of his life. What else has he had a hand in that Sebastian doesn't know about? How long has he been working like this to gather material with which to control or blackmail Sebastian? And why?

Overwhelmed with a feeling of warmth, so welcome amidst the days spent wallowing in bleak emptiness, Sebastian clenches his hand tightly into a fist.

"Where are they now?" he asks, his voice sounding choked. Rosie's face relaxes into a sorrowful smile.

"They passed away naturally about six years ago," she tells him. "They were good dogs, and they missed you the whole rest of their lives."

The words hang in the air between them for a moment, heavier than Sebastian can bear. He takes an uneasy breath, teeth wearing tightly into his bottom lip. Rosie perks up a little, reaches across the table to pet the back of his hand.

"But like I said, I was able to breed them. Donnie was the runt of that litter. I sold his brother and two sisters, but couldn't bear to part with him," Rosie explains, giving Donatello a comfortable scratch behind his ears in recognition. He lets out a grunt before dropping off her thigh and curling up at her feet happily.

Sebastian almost feels light-headed with the news. A thought occurs to him then, and he says it in place of finding anything else meaningful to add to the conversation.

"Pip said you named them after the Teenage Mutant Ninja Turtles," he says. "Even the girls?"

Pip snorts.

"I told you she was a nerd," she tells him, blowing smoke at her sister again. Rosie throws her an annoyed glance, but laughs at Sebastian.

"Yeah, the girls were Raphie and Leo," she explains. "But all show dogs have weird names, so I swear it's not that bad!"

The waitress brings her coffee then, which Rosie thanks her for as she adds cream and sugar. She makes light conversation with Sebastian; how long has he been going to school here? How is he finding it? How did he meet Pip? (this question, Pip has no problem answering in graphic detail, much to Rosie's disgust—she graciously leaves out the part where Sebastian tried to pretend he remembered her name after all a few weeks later). Eventually, Rosie folds her hands together on the table and gives Sebastian a soft but intense look.

"It was awful what happened to Lydia," she says quietly. Sebastian nods, thinking back to Ren apologising for his mother's death in the hallway of his apartment, moments before disaster. It makes his heart sink a little again. Pip listens intently as her sister continues. "Your mother was always nice to me."

"Was she?" Sebastian asks, genuine surprise in his tone. "She was always drunk when I saw her."

Rosie winces a bit but nods in agreement.

"I think she was always drunk when I saw her too, but she was always nice. I tried to convince her to try a different clinic the last time she went, because clearly the one she'd been going to wasn't working. She tried to warn me about your dad. She tried to warn me about Ivan too, for that matter," Rosie adds, her expression darkening. Sebastian perks up at this. He frowns.

"That's weird," he says. "She was always singing Ivan's praises to me."

Rosie shrugs, suddenly looking uncomfortable.

"He was very intense. Lydia always said he knew more than it seemed. Maybe she wanted you to stay on his good side," Rosie suggests, looking a lot like she wished she hadn't brought the conversation around to this place. She lets out a long sigh. "To this day, I'm convinced he's the one who leaked that story to the press."

Sebastian feels his blood run cold.

"... My father told me you went to the press. To try and expose him. And that it backfired," Sebastian tells her blankly, watching as Rosie shrinks back in her seat. She's blatantly uncomfortable now, causing Pip to lean forwards in her seat, eyebrows pitching together in concern.

"Leaked what story to the press? What happened?" she asks.

Rosie ignores her, just stares steadily back at Sebastian and shakes her head.

"I just wanted to quit when it happened. Move on with my life. The next thing I knew, I was front page news. Painted as some kind of nymphomaniac, even though I—" she cuts herself off, shakes the thoughts away. "I haven't been able to get work in the state since it all happened."

Sebastian lets Rosie's revelation sink in. He knows his father attempted to assault her in their home; he'd been present in the room when it happened, just back from a walk with his dogs and their trainer. The tabloids had spun it out into an affair, an attempt by Rosie to move in on his addict mother's home and take her place. His father had said she'd gone in the first instance to try to expose him as a predator, that it had backfired because *women are idiots who don't know what it is they want.*

So if Rosie had simply wanted to quit and move on with her life, why would Ivan have a need to leak it to the papers? Why spin it in such a way her career and her livelihood would be destroyed along with it?

Sebastian considers what Rosie had said about his mother. That she had tried to warn Rosie about Ivan, despite the fact in the brief moments of lucidity she'd had with Sebastian, she'd emphasised the need to *rely* on Ivan—to stay on his good side, to trust him. Did she suspect Ivan was meddling beyond his position? Had she been trying to protect Sebastian amongst it all? Then there was the question of why Ivan would go out of his way to give Rosie the dogs instead of just disposing of them, as Sebastian had expected him to do? It doesn't make sense that he would give himself extra work like that; unless one day he hoped to use that fact to win favour with Sebastian...

"Look at the time," Rosie interrupts his quickly derailing train of thought with a glance at her watch. Her expression is a little strained. "I need to get Donnie home. It was lovely seeing you again." She offers him a warm smile, stands and calls Donatello up along with her. She pauses for a moment, her eyes glossy as she chews on the inside of her cheek, contemplating Sebastian.

"I'm sorry I left you there, Sebastian," she says finally. "I knew what those people were capable of. I saw… I always saw the bruises you had. And when you would turn up to training with your little wrist in a sling, I knew you didn't fall off your bike. But I was afraid. I was young and stupid and afraid, and I left you with them. I took Poppy and Nuca because I was guilty about that. I wanted to make sure they were happy, because I knew you'd want them to be. I hope—" her voice catches, as a tear escapes and she brushes it away. She takes a deep breath. "I hope someday you can forgive me."

Rosie glances quickly at Pip, who is staring, open-mouthed, at her sister.

"I'll call you later, Philippa, okay? I just need to be alone right now."

With that, Rosie turns, leading Donatello back down the promenade beyond the campus lawn. She wipes another tear away as she goes. Donatello nuzzles the side of her leg.

Pip watches her alongside Sebastian, before finally sighing deeply and giving him a bizarre look. She's acting like he might spontaneously combust at any moment. Sebastian supposes the revelations she's faced this afternoon are on a level with that.

"Well, Sebastian," she says, calling over the waitress to get their bill. "You're in luck. It seems like you and I have a lot to talk about in the end."

Seventeen

The unexpected encounter with Rosie has done little to stop the constant pain in Sebastian's head.

Rosie had not gone to the press claiming his father assaulted her as he had led Sebastian to believe. That implied that his *father* thought that to be the truth too, which meant he clearly isn't as well informed by Ivan as Sebastian had once feared.

That, coupled with Ivan's slick involvement with the publishing of the photos of Sebastian and Ren, suggested he was the one pulling the strings in what did or didn't make it to the tabloids. He was careful to pick and choose how these stories were angled too. It was just enough to stir outrage in the president, most likely resulting in some kind of punishment for Sebastian, and serving to put Ren in his place.

But why bother with any of it? What benefit would befall Ivan, in the end of it all, with Sebastian sufficiently collared? What did Rosie or his mother have to do with it?

And then there were the dogs. He hadn't lied then, all those years ago when he'd told Sebastian they weren't dead. They'd been with Rosie, safe for the remainder of their lives.

Every time Sebastian thinks of one question, another crops up. And amongst it all, his brain always ends up cycling back to Ren. Rosie's revelations relating to Ivan only serve to further throw into question how much Ren knew while agreeing to his demands. He'd said he needed the money when Ivan approached him. He'd been cagey about it, of course, but he'd alluded to the fact his father had left behind debts to people who demanded to be paid. He'd seemed so earnest when he said he didn't know about the other pictures. In Ren's mind, with the frat party images safely in his possession, Sebastian was in no real danger.

Maybe it hadn't all been a lie.

How could someone touch him like that and it all be a lie?

Sebastian pinches himself tightly on the inside of his wrist, berating his unconscious mind for arriving back at that same foolish hope. Still, he's letting those thoughts guide him even now.

Pip pokes him as the cab slows down.

"Are you serious?" she asks, her face a mask of disapproval. "A gay club at five o'clock on a Thursday?"

Sebastian hands the driver his fare, shoots her a blank stare.

"I told you. Ren used to work here, and his friends still do. I need to talk to them," Sebastian insists, opening the door and stepping out into the barren street. It's completely different to how it had been that Halloween night. The neon lights still flicker, but they've lost their radiance without the varying glitter studded costumes reflecting across the dull walls. Nonetheless, the sign above the basement door indicates *Rain* is open.

There's no one on the door, as early as it is, so Sebastian ducks down the steps and heads for the entrance. Pip grumbles as she follows.

"I thought you were going to take me somewhere fancy," she insists. "Are straight women even allowed in gay bars?" She raises a coy brow in Sebastian's direction. "Are *you*? I thought you weren't gay."

"Are you always this insufferable or am I just special?" Sebastian asks sweetly, turning to angle a warning glance in Pip's direction. She returns his smile just as delicately, the dimple on the side of her face puckering.

"You know a good way to get me to shut up? Buy me a drink," she orders, marching past him and straight up to the bar. She leaps up onto a stool (Sebastian notices for the first time just how short she really is), swinging her legs expectantly. As Sebastian joins her at the edge of the bar, Ricky emerges from a door behind a metal fringe.

He's traded the Baby Spice getup for a white vest and a pair of denim shorts which don't leave much to the imagination. His curly hair is held back with a colourful bandanna, his eyes rimmed with smoky kohl. He's wearing a pair of earrings with plastic green gemstones dangling from his lobes. He recognises Sebastian right away.

"You're Birdie's friend," he says, toying with a metal ring which is punctured through his full bottom lip. Without the pound of the music, Sebastian can hear the way his words curl in an accent he can't place. "Sebastian, right?"

Upon hearing Ren's nickname, Sebastian's stomach does an odd sort of flip. He nods, easing himself onto the barstool next to Pip.

"Yes. Hello. Ricky, wasn't it?" Sebastian reaches into his wallet, produces a wad of cash, and slides it across the counter. "Make her something to keep her quiet, will you? You can keep the change."

Ricky's eyes nearly bug out of his head as he takes in the sight of the cash, Pip making a soft scoff from Sebastian's elbow.

"Do you always carry that much cash around? Your bodyguard's on sabbatical, remember? And I'm not going to help if you get jumped," she swivels in her seat a bit, before producing a pack of cigarettes from her pocket. Sebastian wonders where it had been earlier when she was smoking all of his. She pops one in her mouth before glancing at Ricky. "Can I smoke in here?"

Ricky gives her an amused look, his mouth twitching at the edges.

"You can do whatever you want, honey, so long as you're out of here by nine. If the boss comes in and sees a lady sitting at my bar, he'll flip," Ricky tells her, placing a hand on his hip. He's chewing gum like he'd been doing on Halloween too. He blows a big pink bubble as Pip nudges

Sebastian. It makes a satisfying pop before he drags it back into his mouth.

"See? I told you straight girls aren't supposed to be in gay bars," Pip mutters. Ricky reaches down onto the bar to tap his fingers on the cash Sebastian left there.

"And as for this, mister bigshot," Ricky says smoothly, "I'm not usually one to turn down a generous tip, but something tells me you're expecting a little more than just drinks for that kind of cash. What are you after?"

Sebastian frowns, feeling as if Ricky's caught him under a microscope and is poking at his limbs to see which one will fall off first. He sighs.

"I need to talk to you about Ren."

The name sounds alien now, nearly a whole week gone by since he'd last said it. Still, it makes him ache with longing. Sebastian has to grit his teeth at the end of the sentence just to stop himself from wincing.

Ricky's shoulders fall as he lets out a mighty sigh.

"Usually I wouldn't agree to talking about any employees, former or otherwise," Ricky tells him. He softens a little, leans his hip against the bar. Sebastian can see some kind of tattoo peeking out, turned blue against Ricky's warm brown skin. "But Birdie was here the other day and told me what happened. So I guess if it means you'll consider talking to him again…?"

Sebastian stares at Ricky for what he knows is a moment too long, but he can't seem to respond. He wants to say yes. *Fuck*, he wants to see Ren right now, and skip the talking—go straight to holding him again and kissing him and touching him.

But the hurt still snags on that want. Every time Sebastian yearns for Ren, he thinks of a time they'd been together and wonders how much of it was real. How much was to subdue him into being an obedient pawn in Ivan's game?

"I just… I need to understand him better," Sebastian says finally. Ricky seems satisfied with that response in any case, nodding as he picks up a cocktail shaker and starts loading it with ice.

"I hear ya. If it helps, I chewed him the fuck out for being an idiot and getting so involved with you," Ricky sighs as he pulls a martini glass from above his head, sets it on the bar. "But that's Birdie. He's a fuckin' sap, let me tell you, real hopeless romantic. I love the guy, but he has this real bad habit of getting too involved." Ricky glances at Pip and gives her a wide smile. "You like sweet or sour, honey?"

Pip pouts for a moment as she thinks.

"Sour! Like a Lemon Drop," she says, before taking a quick drag on her cigarette. "What do you mean, hopeless romantic? He seemed pretty serious any time I saw them together."

Sebastian glances at her briefly, mouth set in a thin line. Pip rolls her eyes.

"Here, take a puff," she offers the cigarette to Sebastian. "You're all white knuckled and tense. Chill out."

Briefly considering that perhaps he fell asleep in the car on the way back from the cabin and is still somehow embroiled in a product of his own sick imagination, Sebastian does as she instructs. The nicotine does help to calm him down a bit. It places him firmly in *Rain*, Pip at his side, Ricky making some kind of heinous cocktail with the cheapest liquor he can find.

"Look, he's a professional through and through, don't get me wrong," Ricky concedes. "Most of the time he's as straight as they come," he throws Sebastian a wink. "Well. In all aspects relating to his work. Right, Sebastian?"

Sebastian feels his cheeks immediately roar red and resists the urge to slide off the stool and hide below the bar. Pip lets out a scandalised gasp.

"Oh my god, you two were *totally* fucking!" she declares, eyes wide as she points an accusatory finger at Sebastian. He grits his teeth and grabs her hand, shoving the offensive digit away.

"Can we stay on topic, please?" he pleads, ignoring Pip's cackle of laughter as she throws her elbow up on the bar to watch with rapt fascination as Sebastian tries to control his embarrassment.

"Sure. What was I saying? Oh yeah, Ren's a hopeless romantic. He takes his work seriously, but once he takes a shine to you, there's no going back. You know what I mean, right?" Ricky lifts the cocktail shaker and begins vigorously mixing the cocktail as Sebastian considers his words.

That night they'd left *Rain* and gone to Ren's apartment—he'd been so patient with Sebastian. He'd taken his time to prepare him, showered him with praise and encouragement. Even after that night, as their relationship progressed, Ren had taken his time over every kiss he'd given Sebastian. Each one was carefully thought out, composed, but laced with an intensity that made Sebastian feel like Ren needed each kiss to carry on breathing.

Sebastian has never in his life encountered someone described as a 'hopeless romantic,' but finds the term inexplicably fits Ren the more he considers it.

Sebastian nods.

"Yeah," he agrees weakly. "I think I know what you mean."

Ricky finishes pouring Pip's cocktail and slides it over to her. She makes an excited noise and thanks him before slurping delicately from the end of her straw. Ricky nods at Sebastian.

"You want something?"

He shakes his head.

"I'm trying to ditch a five-day hangover," he groans, the numbing headache that's been following him around all day throbbing for added effect. Ricky nods knowingly, reaching under the bar for a plastic bottle full of brilliant blue. Probably some kind of sports drink.

"I got something for that too, hang on."

As Ricky makes Sebastian what looks to be a cocktail of orange juice, Gatorade and Alka-Seltzer, Sebastian squeezes his fist tightly.

"So," he continues. "How long have you known Ren?"

Ricky slides Sebastian his drink and throws a rag over his shoulder.

"I've known Birdie since we were kids. We started working here around the same time... I think he was sixteen?

The boss has a soft spot for him," Ricky explains, yanking over a cardboard box full of limes and proceeding to start chopping.

"Sixteen?" Pip asks, teeth clenching the end of her straw. "Is that even legal?"

Ricky shrugs.

"A lot of us have been here since we were a little on the young side. Ren's mama kicked him out… mine refused to stop calling me Ricarda…"

"Ren was kicked out?" Sebastian asks, clenching his glass. The ice sinks a little further into his drink, snapping as it's submerged in liquid. Ricky nods, instantly becoming more resigned.

"That's not really my story to tell…" he begins slowly, staring at the tip of his knife, poised above a lime. He sighs. "But… it was 1986. She found out he was gay and… AIDs was starting to freak everybody out. He's been trying to get back in her good books ever since. She's the only family he has."

Sebastian recalls the way Ren had clammed up when discussing his family. He'd seemed strangely distant at that moment.

"He said his dad ran up debts and left before he was born," Sebastian says slowly. "And that his mother had to move away from the city." Sebastian forces himself to revisit those moments in his bedroom, Ivan watching from the window, Ren desperately trying to make a case for why he'd posed those frat party pictures in the first place. "He said he really needed the money. Do you think he's trying to pay off his father's debts? So his mother can come back?"

"Maybe then he thinks she'll talk to him again," Pip offers quietly, gazing into her drink with an air of defeat. "Man, that is so horrible. Poor Ren."

Ricky watches her for a moment, chewing on his lip ring in thought. His mouth stretches into a non-committal frown.

"Maybe. He was trying to get together a bunch of cash, though, I know that much. He wanted a change of pace from here too, after what happened during the summer."

Sebastian raises a brow.

"What happened during the summer?"

Ricky throws the limes he's chopped into a bucket, mouth pressed into a thin line.

"There was an incident a few months back," Ricky says tightly, slicing more harshly into the lemons he's now procured. "A guy pulled a gun in here and managed to get a round off—he was yelling all kinds of shit, real nasty stuff. He didn't manage to hit anyone thankfully. Second bullet jammed and then Birdie came outta no where and knocked the fucker on his ass. All it took was that one second of distraction. Wrestled the gun off him while Darius beat him half to death." Ricky shivers a little, eyes wavering over to the dancefloor as he speaks, like he can see the events recurring before his eyes. He nods at Sebastian then, pointing his knife lazily in his direction. "That was around the time that creepy old guy started trying to recruit him to work for you."

"Creepy old guy?" Sebastian asks. His stomach is already beginning to sink once again, an unprovoked pang of pain surging through his head from behind his right eye. Ricky nods.

"Yeah. He'd been hanging around for a month or so before the gun thing happened—he would come in and buy, like, a magnum of champagne and then just sit at the bar and not drink it. Creepy bastard, always asking questions, but he brought in a lot of cash on slower nights, so the owner said we weren't allowed to kick him out. Started pursuing Ren for the job babysitting you after he saw him in action."

"What did the guy look like?" Pip blurts out when Sebastian doesn't say anything. His jaw feels like it's been wired shut. Ricky makes a face, his nose wrinkling in distaste.

"Like I said, creepy. Not gay either. Had these pale bluish eyes, real shifty like."

"Like a shark?" Sebastian says quietly. Ricky's mouth falls open and he nods enthusiastically.

"Oh my god, now you mention it, yeah! And always smiling... no, *leering*. Half expected his fucking teeth to be pointed."

"Ew," Pip says loudly, before poking Sebastian in his bicep. "Well? You know him?"

Sebastian takes a deep gulp on his hangover cure, the sting of citrus making his tongue pucker in protest. He nods.

"Yeah," he says grimly, "I know him."

*

Ricky has prep work to finish, so Sebastian and Pip move to a booth in the back. Pip drinks espresso martinis while Sebastian chain-smokes and divulges everything he knows.

"Okay, so let me get this straight," Pip says, cigarette poised between her fingers as she leans across the booth. She has bright pink splotches on her cheeks, but despite the copious amount of alcohol she's put away this afternoon, she's faring reasonably well. Sebastian decides that perhaps he was right to be wary of her.

"My sister Rosalind comes to train your dogs when you're ten," she says. "Your mother, Lydia, is still alive. Lydia and Rosie talk, and Lydia warns Rosie that this Ivan guy, who's worked security for the family since before you were born, is bad news. Your mother makes sure to tell *you*, however, that you should rely on him more. Your dad tries to assault my sister," Pip draws in a sharp breath as she says it, her face going a bit pinker with outrage, "and Rosie tries to quit. Before she can, the story is leaked to the tabloids, and your father is under the impression that *she* leaked it, but that's not true. We think *Ivan* leaked it. All good so far?"

"Yes," Sebastian agrees, drumming his fingers along the table to try to counteract the amount of nicotine racing through his veins.

"Lydia kills herself while you're at boarding school," Pip presses on. Sebastian is surprised at the almost callous way the girl can list off the many horrendous happenings in his past without wincing as so many often do. "You start experimenting with guys. Ivan finds out, but tells your father you just kissed the other boy, not that you sucked him off."

"Your way with words is simply exquisite, Pip," Sebastian says dryly, as Pip flails her hands at him, insisting he be quiet.

"Just summarising the events. Okay, so your dad beats the shit out of you," Pip does hesitate a little at, but doesn't let it derail her any further. "And you're in the hospital for a while. Instead of disposing of your dogs, Ivan gives them to my sister, even though he clearly hates her for some reason. Some time passes, and Ivan starts looking to acquire a new bodyguard for you."

"He comes to this place, presumably because he knows you're into guys and he wants to blackmail you with that. He sees Ren disarm a gunman, thinks he'd be a good fit. Finds out through creeping around the bar and asking questions that Ren's trying to clear his dad's debts to try and repair his relationship with his mother. Offers him a fuck load of cash to come work for you, and specifically to pose for pictures taken at a frat party, which he then gives to Ren."

The emptiness in Sebastian's chest pangs uncomfortably at the reminder. He frowns.

"Ren thinks that means you'll be safe, it's just insurance to keep you in line and stop you sowing your wild oats too hard," Pip continues, wiggling her eyebrows suggestively. "But in actuality, Ivan has someone else following the two of you, taking more pictures. He makes sure these aren't explicit, no kissing or whatever, but suspect enough they could raise questions. He finds out via this info that you guys have started hooking up. He decides enough is enough and publishes the pictures. Exposes Ren for working with him, puts him on sabbatical for insubordination, breaks your heart into little tiny pieces."

"Don't be so dramatic," Sebastian snaps defensively, rubbing at his right eye to try and diffuse some of the pain which has been twanging there non-stop. All of this nonsense seems to be triggering the discomfort caused by his old injury more than usual. He wants nothing more than to crawl into his bed and fall asleep for the next month, but he knows Ivan has eyes everywhere at the apartment. If he wants to talk to Pip about this, *Rain* is probably the safest place to do so.

"I'm not being dramatic," Pip retorts. "Did you look in a mirror before you left the house today? When I came up to you at the coffee place earlier you looked like your entire family had died."

Sebastian snorts with laughter.

"I would probably look much happier if that was the case," he says blithely. Pip rolls her eyes.

"Oh haha, sorry, I forgot how deep your daddy issues run," she responds, before seemingly catching herself and fiddling with her straw. She watches Sebastian for a moment, chewing on her lip carefully. "That's not fair. Sorry. I shouldn't be... Rosie seemed really upset when she was explaining what happened to you when you were a kid.

And I guess if you were in the ICU for so long, your dad must have been pretty rough with you, huh?"

Sebastian thinks about it for a moment, finding he can't quite answer.

Was his father rough with him? That was just how he was, how he'd always acted. It was less the physical pain that Sebastian had learned to endure which had caused him to panic growing up. He knew how to compartmentalise it as it was happening. He was able to bear it, knew how to react to ensure that it ended as quickly as possible.

It was more the threat of what *could* happen which had caused him concern. It meant he was rarely able to actually commit to the moment if something good was happening to him. It meant that even if he did succumb to his desires, and give a guy head in the bathroom at a nightclub, he was only ever really half in the moment. The other half of his brain was buzzing with the possible outcomes if he were to be found out.

Except with Ren. When he was with Ren, kissing Ren — he wasn't able to think of anything else at all.

Shoving that thought to one side, Sebastian supposes, by definition, all the broken bones must have been caused by an action that was fairly 'rough.' So, after what he senses to be too long a pause, he looks at Pip in the eye and nods.

"Yes. But you don't have to make it a big deal. I'd rather you didn't," he says honestly. Pip puffs up her cheeks and blows out a long breath, leaning back in her seat and stretching. She shakes her head, staring into the dregs of her last espresso martini.

"*Why* though?" she asks, and it's quiet, almost as if she doesn't want a response. She tugs her bottom lip back and forth between her teeth. "Like, why would any of this benefit Ivan? Why would he go to these lengths over all these years?"

Sebastian sets his elbows up on the table, steeples his fingers together. He surveys Pip through the middle of them, clenching his right eye shut.

"I don't know," he admits. "I mean, I was always threatening him that as soon as I became president I was going to fire him, but to be working like this since I was a child? It doesn't seem likely that's his only concern here."

Pip reaches across the table and settles her palms on the backs of Sebastian's hands, holding him in place. Her hands are smooth, her nails well-manicured and polished cherry blossom pink. She gives him as serious a glare as she can muster.

"You know you have to ask Ren about it, right?" she says. "He's the only one who's been behind the scenes in all this. Maybe Ivan's let something slip that makes all of it clearer."

Sebastian wriggles his elbows uncomfortably, but Pip doesn't relinquish her grip. His temper flares.

"I don't want to speak to Ren," he says sharply. Pip squeezes his hands with her fingers again, cutting him off before he's even finished speaking.

"Look, I know he shouldn't have agreed to pose for those pictures, that was fucked up. But think about it; that was way back when you first met. For all he knew, you were just some pompous little rich boy who tries to fuck girls when he can't even remember their names," she finishes with a knowing look. "Do you believe him? That he didn't know about the other pictures?"

Sebastian feels sick just thinking about it again, the seed of doubt planted in his mind, having rooted too deep to disregard.

"I don't *know*, Pip," he says, his voice clouded with exhaustion. Pip lets go of his hands.

"Well you never will if you don't *talk to him*," she says. "I'm going to go ask Ricky for his phone number."

Sebastian watches Pip jostle her way out of the booth.

"Why do you even care?" he asks suddenly, markedly aware that Pip has just spent the afternoon deducing the timeline to his family security guard's illicit goings on. It occurs to him that he's spent the entirety of their fledgling relationship underestimating her. First, assuming she was just another brainless sorority girl he could fuck to keep up appearances. Second, when he thought he could pull the wool over her eyes and make her feel bad by implying he'd known her name the entire time. Third, as she'd sat in front of him and successfully picked apart the vast web of lies and underhanded dealings that had gone on within his family to bring them to this moment in time.

Sebastian feels regret—alien and unnatural to him, but he's able to name the emotion with relative ease.

Pip grins, shrugging her shoulders.

"I feel like Nancy fucking Drew! This shit is a journalist's bread and butter!" she exclaims. She sobers, her sharp green eyes bright with intent. "And I wanna help you get even for Rosalind's sake. Plus, when I graduate and get a job at one of the big papers, being friends with you might actually prove to be useful!"

Sebastian watches Pip flounce off into the bar, and wonders if, had Rosie stuck around in his life, they'd have become friends sooner.

Eighteen

Despite the fact Ivan is still ostensibly abroad with the president, Sebastian knows he has eyes everywhere. The maids in his apartment can't be trusted, as evidenced by the abrupt telephone call chasing him from his hangover pit. Sebastian doesn't know who Ivan had employed to take those tabloid pictures, but they could still be tailing him. For that reason, he doesn't think it's safe to meet with Ren anywhere to talk, as Pip had suggested. When he lays this all out to her nearly a week on from their trip to *Rain*, her eyes narrow suspiciously, but she reluctantly agrees he's probably right.

They've taken to meeting up nearly every day now, sometimes at the campus coffee spot, sometimes for a walk with Donatello in the park. Rosie is away for work again, and Pip reveals (as if it's a surprise) that she hasn't much of an affinity for dogs in the first place, so she's more than happy to let Sebastian wrangle Donnie. It stirs something warm inside him, something soft which cushions the sharp pangs of loss that stab at his stomach when he thinks about Ren.

"So I'll meet up with him," Pip suggests, kicking at the last stray autumn leaves which haven't turned to mush in the November damp. "I got his number from Ricky. Why don't I arrange to talk with Ren in *Rain* or something, and I'll call you from my cell. That way, you can listen in on the conversation and decide once and for all if you really believe he's telling the truth, but whoever might still be tailing you thinks you're in your apartment. You don't have to talk, just listen, so the maids won't know who you're on the phone to."

She folds her arms, looking very pleased with herself. Sebastian frowns, shooting her a sideways glance.

"Why are you so sure he knows anything worth telling?" he asks tightly, pausing as Donatello sniffs at the base of a tree. Pip shrugs.

"I already called him and asked," she says.

"You already called him and asked," Sebastian repeats blankly, shoving a hand into his pocket as it reflexively curls into a fist. "Who do you think you are? Why are you trying to get involved in this mess any more than you have to?"

Pip nudges him playfully with her elbow as Donatello begins to walk on.

"Keep your underpants on, sweetheart," Pip says coolly. She's become increasingly familiar with him over the past week. This in itself is annoying, because she seems to have always been able to see through any mask Sebastian has been wearing. It's why she stopped him that first night they tried to fuck. It's why, despite how much it annoys him, he finds some comfort in her presence. She's almost like Ren. Except shorter and more inclined to steal his cigarettes and tell him he looks like he needs to shower. Pip continues: "I told you—this weird shark-man everyone seems so afraid of fucked with my big sister. You might be happy enough to live under his thumb forever, but Ren certainly isn't."

"Ren needs to get a grip," Sebastian replies sharply. "Ivan is his boss. Whether he likes him or not—"

"Sebastian," Pip cuts him off, impatiently rounding on him in the middle of the path. Her cheeks are pink with the cold, her bright eyes pinning Sebastian harshly in place. "I get it. You're upset. You're allowed to be upset. What Ren did to you was fucking slimy," she cuts Sebastian's attempt to speak off by raising her gloved hand in his face. "—and I don't just mean posing for the pictures and letting you think they were a potential liability when he had them the whole time. I mean the whole getting involved with you part."

Sebastian lets out a low breath.

"He told you about that?" he asks through his teeth. Pip nods.

"I asked him directly if you two had been involved and he said yes. He didn't go into all the nasty details because I do not need those mental images," Pip mimics gagging before straightening back up and offering Sebastian a sympathetic smile. "But he said things were pretty... he said yes, you were involved. So he has a lot of grovelling to do to make that up to you. But this problem is bigger than just that. Ivan screwed Ren too with those pictures—even if he wanted to leave and find other work, he's been implicated as some kind of gay-romancing-bodyguard. He's trapped now, just like you. And that's probably what Ivan wanted all along. *He's* the problem here. The two of you need to put your shit to one side for now and figure this out."

"You're not going to let this go, are you?" Sebastian asks quietly. Pip shakes her head, curls bouncing about her shoulders as she grins.

"Nope! So when works for you? If I set up a meeting with Ren, when can you listen in?"

Sebastian sighs, checks his watch for the date.

"My father and Ivan will be back from their trip the day after tomorrow. It has to be before then."

Pip lets out a whistle, which causes Donatello to jerk around to see what she wants.

"Tomorrow then?" she says, as she hunches over to ruffle Donatello's smooth ears atop his head. Sebastian nods, his stomach twisting uneasily at the prospect of being in contact with Ren for the first time in ten days.

"Tomorrow," he confirms.

*

It's not the first time in his life Sebastian has locked his bathroom door and curled up on the floor tiles. There's underfloor heating, but he keeps it turned off when he's not in the shower, preferring the cool press of marble on his skin. When he was younger, and his father's hands could still fit around his biceps and clench until they blossomed purple, he would lie down on the bathroom floor to leech some of the heat from the bruises. It would make him shiver sometimes, so violently his teeth would chatter, but it provided a welcome distraction from the pain. When he was a little older and the pain behind his eye would flare up in the aftermath of an altercation with the president, he would rest his forehead there too.

When his mother died, and he hadn't yet been prescribed enough tranquilisers to fell an elephant, he would lie down on the floor to chase away the nightmares. He'd started smoking cigarettes around that time too, just for something to do other than sleep. Lie on the cold floor, let the warmth seep from his body like his mother's interred in the family mausoleum. What was left of her, anyway. She'd been inside a closed casket, what remained of her face that they'd scraped from the pavement too damaged to look upon. He would have nightmares about her on the ledge of the roof, thinking how cold she must have been up there above the clouds. It hadn't necessarily made him upset to think of—just empty.

I miss feeling like that, Sebastian thinks, as he lies on the floor awaiting Pip's call. He doesn't feel empty anymore. He feels full of conflicting, rotted emotions, none of which he can pin down properly. They're so heavy they make his limbs feel glued to the tiles. He aches and yearns and foolishly desires for Ren to touch him again, to just be near him. This is accompanied by the constant weight of remembering all the things they'd done. That he let Ren touch him in the way he did, that he *enjoyed* it. That despite everything, he'd give anything to feel it again. Even though the entire time, Ren knew where those pictures were. He knew how the panic over them being sold off had eaten away at Sebastian's insides, and still he'd whispered sweet things in his ear. Kissed him tenderly, like no one else ever had.

Praised him, worshipped him, knelt before him, and lavished his body with affection. Now it's all tainted. Drenched in the knowledge that Ren had *lied*.

What's more shameful is how much Sebastian hopes amongst the lies, he's telling the truth. That he didn't know about the other pictures, that he wasn't working alongside Ivan this entire time to further ensnare Sebastian. He hopes Ren is telling the truth and that all of the embarrassing things Sebastian allowed himself to partake in weren't all for nothing.

He misses him.

Sebastian misses Ren more than he ever missed Poppy or Nuca, or Rosie, or his mother.

He hates it.

Sebastian's phone rings once, twice, battering the ceramic walls with its shrill buzz. He'd had to go and buy a new cellular phone yesterday afternoon, having smashed his last one to bits following his conversation with Ivan and attempting to have Ren fired. He answers just to make it stop, lifting the device to his ear and holding it close.

"Sebastian?"

It's Pip. He swallows tightly, trying to force himself to respond. Nothing comes.

"Sebastian? Are you there?" Pip sounds a little unnerved. Sebastian lets out a shaky breath, finds his voice cracking in protest.

"Yes. I'm here. I'm not talking to him," he says finally. He wants to talk to Ren. So badly he wants to hear him say his name, softly, whispered wet against his neck. He knows however, that as soon as he does, he'll lose any sense of control over the situation he has. He'll fold right away to whatever Ren says, believe him no matter what.

The bathroom tiles are cold below Sebastian, where his cheek presses against them. They help with the tempest still raging endlessly where a hole has been left in his chest. The feeling keeps him grounded as he refuses to let himself surrender to Ren's flimsy excuses.

Pip gives him a short sigh, but her voice sounds a little more distant and tinny when she speaks again.

"He's there. He's not talking to you. So you'd better get explaining," she says.

There's a moment in which Sebastian holds his breath, preparing himself for the inevitable waver in his determination when he hears Ren.

Another sigh, deeper, masculine, different from the ones Ren made when Sebastian had his mouth wrapped around him.

"I understand," Ren says.

Sebastian grips the phone tighter, listens as there's a creak from a barstool. Pip readjusting herself—he can almost imagine the exact scene playing out. Both sat in the quiet booth at the back of *Rain*, Pip leaning forwards in her seat like some kind of hungry reporter, Ren with those hollow, hollow eyes of his.

"So when we talked you said you had information for Sebastian that will prove you're not still working with Ivan," Pip says, the subtle click of Ren's Zippo in the background of her words indicating she's lit a cigarette.

"Do you remember the day you met Sebastian in the park with Donnie the first time?" Ren says. Pip makes a noise of affirmation, her lips otherwise occupied around her cigarette filter, Sebastian thinks.

Ren continues. His voice sounds just robotic enough through the thin static of the cellular phone that the familiar timbre doesn't catch too hard in the back of Sebastian's throat. He listens intently as Ren begins his explanation.

"I had already started to suspect something weird was going on with Ivan," he says. "He was offering me crazy money. The initial salary to come on board was decent, but the amount he offered me to pose for those pictures at the frat party was significant. Yet he kept assuring me the president wasn't aware he was having those pictures staged. They were purely for... our benefit, he said. To make sure Sebastian continues to walk the line the president expects."

Ren pauses to draw breath. Sebastian tries not to linger on the way his mouth curls around his name.

"But the more I thought about it, the more I realised that if the president didn't know about any of the pictures, then surely he wasn't aware of the cash on offer."

Pip snorts.

"I doubt Mr Clarence Senior has any idea how much cash he has on offer, Ren. Those types of people don't even think about what's going in and coming out. Why would it matter?"

Sebastian releases his grip on the phone a little, an almost overwhelming wave of gratitude washing over him. Pip had highlighted exactly what he had been thinking, her tone flippant and almost accusatory.

"I know that," Ren acknowledges quickly. "But still, I thought it was strange Ivan had that kind of input into how the president's money could be spent. So that day I left Sebastian in the park to go to the bank. I used my company card to ask for a statement."

A beat.

"Okay so...?" Pip drags the word out, indicating Ren to continue. Sebastian can almost see her waving her wrist distractedly, urging him to drop the mysterious act.

"So, it seemed reasonable enough at first—just the usual transactions I expected to see. Gas for the drivers, lunches and dinners, monthly outgoing for my salary and Ivan's. Then, I noticed the hush money payments."

Sebastian sits up straight then, concern flooding his veins with its familiar icy touch. It makes the bathroom floor suddenly too cold to bear.

"I knew that's what they were because Ivan had given me strict instructions when I took the job. If Sebastian hooked up with someone, I was to arrange a payment to them to ensure that they didn't share that information with anyone. An NDA of sorts. One night that happened and I saw the guy out. Made him an offer he couldn't refuse when I called him a cab. I took his info and passed it on to Ivan, just as he'd instructed me."

Sebastian recalls Jerome Godoy and his fiery red hair amongst the sea of faces at the Halloween party. He'd mentioned Ren had seen him out that night—that he seemed professional. Sebastian inches a little closer to the toilet, worried he might vomit at the sheer memory of Jerome throat-fucking him until his mouth was raw and his jaw locked. Ren continues.

"There it was on the statement—JG was listed as a payment reference, but the account information the money was going to wasn't what he'd given me. All of them, every single one had different initials, I guess relating to different people, but all the money was being funnelled into one account."

"The same account Ivan was getting paid into?" Pip says excitedly, rushing in to speak before Ren's even finished his sentence. Sebastian winces a little at her enthusiasm, leaning his head back so it rests on the wall of the bathroom.

"Obviously not," Ren says. "He's not that stupid. So, I asked the girl at the bank if she could trace the account number and see who it was originally registered to."

"And?" Pip prompts, her voice barely above a scandalised whisper.

"And she said that would take some time because it was an old account, but that she'd let me know when she found it. She called me on Monday to fax it over to me,"

Ren takes a deep breath, his next words sounding clearer, as if he's moved in closer to Pip and therefore the phone. "The account was in the name of Lydia Clarence."

The name falls from Ren's lips like sudden heavy drops of rain. Unexpected, chilling, as they race down your neck past the collar of your shirt.

"Sebastian's mother?" Pip squeaks out.

"The first payment made into the account was the week before she died. The payment reference was 'For the future.' It was a lot of money."

Sebastian tries to piece together the information alongside what they already know, trying to force it all to fit together properly.

"So… Ivan's been stealing money from Sebastian's dad all these years under the guise of keeping people quiet about…?" Pip talks slowly, as she undoubtedly tries to connect the information as well.

"Yes," Ren says solemnly.

"Which means… those guys weren't actually receiving any money, so they could have gone to the tabloids at any time?"

"I doubt it," comes Ren's grim tone through the phone. "Even before I offered that guy the money, he said something weird. He said it was a nice offer, but he knew better than to antagonise the shark that works for the Clarences. Ivan's reputation precedes him."

Silence. Dull and damning, it hangs on Ren's last words. Sebastian stands up, flips the faucet on so the shower starts running. The rush of the water is brisk and immediate, swallowing the echoes of the bathroom up with it. Sebastian takes a deep breath.

"I want to see those statements," he says into the phone, proud of the cool tone of his voice. It helps if he pushes the warm feelings he associates with Ren to the bottom of his person. Focuses as though he's talking to his father.

There's scrabbling on the other end of the call as if the receiver has been snatched up and away from the table.

Fraught breaths meet Sebastian's request.

"I can bring them tonight," Ren says, closer than before, like he's whispering in Sebastian's ear.

Sebastian grits his teeth, shakes his head even though Ren can't see.

"You can't come to the apartment. Send them with Pip instead," he replies tonelessly. He's certain to make his words ambiguous, on the off chance he is being listened to.

"I know another way in," Ren answers right away. "An escape route, in case there was ever an attack on the building and we needed to extract you or the president. I can come without being seen."

"And I'm not your fucking lapdog, Sebastian, I'm not just ferrying shit to your house because you order me," Pip interjects from the background, voice laced with contempt. "I didn't mind helping out with this, but if Ren can bring you the stuff you need, he should."

Sebastian taps his foot deliberately to avoid snapping at Pip. It's not her fault. None of this is her fault. If anything, she's been bizarrely helpful in the past week, given his history of insulting her.

He wants to see those statements for himself. Find out the exact extent of Ivan's embezzlement. If he can provide his father with tangible proof that Ivan's been fucking him like this for years, then there's a chance he can soften the blow surrounding the tabloid pictures.

He doesn't want to see Ren.

(He very much wants to see Ren, but he doesn't know what he'll do if he does).

Sebastian hates not knowing.

"Fine," he says at last. The longing wins out against his better judgement. "Bring the statements tonight. If you're seen then there's nothing I'll be able to say to save your job." He adds, as a legitimate afterthought; "And my father will probably break my fucking arm, so keep that in mind, too."

Silence on the other end of the phone as Ren no doubt digests that last statement. Good, Sebastian thinks grimly. Let Ren ruminate on the shameful interaction between Sebastian and his father that he'd witnessed at Halloween. Let him despair over how his actions will contribute to more of the same.

"I'll be there late—after 9," Ren finally says.

"I can hardly wait," Sebastian responds icily. There's more silence, the gentle clink of glasses in the background of the call indicating Ricky starting to open up the bar.

"I'll call you tomorrow, Sebastian," Pip says, somewhat bleakly, Sebastian thinks.

"If you want to," Sebastian responds without thinking, earning a huff of displeasure.

"Or I'll just go fuck myself," Pip responds haughtily, before she disconnects the call. Sebastian feels a pang of regret. Reminds himself again none of this is Pip's fault.

It's too late to say anything else, however, so he just folds the cellular phone closed and reaches up to undo the collar of his shirt. The shower is still running, and he supposes he'd be best to at least appear like he'd used it. He finishes undressing, leaving the cellular phone on the pile of clothes.

He thinks of Ren stumbling up a fire escape somewhere in the dark to come and see him. Like something out of a movie, some wet behind the ears romance novel where the heroine crumples as soon as she's reunited with her love. Sebastian thinks of the shower in Ren's apartment—standing room only, as he always jokes—his chin on Sebastian's shoulder as he lathers him with soap. As he whispers sweet praise in his ear. As he strokes him until he finds release, almost second nature now, like touching Sebastian is the same as when Ren touches himself.

It stirs intrigue in Sebastian's belly and he presses the front of his body to the chilly tiles, hoping to shock the arousal from his groin. It doesn't work.

He touches himself instead, disgust draped across his shoulders now instead of Ren's warm form.

Nineteen

Sebastian sits in the chair by the window chain smoking until the soft rap of knuckles sounds at his bedroom door. He'd bought himself a disposable lighter alongside Pip earlier in the week. It barely works, the plastic ugly and warped from repetitive use. It leaves a dark grey residue on the tip of his thumb.

It's just gone 11:30pm, and his eyes feel heavy and his limbs listless. This empty feeling in his chest has been leaving him increasingly exhausted, dark bruises appearing under his eyes. He wonders vaguely when the last time he properly ate something was.

He doesn't say anything in response to the knock at the door, just waits until it softly opens and Ren slides through the gap there.

The hallway beyond is dark, so the only light which catches his face is from the twinkling city beyond the window. Sebastian wonders how long he's been sitting there in the dark.

The city lights caress Ren's high cheekbones, the shine of his ink black hair where it hangs limply across his forehead. His eyes look strained too, but they aren't hollow.

They're full of something, dark brown and searching, as he comes closer to Sebastian like he's approaching a feral cat. Beyond that, he's once again reapplied his mask of professionalism, so reminiscent of those first few weeks spent in each other's company. It's almost comforting, a return to something Sebastian can cope with.

Ren's dressed all in black, a backpack slung over his elbow where it slid down from his shoulder. He clears his throat, breaking the frigid silence which stretches between them like the frozen lake they'd watched from the cabin upstate. They'd sat huddled together, a blanket slung over their backs, and Ren had interlaced their fingers. Sebastian thinks he can still feel the burn of his palm at the touch, like muscle memory, like something which has left its mark on him forever. He hates it.

"Hi," Ren says quietly.

Sebastian nods his head tersely. He doesn't trust his voice. His throat feels tight.

Ren takes the nod as a sign Sebastian isn't completely without his faculties, and moves further towards him. The backpack slips down into his hands, where he scrunches the strap between long fingers.

"I'm sorry I'm so late," Ren continues. "I wanted to make sure it was as clear as possible. How—" he stops, clears his throat again, glances at the floor and takes a deep breath. When he looks at Sebastian again, a nerve in his jaw jumps. "How are you?"

Sebastian clenches the arm of the chair tightly.

"Let's skip the niceties, shall we, Ren? I want to see those statements," he says briskly, offering out the hand that isn't clenching the armchair for dear life to jerk the tips of his fingers expectantly. Ren nods, his jaw releasing. His eyes appear less full of whatever searching emotion they'd held. Hollower.

"Of course. My apologies, sir," he says sternly, unzipping the backpack and producing a manila folder. Sebastian lets the detached title wash over him, lets the alienation sink in. It's worse than when he'd said his name down the phone earlier. Somehow, it makes him feel even more foolish.

He doesn't say anything, taking the folder and flipping it open to review the account.

It doesn't take him long to identify the payments, as Ren has taken time to circle every one with a red pen, each accompanied by a set of initials and varying large amounts. As Ren had also highlighted, each one is paid into the same account, differing from the Ivan Jovanović account his salary is paid into each month. Sebastian scans the accompanying fax from the bank, the account set up by his mother, her name signed at the bottom. Lydia Clarence. A six-figure lump sum lodged at the account's opening, the accompanying reference reading, 'for the future.'

There's at least twenty payments Sebastian can spot just from scanning the statements, each one with differing initials. He wonders if he's ever even actually been with this many men. Were some of them the boys from school? Were all of them even genuine? He'd been so careful when it came to anyone he was hooking up with, usually keeping it to dingy bathrooms in clubs or pool houses at parties. He'd only started venturing out properly a little over a year ago anyway, in anticipation of his twenty-first birthday and his father's stern suggestion that he should stop holing himself up and studying so much.

"Some of these have to be fake," Sebastian says, more to himself than to Ren. "Which works in our favour. I'm sure if we match some of these dates up, we could find alibis as to where I was or what I was doing. That bodes well for the whole thing; we could paint it all as nonsense, imply Ivan's been lying this whole time. It might make my father trust me more."

"That's a good idea, sir," Ren says blandly. "I thought it would be too risky to ask accounts for any of the annual statements to review, in case Ivan has someone there collaborating with him, too. It's likely—someone would have noticed this money going missing eventually, even if the president didn't."

Sebastian feels his skin prickle uncomfortably as Ren refers to him by title again. His grip tightens on the paper a little.

"I suppose I could take a sudden interest in the accounts," Sebastian agrees reluctantly. "I *will* be taking over this company at some point." He studies the numbers again, totting them up quickly in his head. "This isn't an insignificant amount of money. How the fuck didn't my father realise this? What must the rest of the fucking accounts look like?"

"A good point, sir," Ren replies robotically.

Sebastian's patience evaporates.

"Will you stop that?" he snaps, throwing the paper down on the table to avoid denting it any further with his ire. Ren blinks at him, his jaw tensing again before he speaks.

"Stop what?" he asks, belligerent. Sebastian's eyes narrow.

"You know what," he says, voice low and dangerous. "I know how much you must enjoy making me feel like a fool, but the incessant chirps of 'yes sir, no sir, three bags full sir,' is quite unnecessary."

"What am I supposed to call you then?" Ren asks sharply, stepping forwards again. He's only a foot from the edge of Sebastian's chair now. His shoulders look broader than Sebastian remembers, the sculpture of his muscles through the dark turtleneck he's wearing almost distracting.

Sebastian rolls his eyes, offers Ren the sourest smile he can muster.

"Oh, you're enjoying this aren't you?" he asks quietly. Ren jerks his head in a barely there refusal.

"I'm not enjoying any of this," he answers, and his voice sounds strange. Dry and choked, like he can barely get the words out. Sebastian frowns.

"Spare me," he says slowly, deliberately. He means for it to come out flippant, disinterested. Rather, it sounds very much like he's begging, the words hanging on the end of an almost sob. Emotion rages up in the tattered hole which has burrowed its home in his chest over the past week, threatening to spill out all over the floor at Ren's feet. Sebastian takes a deep breath, forces it down. Tries to pretend he's talking with his father, and that letting a trace of concern translate to his face will mean punishment.

When he looks at Ren, however, teeth worrying at his bottom lip, hands clenched into fists at his sides, Sebastian finds his ability to compartmentalise slipping away. The loss of control makes him feel more naked, fully dressed sitting before Ren, than he's ever felt lying beneath him.

"You have to believe that I didn't know about those other pictures," Ren says finally. Sebastian shakes his head.

"I don't *have* to believe anything you say," he responds, and his words tremble, and he's lost whatever veneer of detachment he'd possessed when Ren had entered the room. He doubts very much he ever really had it. Regardless, Ren's always been able to see through him anyway. Sebastian glares up at Ren, spits the next words out. "You made me trust you. You said I could trust you. I told you I—I don't think I've ever—and the whole time you *knew*."

Sebastian takes a deep breath, tries to formulate a thought that isn't just an outpouring of the emptiness he feels.

"I believe you when you say you didn't know about the other pictures. Ivan implied as much. But I don't fucking *care* about the other pictures," Sebastian hisses, running a hand through his already dishevelled hair. He must look like a man on the edge of madness, bruises beneath his eyes, gaunt cheeks, unkempt hair—when was the last time he shaved?—"You should have told me that you had the frat party pictures. You should have been honest with me about what happened as soon as we started to—as soon as I started to..."

Sebastian falters, mouth moving fruitlessly as he tries to finish the sentence, but he doesn't quite know what he wants to say. As soon as he started to what? Develop feelings for Ren? What feelings were they? Lust? Desire?

Something more, perhaps. That's why it hurts so much. That's why he hasn't eaten a proper meal since last Wednesday, and hasn't slept a full night since the cabin with Ren at his side. Suddenly, he remembers it all.

"I know," Ren says, and he drops to a crouch, leaning in as if he's going to take Sebastian's hands and stopping his movement at the last second. Sebastian is glad. He knows if Ren touches him, he won't be able to resist. He won't be able to stop touching him back.

He wants Ren to touch him.

"I know. I should have told you. I wish I had. I thought I was protecting you from it, but I was just keeping it from you and justifying it to myself," Ren says quietly, fingers spreading uneasily where they rest on his knees.

"I don't need your protection," Sebastian says immediately, to which Ren sighs.

"My job is protecting you," he responds.

"You know what I mean," Sebastian bites back. "Keep the paparazzi at bay, sweep the venue for potential assailants, threaten whoever you need to to keep their mouths shut. *That's* your job. I don't need you to protect me… emotionally or whatever you think you were doing. I can handle myself. I've been doing it on my own for twenty-one years."

"I know you have," Ren says softly, and it's sad, and it's laced with pity and Sebastian *hates* it. He hates how it makes him feel seen, he hates that Ren is under his skin, pulling him apart fibre by fibre and dissecting him without his consent.

Was it without his consent though? Hadn't Sebastian opened up enough to relinquish his body to Ren? How much of a distinction could be made between offering up his body and offering up his thoughts? His feelings? Sebastian tries to pick apart the conflicting thoughts raging through him, but can't seem to get a grasp on any of it. This indecisiveness makes him impossibly on edge, every movement he makes or word he speaks chased with a barrage of self-doubt.

"We should never have done this," Sebastian finishes, gesturing between the two of them. Ren nods. He leans in a little closer.

"I know. You're right," he agrees. Sebastian watches the way Ren's eyes flicker to look at his mouth. The way he licks his lips thoughtlessly before forcing his attention back up to meet Sebastian's gaze. Sebastian swallows back the wave of attraction that threatens to overwhelm his every conflicting thought.

"We'll just have to go back to the way things were be-fore," he says, untrusting of the waver in his voice. "It's for the best."

Ren edges ever closer. Shakes his head.

"I can't do that," he says definitively. "I can't go back to the way things were before. In future, I won't keep any-thing from you. I don't care what Ivan says, I work for *you*. I report to *you*," he insists. He pauses, chooses his next words with precision. "But… if you'd rather we returned to *just* that. A purely professional position. I can do that. If that's what you want, Sebastian."

His name out of Ren's mouth is like poison, like honey, sweet and deadly all at once. It makes Sebastian's chest constrict tightly, his palms sweat with want. He watches Ren with trepidation.

"And what do you want?" Sebastian asks slowly.

"… I want whatever you're willing to give me," Ren says after a moment of hesitation. "Whatever that is, even if it's just this job protecting you. I'll endure it. I just can't… I can't leave you here. With these people. I know you've protected yourself your whole life. I know you think you know what's best when it comes to your father and the way he treats you. I'll… endure it all, if it means I can stay with you. Will you let me?"

"Why the fuck do you care so much?" Sebastian says quickly. Ren's speech makes the hairs on the back of his neck stand up. It's too sincere, too much, all at once.

"Don't answer a question with a question," Ren says wryly.

"You want me to collapse into your arms," Sebastian says viciously. "You want me to fall at your feet and proclaim my thanks, tell you *no one can take care of me like you can Ren*! Well I won't. I won't do it."

"But will you let me stay?" Ren shakes his head like he doesn't care. Like he doesn't care if Sebastian never touches him again, as long as he is permitted to remain at his side. Sebastian wonders what the fuck is the matter with him. Still, he finds he can't bear to refuse.

"... You can stay," he says, so quiet it's nearly a whisper. So quiet Ren almost catches the words on his lips, as close to Sebastian as he is, poised below him, gazing up through long eyelashes. "Yes. You can stay. I don't—"

I don't want you to leave me, is what he thinks, but he manages to curb the pathetic statement at the last second. He'll be damned if he bares himself to Ren again the same way as before, even if it feels like every moment they're not touching is a moment of his life wasted. Even if it hurts, like knives in his belly it keeps the other pain at bay. The pain behind his eye has returned with a vengeance since he's been apart from Ren. He doesn't know how effective Ren's ability to soothe that old wound is in reality, but in Sebastian's desperation to justify this continued association, he'll take it.

Ren nods.

"I won't leave you," he says.

The blare of Sebastian's cellular phone cuts off the end of Ren's words. He glances at it warily. Pip is usually the only person who calls him on this number, but she wouldn't this late. He lifts the phone and flips it open, a trembling breath exiting his lips as Ren furrows his brows in confusion.

"Hello?" Sebastian speaks into the receiver, voice still quiet in the stillness of his room.

"Come to my apartment. I made it back early and I would like to discuss something with you."

Sebastian's father hangs up the phone before Sebastian can even really register it's him, the line going dead and the dial tone ringing loudly against his ear. It makes the pain behind his eye throb in warning. He flips the phone shut, licks his dry lips.

"I have to go and speak with my father. You should go," Sebastian glances at Ren as he stands from the armchair, tucking the manila folder under his arm. "I'm going to try and talk to him about Ivan."

"I should stay then," Ren argues, predictably, his face set firm. "What if he won't listen? What if something happens?"

"I'll deal with it," Sebastian says tersely. Ren stands and follows him as he walks over to his wardrobe mirror, smoothing down his dishevelled hair as best he can. He looks awful, but there's little that can be done to rectify that now.

"I won't come with you," Ren counters, watching Sebastian in the mirror. "But I'm staying here. If you don't come back I'll know something happened. I can't just leave—"

"Aren't you still on sabbatical?" Sebastian asks coolly, trying to take slow breaths to prepare himself for the impending conversation with his father. "You're not getting paid overtime to be here, Ren. Go home."

"I just told you I'm not leaving you," Ren says forcefully, and Sebastian winces ever so slightly with the sudden increase in the tone of his voice. Ren's brows pitch in concern immediately, only further serving to irritate Sebastian's already frayed nerves.

"Ren, you are making this *worse*," he hisses, turning to face him and trying to sound frustrated. The words leave him with the fear that lurks beneath everything, every conversation he's ever had with his own father riddled with it.

Ren doesn't hesitate as he surges up, palms reaching to cup Sebastian's face as he kisses him. It's just like the first time, all at once hot lips and warm breath against Sebastian's face, before Ren's gone, dark eyes watching every inch of Sebastian's face for a reaction. Sebastian can't bring himself to do anything except lean back in and kiss Ren harder. The utter relief which floods through him in the moment is a high he's been chasing throughout their entire separation. Something bright and comforting fills up the gaping hole in his chest, and his fingers tingle with adrenaline as the sheer want nearly completely overwhelms him.

Sebastian pulls away suddenly, realising what they're doing, where they're doing it. He rubs at his bottom lip with his thumb, clinging onto whatever courage the kiss affords him.

"Do whatever you want," he says finally, sternly. "It's not like you listen to a fucking word I say anyway."

Sebastian turns on his heel and marches out of his bedroom, beginning the familiar trek towards his father's personal apartment at the other end of the penthouse. He meets his mother's sad eyes in the portrait by the elevator. What would she think of him now if she were here? What did she think of him then, all those years she knew him? He remembers her rubbing whiskey on his gums to help him sleep one of the nights his father had been particularly enraged with him. The space behind his eye twinges in response, the pain echoing throughout his skull.

That's just how he is, Lydia Clarence had said, as she brushed blonde curls from Sebastian's eyes as his mouth stung with the pungent liquor. *You just have to learn how to deal with him, Sebastian. That's just how he is.*

Sebastian had taken her advice to heart, learning how to endure the torment silently. He tries to imagine how his life would have been different if she'd told him to fight it. If she'd stood beside him and defended him when he was a child; barely taller than her knee, wrist snapped at the dinner table because he'd spilled his soup.

But his mother had learned how to deal with it by drinking herself to sleep. She'd left Sebastian to figure it out on his own, and had abandoned him to his father's primary care when she finally succeeded in killing herself. Sebastian had taken to thinking of her as the *whore* his father insisted she was. Something about it made it easier to stomach the fact she had left him, always, to fend for himself.

Sebastian takes a deep breath before twisting the polished brass knob of the door leading to his father's study. His luggage is stacked in the hallway, a maid already wheeling some of it away to be laundered. Sebastian tucks the manila folder tighter under his arm and enters.

His father is drinking whiskey, seated at his desk and flipping through the very tabloid paper Sebastian is splashed across the front of. He doesn't look up as Sebastian enters the room. He's on the phone.

"That's fine. Do whatever you think is best," he says, before hanging up the phone and inclining his head towards Sebastian. "Drink?" he asks.

Sebastian can think of nothing worse than the taste of whiskey at this moment, but he nods. Part liquid courage, part potential painkiller, he thinks.

"Please," he says. His father doesn't wait for the response, and has already started pouring a finger of whiskey into a crystalline glass. He sets it on the desk, gesturing distractedly at the seat in front of it for Sebastian to sit down.

He does, slipping the manila folder into his lap as he goes, reaching out with tentative fingers to take a sip of the liquor. It's certainly smoother than anything he's been drinking recently. Still, it catches in the back of his throat, almost makes his nose wrinkle in discomfort. His heart thrums a fervent staccato against his ribcage, the empty hole Ren had left in his chest replaced with the urgent flutter of anxious butterflies.

His father leafs through page after page for another moment before turning the newspaper back to the front. Sebastian hasn't looked at the pictures since Ivan had revealed himself in his bedroom. He can see from where he's sitting that while the pictures are clear, both he and Ren's faces have been anonymised. He wonders how much Ivan had to pay them for that little detail. He supposes it adds some layer of intrigue. Anyone who knows him would be able to identify him easily, however the average consumer of the tabloid would simply be caught up in the scandal of wondering who it could possibly be. It does little to help his case right now. The people who matter will know it was him. The people who could actually affect the business will know it was him.

"Do you know I told Ivan this would happen," his father says idly, tapping the first picture as if deep in thought. "I said you wouldn't be able to keep your hands to yourself."

"Sir, please let me explain."

Sebastian hears the backhanded slap ring out in his ear before he feels the sharp snap against his face. His father's signet ring catches on the highpoint of his cheek. Or it must have, Sebastian thinks, when he feels blood begin to slide down his face. It drips off the bottom of his chin, splattering into his whiskey and marring the rich amber liquid with crimson. He can't feel the sting of it yet, the wound too fresh. His temple throbs in protest, the pain behind his eye snapping ferociously.

"Be quiet, Sebastian," his father says. He contemplates the edge of his ring, the onyx too dark to see the pink of Sebastian's blood. His father lifts his whiskey, takes a sip.

"Ivan was very convincing," he continues calmly. "Said he thought you'd made a real effort to act like a normal person. That this would be an excellent test—proof of how capable you are of stepping up to the plate when it really counts."

He swills his whiskey around, lifting the glass to his lips and gulping down the last of it. He brings it down onto the desk hard, the thick crystal shattering as it collides with the mahogany. A prism of colour twinkles up at Sebastian from the shards of glass now strewn across the front page of the newspaper, painting his father's tight expression with colour. He clenches his jaw, his hand trembling slightly as he clenches it into a fist.

"But no," his father adds softly, watching as a bead of his own blood trickles into the palm of his hand. "I was right. My pathetic faggot of a son disappoints me as expected. The one thing you're built for, Sebastian. The one thing you could have done easily, successfully, to ensure the solid reputation of this company, and you're incapable of even that."

Blood is dripping more quickly off Sebastian's chin now, and the wound on his cheek is finally beginning to prickle. He doesn't dare move his hands to swipe some of the blood up, frozen in place as his father produces a handkerchief from his breast pocket and wipes at his own injured hand.

His father is right, of course. All Sebastian had to do was outgrow the sick fascination he has with other men. Instead, he'd only made matters worse. Climbed into bed with Ren. Begged Ren to *fuck* him. Enjoyed every foul second they'd spent wrapped around each other.

Still, if he admits to that much, he isn't sure his father will let him leave this study in one piece. He grips the manila folder in his lap, tries to find the strength to speak.

"I don't know what to do with you," his father continues. "Your whore mother did far less in the way of causing me trouble and look how she ended up. You always were too much like her. She enjoyed letting other men fuck her just as much as the useless child she birthed."

Sebastian opens his mouth to retort but his father has leant over the table to snatch up his right arm with speed Sebastian didn't know he was still capable of. He twists on Sebastian's wrist, the way he always has, the way he's perfected across the twenty-one years of Sebastian's life. The only sound Sebastian can make is an aborted yelp, one he quickly tries to cover with a sharp intake of breath. His father hates it when he makes noise. He only twists harder then, makes the pain last longer. Sebastian's fingers tremble, his limbs numb and cold.

"I don't know what to do with you, but I've told Ivan he can do what he wants with the other one. I thought he'd been told to stay away from this place, but I just got off a call with Ivan and he seems to think he'd slipped in another way. Were you making the most of the entertainment while I was gone, Sebastian?"

His father twists his wrist tighter, the pain burning through Sebastian's nerves. Spots are starting to appear in his vision, bright white and making his head swim as he tries to catch what his father is saying past the pain.

"What?" he manages to huff out, brain trying to make sense of the words. His father almost growls, mouth twisted in an unpleasant snarl.

"Were you having that faggot bodyguard of yours sneak in at night when you thought no one was looking?" his father asks, voice dangerously quiet, almost too soft for Sebastian to catch past the repetitive bursts of agony. "Is that why he was in your room tonight?"

The mention of Ren seems to shock Sebastian's nervous system into overdrive, the words all colliding at once as he realises what his father means.

"No!" he manages to yelp. "No, I—Ivan's been lying to you! He's been stealing money from you, funnelling it through the security account. Ren and I never—we never—Ivan's been setting this all up, he's playing you for a fucking *fool*!"

Sebastian thinks it's perhaps the longest speech he's ever given his father trapped in this position. It seems to shock his father as much as it does him, because his grip on Sebastian's wrist goes a little slack before he tenses it again and twists tighter. Sebastian can't hold back the cry of agony this time, his vocal cords loose once again.

"You're a lying little piece of shit," his father mutters, but Sebastian shakes his head, clutching blindly for the folder in his lap with his other hand.

"It's true!" he insists. "It's true, please, you have to believe me! Look at the accounts, Ivan's been stealing hush money—there never *was* any hush money, he's been taking it all, for who knows how long! He framed Ren, he's framing me, he's trying to *destroy* the company!"

Sebastian isn't sure if it's the fact he's never once in his life fought back like this, or how incredibly unhinged he must look right now, but his father lets go of his wrist. In the moment of freedom, Sebastian fumbles to produce the statements Ren had collected, shoving them in his father's face.

"Look, if you just *look*—the money's been going to one account, one in my mother's name. She—I don't know why, but she set this account up for Ivan before she died and he's been skimming cash into it for years. He's been lying to you! He's been lying to both of us! Ren found out, so Ivan tried to frame him—"

Sebastian stops dead, the scattered edges of his train of thought grasping something his father had said minutes ago.

"Wh- What is Ivan going to do with Ren? Where are they?"

His father is grasping the edges of the statements, eyes scanning the contents quickly. He can see the red pen marking each damning deposit, digesting the information far too slowly. Sebastian jerks up and out of his seat, urgency causing the pain in his arm and his rapidly swelling cheek to almost vanish entirely.

He looks down at his father as he stares at the statements. Sebastian realises for the first time in his adult life how much smaller than him his father is now.

"Where the fuck is Ren?!" Sebastian yells the words in his father's face, his stomach churning so hard he has to bite back a wave of nausea. He can't lose control, not now, not when Ivan has Ren and they could be anywhere.

His father looks from the statement back up into Sebastian's eyes, doubt flickering in the depths of his cold expression. *It's enough*, Sebastian thinks, as his father shakes his head.

"The roof," he says. "They'll be on the roof. But you won't make it in time."

Sebastian doesn't hesitate for another second. He reaches onto the desk and grabs the largest shard of broken glass that he can find, the keen edge burying itself in the meat of his fingers as soon as he picks it up. He turns and runs from the room, sprinting towards the fire escape stairs which lead to the roof of the building.

His heart is in his throat as he runs, and all he can think of is *Ren*.

Twenty

The bang of the fire escape door is just enough to distract Ivan so that he redirects the gun from the small of Ren's back to face Sebastian.

The freezing air slices its way through the wound on Sebastian's face, the wind on top of the building disconcertingly still in the cold November night. Ren's face is pale where he stands on the precipice of the building's edge, moments from being forced up onto the ledge of the roof.

When Ivan realises it's Sebastian, he swivels around, planting the gun firmly in Ren's side and holding up his other hand in a motion for Sebastian to stop. His face is tight with frustration, gone the ever-present smile and glint of sharp, grey teeth.

"Don't come any closer, Sebastian. Stay right where you are," Ivan says. It sounds like any instruction he's ever given Sebastian, unperturbed as he is by the damning situation they now find themselves in. Unsure what else to do, Sebastian brandishes the broken shard of glass in Ivan's direction, shaking his head.

"Let him go," Sebastian tries to replicate the deadly coolness of Ivan's tone, but his voice is in tatters. He can feel his throat threatening to close entirely, his eyes burning in protest as he tries not to look at Ren. If he looks at Ren, really *looks* at him, he knows he'll give up, and fall to his knees, and beg and it will all be over.

Ivan shakes his head.

"You're being silly," Ivan says coldly. "Look, your hand is bleeding. You're pale, you're shaking—you can't do this, Sebastian. Stop it. Now."

Sebastian knows he's right, but he also remembers what Ricky had told him in *Rain* that day. Ren had managed to apprehend a gunman, stop him before any of the patrons in the bar had been injured. Sebastian knows Ivan is right, that he can't do this—but he knows that Ren can. He swallows back another wave of nausea and tries to buy time.

"You've been stealing money from the company for years," Sebastian yells. "Why? Why did my mother set up that account and give you that money to begin with? What did she mean 'for the future'?"

Ivan stares back at him blankly, so Sebastian does the only other thing he can, and lifts the shard of glass to his own throat. The tip of it nicks the thin skin at his jugular, another river of blood working its way down his neck, the collar of his shirt blooming with drips of ruby red.

"Start *fucking* talking, Ivan!" he cries, voice trembling with panic. "I swear to fucking god, I'll do it, and then what will it all have been for, hm? You've kept me alive all these years, what if I just finish it all now? It'll have been for nothing!"

Ivan lets out a deep sigh, frustration colouring his stern expression.

"Calm down, Sebastian. We both know you haven't got it in you—"

"Don't I?" Sebastian yells back, dragging the edge of the glass a little further across the skin of his neck. He doesn't press any deeper, just lets the jagged edge of the crystal do its work. He laughs, and it sounds manic even to his own ears. "Everyone keeps telling me what I'm *not* capable of! I could surprise us all, right here, right now! Finally make something of myself! But not if you tell me the *truth*. Why did my mother set up that account?!"

Ren's eyes are wide with horror, but Sebastian doesn't dare observe him in anything closer than his peripheral vision.

Ivan presses the gun tighter to Ren's side.

"She set it up just as the reference says," Ivan says. "For the future."

"Who's future?" Sebastian demands. "Your future? Her future?"

Ivan shakes his head.

"It was for all of us, Sebastian," he says. "It was for all of us, but she ruined it."

"I don't understand," Sebastian bites back, hand trembling now from the blood loss as he continues to grip the edge of the glass. Ivan sighs again, shutting his eyes for a moment and seemingly gathering the strength to continue. When he does, he looks tired, as if the truth has been strangling him this entire time, slowly sapping the life from his veins.

"Lydia was never supposed to be a mother," Ivan says. "She always knew she wouldn't be any good at it, but it happened by accident. Your father forced himself on her around the same time she found comfort with me. She let the president believe you were a Clarence, but she and I both knew you were mine."

Sebastian feels as if all of the air has been sucked out of his lungs, the scream of panic in his ears dulling to a quiet drone.

"You're lying," he says automatically. Ivan shakes his head again.

"You wanted the truth," he says. "This is it."

Sebastian watches dumbly as Ivan readjusts his grip on Ren, thumb hovering over the hammer of the gun. He takes a deep breath before he continues.

"When you were born, she was always apologising for being such a bad mother. She didn't want to be one. She didn't know what to do with you, how to look after you. But you were so beautiful when you were a baby, she couldn't help but love you. And what's more, she loved that you were *mine* and not *his*," Ivan smiles at that, like he's proud. Like he's never been more proud of any fact in his life, his sharklike grin returning with vigour. It fades just as quickly, a sour turn falling across his features. "The first time the president broke your arm, you were three years old. You won't remember, but I do, and Lydia *always* did. She realised that night that there was nothing she could do to protect you, not when he broke your arm and then held her down in the same room and assaulted her. That just made her worse. She drank every waking hour of the day, took whatever that quack doctor prescribed her to numb herself to it all. She was a fucking mess, and she didn't care about either of us."

Ivan takes a deep breath, watches Sebastian closely.

"In the brief moments of sobriety between clinic stints she started to act like she wanted us all to run away. She acted like she still loved me, that she wanted us to leave and be a family. But she never saw it through. She went back to the bottle, she let you be beaten time and time again by your supposed father. Eventually, she went rogue and started telling the president you weren't his, that she'd had an affair. Around the time that fucking dog walker started interfering along with her bleeding heart, telling Lydia she didn't have to stand for it all. And that simply wouldn't do."

"What do you mean?" Sebastian asks weakly, the onslaught of information failing to sink in. It sounds like Ivan is talking about someone else, a character in a story, and in some ways, Sebastian thinks he is. All of this happened to a little blonde boy, someone who Sebastian has long since locked away to avoid revisiting what he remembers.

"If the president thought you weren't his, you'd be disowned. You were the only child of his legal wife, but we both know he's got plenty of other little bastards available. What would be the point of you and I enduring all those years of pain if you saw nothing of it in the end? No. Lydia became a liability. So when the president told me to teach the cheating little whore a lesson, I called her suicidal bluff and pushed her off the roof."

Ren makes a noise then, somewhere between a gasp of outrage and a yelp of pain as Ivan shoves the gun deeper between his ribs. Sebastian lets his gaze flicker to meet Ren's for just a second, the fear he expects to see in his eyes failing to materialise. He looks more horrified, outraged at what Ivan's just admitted to.

"You… you killed my mother?" Sebastian asks brokenly.

Ivan shakes his head again, as if Sebastian doesn't understand.

"I did what had to be *done*, Sebastian. For you. For the beautiful little baby that Lydia loved, despite it all. I had her set up that account and transfer the starting funds; let her believe we would run away. After she was dead, I kept putting money aside for us, just in case the president ever found out about you or the company he barely knows how to run went belly up. I did it all for *you*."

Sebastian is struggling to hold the glass to his throat now, the pain starting to catch up with him and the adrenaline keeping him upright, causing his fingers to shake.

"But you let him hurt me," Sebastian argues. "*You* told him about those boys in school. You were always telling him things and doing things that made him hurt me more. That just… *hurt me more*."

Ivan frowns.

"I had to keep him on my side, Sebastian," he says calmly, as if he's explaining something to a child. "I had to make him trust me more than anyone—he never once suspected I was siphoning that money, he never once suspected I had been the one Lydia had an affair with." He pauses and frowns, appearing a little disappointed. "And I didn't *always* do things that hurt you. I only told him bits of the truth, especially after that first hospital stint. I learned where to leave certain details untold. I even gave that fucking nosy dog walker those mutts you cared so much about! And you didn't even believe me."

He shakes his head sadly, backing up a little and tugging Ren along with him.

"You've tried your best to fuck up all my hard work. But I will let you go back down there and tell the president you were making it all up. We can dispose of him together, it won't be difficult. I very nearly managed it at your birthday, but you shouldn't trust something so important with a random grunt of a hitman that already failed in shooting up a bar full of queers. Just think; with the president gone, you'll have everything you've ever wanted. Doesn't that sound better than doing anything drastic? Put the glass down Sebastian. Take a deep breath," Ivan tugs Ren back further, away from Sebastian. It only serves to make the panic surge more violently in his stomach and he jerks his hand out, desperate.

"Stop! Stop, okay, I'll do what you want, just—please, you don't have to hurt Ren. Let him go, just send him away or something, but please don't hurt him," Sebastian pleads. His eyes sting harder now, and he feels something hot drip down his face, through the streaks of dried blood which cake his skin. Tears, salty and completely alien, breaking the barrier of his dry eyes. His lower lip wobbles in protest as he tries to gasp out another plea. "Please, Ivan, I promise, I'll never speak to him again, I'll do whatever you want, just let him go."

Ivan shakes his head.

"You need to learn your lesson, Sebastian," he says simply. "You need to understand what will happen if you try to cross me again. I alone know what's best for you. You need to realise that, and I'm afraid this is the only way the message is going to hit home."

"Sebastian, it's okay! It's going to be okay!"

Ren's voice is hoarse from disuse, his own eyes red raw at the edges. He gasps in pain again as the barrel of the gun is thrust again into his flesh.

Sebastian shakes his head, the tears catching on his words and making him unable to speak. Ren's eyes are deep, dark, so brown and so full, so far from the hollow emptiness he'd first watched Sebastian with all those months ago. Sebastian remembers what Ricky told him about the shooter in *Rain*—the one it appeared Ivan had instigated in the first place, something to test if Ren was right for the job.

All it took was that one second of distraction, he'd said, and Ren had wrestled the gun free of the attacker.

Sebastian takes a deep breath, thinks of the dreams he'd have as a child of his mother on this roof. It is as cold as he'd always thought it would be, despite the lack of wind. He thinks now of the press of a hand on her back, perhaps as she'd looked to Ivan for comfort in her last, helpless moments. Begged him to spare her. Maybe even told him she still loved him.

Sebastian throws the shattered crystal to the floor and sprints in the opposite direction, aiming for the edge of the roof as if he's going to leap off the side.

One second of distraction, he thinks, as he runs. He hears Ivan begin to shout his name before the word dies in his throat, cut off with a sudden expulsion of the air from his chest. Sebastian tries to come to a halt, but his legs are trembling so violently that he trips and falls, elbows colliding with the rough tiles of the roof. He drops the viciously sharp broken crystal as his hand finally seizes up with the pain, the edge of it lodging in the tense flesh of his biceps. Pain erupts in his arm, no sound escaping when he cries out, as the jagged edge of the crystal embeds itself deeper in his body. Sebastian can hear the grunts of a struggle behind him, trying to twist to see what's going on and finding his whole body unresponsive.

One second of distraction, he thinks desperately, as he hears the telltale ring of a gun exploding from the other side of the roof. His entire body ricochets with unspent energy as he violently throws up, somehow managing to roll up onto his knees as best he can in an attempt to expel it all. He finishes quickly, dry heaving into the tar the roof tiles are held down with, nothing in his body but a mouthful of whiskey.

He tries to call Ren's name and nothing comes out as another gunshot roars through the air. Then, everything is quiet, the lack of wind on the roof deafening in Sebastian's ears as they ring in answer to the gun going off.

Sebastian's vision is fading at the edges as he feels a pair of strong hands grasp his shoulders and tug him over onto his back.

A man's narrow, hooded eyes meet his from above, pupils blown wide in alarm past glossy dark irises. Not black, *very dark brown*, he thinks.

Sebastian is vaguely aware that warmth is blooming across his shirt now, the blood gushing from the wound in his arm tacky and wet.

"Just hang in there, Sebastian," a familiar voice begs. He feels the press of dry lips to the corner of his mouth, tries to recoil in protest because he's just been vomiting.

"Don't leave me," he manages to croak, fingers trying to grasp weakly for the comfort of Ren's touch.

Instead, he succumbs to the cold and the dark, and thinks of his mother.

Twenty-One

"He couldn't have arranged this press conference for the day *after* I'm discharged from the hospital? It has to be right now?" Sebastian asks through his teeth as he tries to squint into the shitty hospital mirror and do up his tie. The stitches on the palm of his hand came out yesterday, leaving behind a tender stripe of shiny new skin. It's still a little delicate, even against the smoothness of the silk. His right arm is still bound up too, both around his biceps where the broken glass had lodged itself and tore through the tendons and at his wrist where his father had twisted it. The hairline fracture there, present from the stress put upon the bone in childhood had been re-broken, leaving Sebastian with limited mobility. Ren watches him struggle for an instant longer before raising his hands in offering.

"Allow me, sir," he says, not waiting for Sebastian to consent before he gently pries the fabric from between his fingers. Sebastian scowls.

"I'm all healed up Ren, no need to treat me like I'm made of glass," he grumbles, watching as Ren deliberately ignores the antagonistic tone of his voice. Sebastian tries again for a rise. "Especially considering you were the one who was shot. Should you even be back at work?"

"Grazed, by a bullet, not shot, sir," Ren says clearly, tightening the knot so it rests comfortably below the carefully pressed cotton of Sebastian's collar. He tucks the length of the tie down with a golden pin, stands back to consider it lying flat.

"It looked like you'd been fucking shot to me," Sebastian retorts quietly, remembering the vague moments following the altercation on the roof. All he can really recall is the sheer amount of blood, painting his shoddy memories with vivid scarlet, as the bright lights and whine of sirens accompanied the air ambulance landing on the apartment's roof. Ivan managed to graze Ren with the first shot, but by the time he pulled the trigger for the second, Ren had wrangled his arm halfway behind his back. The gun slipped, Ivan shot himself in the leg and hit his femoral artery. He bled to death there on the roof.

"Well, it's a good thing you're not a doctor," Ren says, stepping out of Sebastian's space entirely and directing a few other men in dark suits to collect his bags. "Ready to go? The car's waiting."

Sebastian nods, waiting until the other security guards have shuffled out of the room with his things, before he takes a deep breath.

"How do I look?" he asks, standing up straight.

To Ren's credit, his eyes don't linger on the scar on Sebastian's neck, nor the one on the apple of his right cheek. His bandaged right arm is carefully concealed with his shirt and suit jacket. Ren offers him a careful smile, dark eyes full of warmth. It makes heat rise in Sebastian's cheeks.

"You look as impeccable as ever, sir," Ren hums, stepping to the side of the door and gesturing for Sebastian to exit the room first.

"Save the ass kissing for later, Ren," Sebastian mutters, embarrassment colouring his neck instantly as he ducks out of the room. He makes sure to graciously thank the nurses who cared for him on his way out. They're standing in a line down the corridor, Nancy, Hilda and Gabriel, shaking his hand and offering shy smiles as he makes his way to the elevator.

As he and Ren stand side by side, Ren clears his throat a little awkwardly, catching Sebastian's eye in their reflection on the industrial steel interior. Sebastian raises a brow in question.

"That Gabriel guy certainly had a good look at you," Ren says, hands folded neatly at his front. He's staring intently at his reflection now, refusing to look at Sebastian properly. Sebastian throws him a wicked grin.

"Oh dear. Jealousy does not become you," he says smoothly, leaning in closely so his lips are only a moment from the shell of Ren's ear. "Let's make sure to remain professional, hm? Wasn't that the agreement?"

Ren expels the air from his lungs in a gruff sort of protest, but rather than respond, just unclenches his hands and goes to exit the elevator first.

"The press have already gathered outside. Are you ready?" he asks quietly. Sebastian nods, applying his most charming smile and drawing himself up to his full height.

"It wouldn't matter if I said no," he replies cheerily, as the elevator doors slide open and the clamour of paparazzi can be heard at the entrance to the hospital. Sebastian follows Ren closely, maintaining his winning smile as they walk. He can't pick out most of what they're yelling as they scramble atop each other, but some of it feeds through—

— how much money was stolen in the end—?

—feel about your new position—?

—a grave oversight on your part, how will the company recoup—?

—any truth to the allegations of a romantic connection with—?

The car door shuts behind Sebastian, effectively blocking out all noise from beyond. Ren joins him from the other side, tapping the partition between the driver's cab and the backseats, and the sleek, dark car slides off.

"Do you have a cigarette?" Sebastian asks as soon as they've got onto the main road. "I swear to god those nicotine patches they were loading me up with wouldn't be enough to give a fucking five-year-old a buzz."

"You should really quit, sir," Ren chastises lightly, but he reaches into his own dark suit and produces a familiar brand of cheap smokes and his Zippo. Sebastian grins, taking the cigarette between his teeth and letting Ren light it. He savours the first thrill from the smoke in his lungs, tilting the cigarette thoughtfully at Ren between his index and middle fingers.

"Your new job is certainly paying," Sebastian says playfully. "Nice suit. Did the lady at the department store pick it out for you?"

Ren offers him a bland look, unbuttoning the front of his jacket as he leans back in his seat.

"The president said he didn't want his new head of security looking like he's paid pittance for the job," Ren responds, his words harbouring just enough distaste that Sebastian drops the teasing smirk from his own face. He glances up, ensures the partition is in place again just to be safe, before he reaches across to Ren's hand and threads their fingers together.

He doesn't say anything, just in case the driver can still hear them. Ren doesn't either. But his fingers clench the tips of Sebastian's in a grateful squeeze, before letting go altogether. Sebastian takes his hand back, takes another drag on his cigarette.

"Congratulations, by the way," he says.

Ren is quiet still, before he lets out a soft sigh.

"Yes. Thank you, sir," he responds.

They continue along in silence as Sebastian finishes his cigarette, pulling up alongside another gaggle of photographers and reporters. The hotel which served as the site for both of Sebastian's ill-fated twenty-first birthday parties awaits them. Sebastian casts his eye over the tired exterior of the building, and wonders if this is another branch of the company which is about to tumble into bankruptcy.

He sighs deeply, reapplies his shining smile.

No, he thinks. Mustn't think of that today. Must put his best foot forward, keep his father on side.

Ren slides out of the car, heading around to open Sebastian's door and shepherd him into the hotel. He doesn't get a chance to pick out any of these reporters' questions, but doubts they're any different. He flicks his cigarette butt to the floor as they enter the hotel. Reiterates one of his father's favourite useless phrases to himself. *Any publicity is good publicity*.

They head straight to the conference room where his father is waiting, checking his watch. He locks eyes with Sebastian as he enters, sharp gaze daring to skirt across to where Ren stands at his shoulder, head bowed in respect.

"Right on time. As expected, thank you Ren," the president says brusquely. There's a flurry of activity in the room around them as hotel staff bring bottles of water, as publicists and company directors scuttle to prepare for the press conference. Sebastian's father lays a tentative hand on his shoulder. It takes every ounce of self-control Sebastian has in his body not to pull back in revulsion.

"A united front, Sebastian," his father says. "Let's show them what they're up against."

Sebastian searches deep inside himself for the simpering smile which he pulls out and lets take ownership of his face. He nods.

"Of course, dad," he says, reaching for the last dregs of warmth left from the brush of Ren's fingers in the car to appear supportive and dedicated in the face of his father.

The press conference is over as quickly as it begins. Sebastian is announced as the new vice-president. He'll be working to gather the remaining credits he needs for college over winter and spring break, in the hopes he can graduate early and commit fully to the business. After the unfortunate plot by their family's long time trusted head of security to assassinate the current president and to steal hundreds of thousands was discovered, the man had taken his own life. Ren Nakahara, who succeeded in exposing the embezzlement, has been promoted to manage the new security team. He'll be working at the president's right hand from now on to ensure the continued safety of the entire family.

With the shocking discovery of Ivan Jovanović's embezzling, a difficult time awaits the company as a whole over the next financial year, as the impact of the losses is appropriately assessed. The president will be making the necessary visits to head offices across the globe to realign the priorities of each branch of the business, and do his best to protect as many jobs as possible.

The press don't like that. They don't like much of any of it, Sebastian thinks, no matter how many well-meaning smiles he offers, or echoes of his father's empty promises he chimes in with. He sees Pip in the crowd, with the press pass he'd procured for her, scribbling something down in a notepad. He doesn't expect much from the dramatic exposé she's planning to pen for the school newspaper on the slew of revelations from the past month (and he'd told her as much), but admires her dedication to the craft. When she catches his eye, Sebastian jerks his finger towards the fire escape and mimes smoking a cigarette. They need to properly discuss what can and cannot be included in her story.

Pip rolls her eyes and offers a smile so dazzling that he's certain would make him buckle if he were that way inclined. She makes immediately for the fire escape, as Sebastian slips down off the stage to follow her. Ren is pulled to one side by his father, presumably to discuss the plans for joining the president abroad in the coming week—he's needed in the city for the time being to firm up the new security team and ensure Sebastian is properly protected, however. His father has a flight to catch this afternoon.

When Sebastian emerges out onto the fire escape with Pip, she's already lighting a cigarette.

"Spot me a smoke, Pip," Sebastian says playfully, clasping his palms together as if in prayer. She recoils in apparent disgust before handing him the lit cigarette she's just had in her mouth.

"So this is the true state of the Clarence empire," she says as she lights another. "Didn't realise things were that destitute."

Sebastian inhales gratefully on the cigarette, shrugging a shoulder lightly.

"It's on a need-to-know basis," he says simply, skewering her with a serious glance. "Meaning keep it vague in your write-up, won't you?"

Pip makes a hum of agreement around her cigarette filter, crossing her free hand over her middle and shuddering down against the cold. She glances subtly behind Sebastian, ensuring they're alone, before she raises a brow at him curiously.

"One thing still doesn't make sense to me," she says, keeping her tone deliberately aloof. Sebastian smirks as he blows thin jets of blue-grey smoke out his nostrils.

"Do tell," he murmurs.

"Well," Pip begins, gazing out at the cityscape sprawling below them as she chooses her words carefully. "If the president suspected you and Ren were involved… romantically with each other, why make him his new head of security? I get they're framing him as the guy who uncovered Ivan's master plan, but you and I know better…"

Sebastian takes another deep drag on his cigarette, the crackle of the paper burning away between his fingers the only sound between them, save for the rustle of the wind.

"We managed to convince him most of what Ivan told him was a lie," Sebastian begins, "certainly in relation to the sheer number of hush money payments that were being made. The same went for the tabloid pictures. None of them were explicit in any way, so there was no actual proof anything went on between the two of us. All those pictures showed was a bodyguard staying close to his charge, which is to be expected." Sebastian pauses, stubbing out his cigarette as Pip leans in expectantly.

"Still," he continues, "Ren knows too much. He knows how fucked the finances really are; he knows Ivan murdered my mother; he knows there's at least some truth to my… experimentation with other men. You know what they say about keeping your friends close and your enemies closer. My father wants Ren to get his hands dirty too, so he's promoted him to head of security to make sure that happens. That," Sebastian leans in sideways so he's whispering in Pip's ear, warm breath against the shiny pearl earring in her left ear, "and I suspect he's a little more suspicious of our relationship than he's leading us to believe. If Ren's his head of security, it'll be much harder for the two of us to engage in any… extracurriculars, if you know what I mean."

Pip jerks her head away from Sebastian, sticking her tongue out in disgust.

"*Please*, spare me the details," she groans, before she stubs out her own cigarette. "Makes sense though. It's going to make things harder for the two of you, isn't it?"

Sebastian shrugs, reaching up to pat Pip good-naturedly on the shoulder.

"Maybe," he says. "But sneaking around is half the fun."

He offers Pip a quick salute of farewell as one of the hotel managers appears and offers to escort him to his room, enjoying the grim smirk she gives in response to his last coy remark.

Sebastian can't bring himself to return to the apartment. Every memory he has associated with the place features shark-like smiles watching him suffer from the side of the room, all in the name of protecting a bond which didn't even really exist. Of course Sebastian's father had had his paternity tested as a child as soon as he knew about Lydia's infidelity. And although the findings were conclusive, perhaps he had held some unexplainable suspicion towards Ivan, because he'd never told him.

Sebastian is his father's son. Ivan had never held any claim to him. Sebastian suspects his mother had always known that to be the case, but had thought leading Ivan to believe as much would provide Sebastian with his guaranteed protection. He's still not sure how he feels about his mother in the aftermath of it all.

Sebastian enters his hotel room, closely followed by Ren, who is still on the phone to someone. He looks exhausted, clenching the bridge of his nose between his thumb and forefinger as he paces back and forth. Sebastian clumsily undoes his tie with his left hand, unbuttons the top few buttons on his shirt, and discards his suit jacket over the back of a chair. There's a bottle of champagne already chilling in a cooler by the window.

For the first time in his life, Sebastian loathes the expense.

If the brief review he'd had of the company accounts during his stay in the hospital (whenever Ren wasn't hovering nearby, insisting he rest) was anything to go by, things are in worse shape than he could have imagined.

His father has clearly been running the business into the fucking ground for years. Firstly, failing to notice Ivan's skimming, secondly failing to question the accounts submitted by finance board members who were obviously taking their own chunk in order to keep things quiet. Thirdly, investing in shoddy, idiotic schemes up and down the country, funnelling money into nonsense to do with *space travel* of all fucking things, and securing government contracts in fields he had no experience in.

Sebastian pours the champagne, as Ren hangs up the phone. He offers Ren a glass, and he refuses. Sebastian rolls his eyes and pours him one, anyway.

"You're off the clock," he declares, raising his drink in mock toast. "Enjoy it. It's the last bottle of champagne this company will be purchasing for a while."

Ren doesn't protest any further, accepting the glass from Sebastian and taking a deep gulp. He throws the cellular phone that has been glued to his hand all day into one of the bags which have already been brought up to the room. He undoes his own tie.

"I fucking hate this," he says, as Sebastian plops himself down on the end of the bed. He raises his eyebrows, watching Ren over the top of his glass.

"I don't think I've ever heard you say you hate something," he says thoughtfully, before snapping his fingers in realisation. "Never mind—I just remembered your utter contempt for the beach."

"Sebastian," Ren says, and his voice is tired. He sighs deeply, watches as Sebastian leans back further on the bed. "I don't want to do this. I don't want to manage your father's security. I told you before everything went down that I work for *you* now. That I wouldn't leave you, that I'd stay with *you*. I can't do that if I'm expected to follow the president across the world and coordinate the rest of these people. I don't want to. I want to make sure you're safe."

Sebastian finishes the champagne in his flute, tilting his head back to swallow the remaining liquid.

"Ren," he says, spurred on by the lap of courage the champagne brings him. "I remember what you said. And it's all still true, isn't it? Your loyalty lies with me, doesn't it?"

Ren nods ardently, coming closer to where Sebastian sits on the end of the bed. Sebastian smiles up at him, as Ren's fingers hesitantly reach for the curve of Sebastian's jaw, dancing along the skin there.

"Of course it does," Ren says. "I promise it does."

Sebastian cups the back of Ren's hand with his own, pulling his palm to his lips and leaving a soft kiss. A shiver seems to pass from his body into Ren's.

"That's exactly why you have to do it," Sebastian says gently, words moist against Ren's warm palm. "My father doesn't know what he's doing. If we leave any more of this to him, he's going to run this company into the ground and ruin any chance I have of getting a handle on it. We'll have suffered all of this for nothing." Sebastian gazes up at Ren, meets the ruthless intent of his deep, dark eyes. "With you on the inside, I'll be able to handle this mess my way. The correct way. I need your help to do it. It won't be for long, I promise you that. You can endure, can't you? You said that you could."

Ren nods, fingers growing increasingly slack around his champagne flute. He swallows down the rest of the liquid, setting his glass on the plush carpeted floor.

"Yes," he says softly, bringing his now free hand up to caress the other side of Sebastian's face. "For you, of course I can."

Sebastian smiles at that, the first proper smile he's offered Ren all day and it soothes the furrow in his brow and the tightness in his jaw. A moment passes in silence, in stillness. Sebastian leans forwards a fraction of an inch.

"Kiss me, Ren," he says.

Ren raises a brow, a coy smile tugging at the edge of his mouth.

"Is that an order, sir?" he asks. Sebastians sighs, watching him carefully.

"It's a request," he supplies, watching as Ren's teeth scrape along his bottom lip in contemplation. He grins.

"So I can refuse?"

Sebastian loses his patience then, jerking his face back out of Ren's touch. He narrows his eyes.

"Do you get some kind of sick satisfaction out of trying to make me beg?" Sebastian demands, flopping back onto the bed and crossing his arms over his chest. "Well, I won't do it. I won't beg," he finishes petulantly, studying the ornate cornicing decorating the ceiling. Another moment passes before he feels Ren's weight settle on the edge of the bed. His knees either side of Sebastian's hips, he crawls up his body, watching his face with an air of amusement.

"Oh, really?" Ren asks, and his voice is low and dangerous, like fire and ice all at once, making Sebastian's skin tingle with anticipation. Ren dips down so his mouth rests in the curve of Sebastian's throat, where he presses a delicate kiss. "You won't beg?"

His tease is followed with the snap of teeth on Sebastian's skin, earning a shout of surprise. Sebastian clamps his mouth shut again in protest, but he quickly feels the loss of Ren's lips on his skin as he pulls back. His face is stoic as he studies Sebastian's face intently.

"Are you sure about this?" he asks, impossibly tender as he's careful not to stroke the scar on Sebastian's cheek. Sebastian frowns, before taking a deep breath and deciding there's nothing else for it.

"I realised something on that roof," he says. Ren leans back a little, depositing his weight more appropriately so Sebastian isn't crushed below him. Sebastian snakes his hand up between them to grab Ren's fingers where they still linger at the edge of his face, gazing up into his hopeful eyes.

"I realised I've spent my whole life living for someone or something else. Always expected to meet unattainable standards. Always set up to fail. Always pushing down what I thought or how I felt because it didn't match up to what I was told I had to be. Even when I started experimenting with other guys, it was only ever really to test the limits of what I could get away with. And then I met you," Sebastian bites his lip, pushes past the embarrassment which is making heat flood to his face. "And for the first time, someone asked me what *I* wanted. And I'm still… not sure what that looks like in the long term. But I do know for sure that I want you. I want this Ren, I want… us. If that's what you want too," he adds briskly, unable to maintain Ren's intense eye contact for a moment longer.

"I want that too," Ren says, leaning his forehead down to press against Sebastian's. He kisses him, slow and careful at first, before deepening it with a gentle tug of Sebastian's bottom lip. The cool metal of his tongue piercing sweeps the roof of Sebastian's mouth, eliciting a shiver he can't hope to suppress. Ren bears down on Sebastian, his torso pressed flush against the weight of Ren's as their tongues slide against one another. Sebastian jerks his hips up, half-hard already and desperate for friction, but Ren maintains a careful distance between them as he pulls back. He wears a smug grin, watching Sebastian with a glimmer in his dark eyes. "However, I also really do want to see you beg."

Somewhere amidst stripping each other down to only their underwear, Ren pulls back and runs a finger down Sebastian's bandaged right arm.

"Can you lie on your front for me?" Ren asks, smiling as Sebastian immediately rolls over and crushes a pillow up under his chest. He positions his weight on his elbows, thinking he'll be able to rut into the bed as Ren preps him. His dick feels tight and neglected from the past few weeks spent trapped under the neon lights of a hospital room (a completely unnecessary length of time in his opinion, but the wound in his arm had been deep and he'd needed minor surgery on it). Sebastian grunts in surprise when Ren grasps either side of his hips and jerks them upwards as he rolls his briefs down his thighs.

"Keep your hips up, Seb," Ren whispers, leaving kisses scattered along the length of his spine as he moves downwards. Sebastian can feel the smug grin on Ren's lips as he scrapes his teeth across his ass. "I can't hear any begging yet."

Sebastian groans in frustration as his dick falls free of his boxers, suspended heavily between his legs as Ren tugs his ass further up. The groan is cut short, however, as Ren squeezes the meat of his ass hard, his fingernails catching and leaving red streaks across the skin there. The pain is chased by the delightfully erotic sensation of Ren's wet breath against Sebastian's hole. Sebastian's thighs shake with the sensation, a whimper lost to the fabric of the pillow he has his face burrowed in.

"Fuck, do that again," Sebastian manages to gasp, turning his face to the side a little so Ren can hear him.

"Do what?" Ren asks coyly. "This?" He kisses his way between the cleft of Sebastian's ass, leaving only the daintiest of licks around the outside of his rim. Sebastian's core is throbbing now, desperate to feel the stretch of Ren's fingers inside him. He can feel it between his legs too, where his cock sits neglected and desperate for stimulation. Ren isn't touching his ass cheeks at all anymore. Sebastian lets a groan of annoyance escape.

"Grab me again, or hit me, do something—!"

His words are cut off as Ren grasps the curve of his ass between his fingers again, squeezing with such intensity that the pain sends a tremor through Sebastian. He follows it with a soothing rub across the expanse of his now aching flesh, sliding his tongue in the wake of his fingers and leaving Sebastian's skin wet and pounding.

"Do you like that?" Ren asks carefully, tracing Sebastian's rim again with determined precision. Sebastian nods into the pillow, his voice trapped somewhere amongst the desperate whimpers escaping as Ren's words brush his centre. "Do you want more?"

"Please," Sebastian huffs. "Please, Ren—"

The crack of Ren's palm connecting with Sebastian's ass is like a clap of thunder, the pain slicing through Sebastian's body, only to be chased by the heady pleasure of Ren's tongue finally, *finally* sweeping across his asshole. He can feel the bright coolness of Ren's tongue stud catch on the edge of his rim, and he can't help the long moan that breaks free as he gasps for air.

"Look at you," Ren hums thoughtfully, between lapping eagerly at Sebastian's hole. "Bent over like this, just for me. Do you like how it feels, Sebastian? This is enough, isn't it?"

As Ren says it, he hits him again, the slap ringing through the otherwise silent room and catching on the metal of the cooling champagne bucket by the window.

Sebastian arches his back up in response to the touch, rewarded with the tip of Ren's finger prodding inquisitively at his hole. He doesn't go any further, however, letting his hand slide down and through Sebastian's legs to ghost the base of his cock. Sebastian whimpers.

"Fuck, you're just torturing me," he cries, as Ren just loosely cups the base of Sebastian's dick, refusing to exert the pressure on it that he's aching for.

"I don't know what you mean," Ren says coyly, taking his hand back from around Sebastian's dick and sliding the flat of it back over Sebastian's ass. He lifts his hand away, and Sebastian takes a sharp breath preparing for the impact of another slap, but it doesn't come. Instead, he feels lube-slicked fingers finally toying with the edge of his asshole, moments from plunging in and filling him the way he wants.

The slap comes after that and shocks him as he cries out again, this time clenching his fists in the pillow for dear life.

"Please Ren," Sebastian whines, imagining the ripe red hand marks across his ass tomorrow, imagining how he won't be able to sit down in the morning after Ren fucks him deep and hard. "Please, do something, please, I need—I need…"

"Just tell me what you need, Sebastian, and I'll give it to you," Ren says easily, like he's offering to make a run to the grocery store. "What do you need, baby? I want to give it to you, just tell me what it is."

"You're a fucking *animal*," Sebastian snarls back, as Ren continues to lazily circle his hole with his forefinger, teeth and tongue only adding to the speckled purple flesh now blooming across his ass.

"All you have to do is tell me what you want," Ren replies, unperturbed by Sebastian's outburst. It's too much—Sebastian can feel his cock weeping in protest, dripping onto the bed as he pushes his ass back further, idly hoping Ren will just take initiative and give him what he wants. Finally, hedonism wins out against his pride. He growls in frustration.

"Please, fuck me, *please*, I need you to *fuck me* Ren," Sebastian lets it out all in one breath, tilting his head to one side so he can glare back at the man in question. He knows his cheeks are roaring red, his eyes wet at the edges from the incessant pain chased by the cusp of true pleasure, but he doesn't care. Ren smiles at him, and it's dazzling, and Sebastian is certain, in this moment, that this is what he wants. Ren is what he wants.

Ren doesn't need any more encouragement, immediately slipping his finger past the tight circle of muscle and beginning to work Sebastian open as he continues to leave sloppy kisses across his ass. Sebastian spreads his knees as best he can, trying to breathe rhythmically into the pillow as Ren works two then three fingers into his hole, before the anticipation is just too much.

This time when he begs Ren to fuck him, he doesn't waste another second, shoving his slick cock into Sebastian's tight hole and clenching his hips hard as he rocks into him. Sebastian cries out at the feeling of fullness, so many nights spent wishing he were here like this. Ren angles his hips just right, like it's second nature to him now, making Sebastian's skin erupt in gooseflesh as pleasure explodes in every corner of his brain. The sound of their bodies sliding together is impossibly lewd, coupled with the increasingly tense grunts from Ren's chest and the gasps from Sebastian's.

Ren starts off as slowly as he can muster to let Sebastian become reacquainted with the sensation. Impatient as ever, Sebastian begins to work himself in time with Ren's thrusts, the backs of his thighs meeting with Ren's hips as he fucks himself back on his cock. Ren seems to particularly enjoy this, barely making sense as he lavishes praise on Sebastian in time with the rapidly increasing pace of his thrusts.

There's little chance for Sebastian to warn him, as Ren thrusts up deep into him and sends Sebastian careening off the edge. He cums, untouched, his dick throbbing with his release as he desperately tries to grasp onto the sheets and ride through the intensity of his orgasm. It sets Ren off too, as he groans not a moment later, his hips coming to an uneasy halt as he collapses down onto Sebastian's back. He can feel Ren's sweat-slick forehead resting at the base of his shoulders, and feels the impossibly chaste kiss he leaves there as he slides out of Sebastian.

They take a moment to catch their breath, Ren diligently peeling the soiled topsheet off the bed and leaving it in a heap on the floor. Sebastian rolls onto his back, accepts the damp washcloth Ren brings him to clean himself up with. Ren collects both of their discarded champagne glasses and refills them, sliding up onto the bed and tucking Sebastian into the crook of his arm as they recline in the warm haze of the room. Sebastian feels sated, comfortable and safe in Ren's arms as he sips on the pleasant fizz of champagne. Ren drops a kiss on the top of his forehead as the sun beyond the hotel room begins to set, bathing them in its amber glow.

"A toast to the future. To us," Ren suggests, tipping his glass to clink the edge of Sebastian's. Sebastian smiles, indulging in the toast as he gazes up at Ren.

"To the future," he agrees, taking another sip and chasing the tang along his bottom lip with his tongue. "Ren," he adds, and it's quiet and thoughtful, in keeping with the request poised on his lips. Ren raises a brow to show he's listening. Sebastian smiles wider, takes a deep breath.

"Ren," Sebastian says again, the name as delicious on his tongue as it's been since the day they met. "I want you to help me kill my father."

About the Author

Having grown upin the North of Ireland, and earned her MA in Creative Writing, Caitlin Bowdenis passionate about telling queer stories, and about leaning into aspects ofqueer characters less palatable to the heteronormative status quo. While thepresence of queer characters is being normalised in today's media, Caitlinfeels they are often sanitised to appeal to an audience less familiar withtheir struggles, and rejects this entirely. She wants to challenge thatnarrative through her work and demonstrate that truly normalising queerrepresentation in media means embracing the fact that just as there's no suchthing as a perfect heteronormative person, there's no such thing as a perfectqueer person either.

Recognising yourself in a character that is inherently flawed and beingable to be inside their head can make you feel seen. Caitlin's hope is that herwork will someday provide that same comfort to her readers.

Excellent LGBTQ+ fiction by unique, wonderful authors.
Thrillers
Mystery
Romance
Young Adult
& More

Join our mailing list here for news, offers and free books!

Visit our website for more Spectrum Books
www.spectrum-books.com
Or find us on Instagram @spectrumbookpublisher